Finch Books by Lanne Garrett

Single Books
The Cinder City Embers: Singularity

A Cursed Crow
The Seven Year Crow

A Cursed Crow

THE SEVEN YEAR CROW

LANNE GARRETT

The Seven Year Crow
ISBN # 978-1-80250-533-7

Interior text design by Claire Siemaszkiewicz
Finch Books

Published in 2023 by Finch Books, United Kingdom.

Finch Books is an imprint of Totally Entwined Group Limited.

THE SEVEN YEAR CROW

Dedication

For Dave, who always has the right word.

And pleasant is the fairy land,
But, an eerie tale to tell,
Ay at the end of seven years
We pay a tiend to hell;
I am sae fair and fu o flesh,
I'm fear'd it be mysel'

– excerpt from *The Ballad of Tam Lin* by Robert Burns

Elphame
~ Alfheim ~
The Golden Court
Spring Court
Seelie Courts
Summer Court
The Court of Blood and Bones
Wildelands
The Gate
The Court of Shadows
The Court of Less
Unseelie Courts
The Hallows
~ Tylwyth ~
Winter Court
Autumn Court

Foreword

Elphame, the land of the Fae, is not without sacrifice.

Every seven years, the Fae pay tithe to the Gods and Goddesses. They sacrifice one member of their courts, priests and priestesses, only the most deserving of an offer to the Gods. Before they are sacrificed, as payment for giving their lives, they are king for seven years. From the day they are chosen for sacrifice to the day they commit themselves to the Underworld, they want for nothing. But the mortal realm, the land outside of Elphame, would not offer sacrifice. They only reaped the rewards of their fertile lands, the rain for their crops, the fish in their nets, children in their bellies, the recompenses of the Fae offerings.

Because of the oaths between Fae and the mortal realm, the Fae could not force mortals to sacrifice one of their own. Fae died every seven years for both worlds to prosper. Soon, to the demise of mankind, Elphame began to refuse an offering to the Gods for the mortals. When the crops of man failed, their fish no longer came and the mortals died of starvation and disease, they agreed to give sacrifice, but only of a halfling bloodline – those birthed of both mortal and Fae blood and seen as lesser in the eyes of mortals.

The Fae, slighted that the mortals would not offer their greatest, their poets and artists, their beautiful and strong, grew angry and vengeful. Since halflings could never rule in Elphame, they would never be called 'kings' or treated as such. Instead, they are Crows, scavenging on the powers and plunders of Elphame, eating the scraps of what Fae have thrown away. The court from which the Crow's line originates is the court that holds the Crow, where they remain for seven years as a sacrifice from the mortal lands, as punishment for reaping reward and offering so little in payment. Upon the death of a Crow, a new Taking begins.

As it has done for decades before and will continue to do for centuries to come, tonight, the Gate has opened once again, spewing Elphame onto the streets of mortals. Solas, leading the Taking, could feel it in his bones, like the fine rusted dust settled on the Gate, the next child of man to be dragged from their home. He could hear the very heartbeat of the next Crow – the pitter-patter of a scared caged cottontail and he the wolf of the night. It was both exhilarating and sickening to feel the fear of another tied so closely to his own heart.

With guilt and hatred hanging heavy on his every step, Solas stalked the streets of Whitwick Gates. Unlike his brethren, he was here for one purpose. He would not dabble in the delights of death, the warmth of a Fae bloodbath. No. He came for the girl. But he knew he would coax her out in whatever hellish ways worked, even if it meant he stood at her door and forced her to see what her delay would cost her people, the suffering life dripping from the hands of creatures, the forced mothers and fathers upon children, the will to live milked from a feeble farmer. Experienced in how very vulnerable mortals were, the Fae would never run dry of ideas. He envied their weakness, their ability to die so quickly. For he could withstand the force of an army without even taking a knee. Mortals were fools to wish for everlasting life, because with it came more life than one bargained for.

His morose loathing blanketed the ground he walked on, casting shadows with each step. Although thick and bloated, his darkness did nothing to dampen the screams of the townspeople. He was birthed for death and war. And yet, he detested the fear that soured the air around him. No matter which side of the Gate he stood, the stench of the dead never appealed to him. To Solas, seven years only went by slowly for the Crow. For him, in every blink of his eye, he was back and Taking another soul, like the devil he knew he was, the devil he had to be. Too much rested on how monstrous he could be, how utterly vile and terrifying he could become. He had nothing but time to perfect his song and dance. That was his curse, after all…to have life everlasting.

"Aoife…" Solas whispered into the night. He felt her heart skip a beat and plunge into her stomach. Her butterflies ran a shiver down Solas' back. Her fear tickled his nose.

He closed his eyes and pushed beyond the stolid dark. His ears twitched at the hint of freight that escaped the Crow's lips. He could sense her desperation, almost taste it, like wafting a fine wine under his nose – a slight whiff of a bottle not yet poured, hinting at what was yet to come. As Crows always had, and likely always would, Solas knew Aoife would test and twist the bindings of her fate until the very last minute. Countless townsfolk would die because one girl would not accept her destiny. They were not brave, nor were they weak of heart. They were, to him, brazen and frail, wishful and so utterly flawed that they died in swaths. They were fools to think they could withstand the torrential force of the Fae. If there had been room for pity, he would feel it for them all. However, there was no space for human emotion when hunting a human.

Prologue

Death rolled in casually, hand in hand with the night. Its purpose hung heavy as a soiled diaper on a lost and starved child. Through the reaching of the fog that crept over the dew-covered ground, its hate slinked along with it and tarnished black every inch it touched. The clouds crawled upon the earth as if the heavens had closed their doors in disgust, leaving mankind to fend for themselves. Even the Gods had turned their backs on the people of Whitwick Gates, the makers of deals with devils. It was no wonder the Gods shut their eyes to our suffering when it was we who had cast our own darkened fates.

Aoife watched as the haze tiptoed around St. Bartholomew's Church. Its hushed footsteps glided around the empty graves of her mother and grandmother. Neither dead matriarch had been returned by the Fae, and both lay dead and twisted on Sidhe land. The markers above their empty graves were nothing more than reminders of why mortals never challenged the Fae, why the Fair Folk came and went as they pleased on the heels of the mists from Elphame. The Sidhe were why mortals feared the dark.

The fog had come again tonight, and its sights were on Aoife's life. She could feel it in her halfling blood. She could do nothing to stop it, as so many had tried and failed in the past. And so, she waited and watched the fog suck the sun from the earth, leaving barely enough light for the shadows. Whether Aoife liked it or not, the night would come, and under its spell, everything in Whitwick Gates would fall prey to its delights, to the sheer pleasures of the abominations called the Fae. As the fog moved, even the moon and stars cowered behind a dense layer of cloud, protecting their eyes from the unfolding night. The air held a tincture to the world before a storm, but it would not be the kind of squall you could simply close the shutters to. No, this storm was anything but the tempest in the wind. The gale rolling over Whitwick Gates carried fate at its fingertips. The destiny of Aoife, the death of many – they would become the puppets of the Fae. Aoife was not yet eighteen, and she knew she, like the other half-blooded in her village, could be selected by the Fae. She'd rather be one of the slaughtered.

Aoife's ears became sharper, like the knife she held in her left hand with cramped fingers. The blade stretched her flesh until her dripping blood echoed against the wooden floor. Each snap of a twig was an aide-memoire, a painful reminder that she stood in her home utterly alone. It was the type of alone that not even the devil himself could instill in your bones. There were no terrors, real or figment, aside from Fae, who could construct such a hell on earth, where death was the mercy.

In the distance, scrapes and scratches were of a predator she knew she couldn't possibly battle against. Every new aroma charged her mind with the most dreadful thing she could think of. As she breathed in the odors, her body prepared for flight, even though it knew she stood no chance against whatever rolled in with the fog. Aoife commanded her feet to be steady, to freeze her on the spot. Running from the safety of her home would surely mean death in a thousand unspeakable ways—or worse, being left to live. She could hear her fellow townspeople run to that very fate, their Fae-drunk laughter cut short, followed by terror and needless, sloppy death. If she didn't die tonight, the screams of her kin would haunt her until her last days. All she could do was wait out the inevitable. The moment she had dreamed for years would come, long before she knew the difference between the waking and dreaming worlds, was waiting in the darkness. The night, printed in the books of destiny, had been set to unfold long before Aoife had been born.

If the Gods allowed her to wait out the blackness still yet to come and bring dawn to her still-beating heart, she would have saved her line for another seven years. Aoife prayed to the Goddesses and Gods for the morning to come. Her heart hammered in her chest. The muscles in her thighs twitched with the need to find a place to hide. But she had been prepared for the moment she now stood in, and her heart could pound all it wanted. She had no plans to move from her home until daybreak. She wished she were braver and could step outside, freely leaving with the Fae and saving the rest of her people, but fear kept her rooted in place. The horrors beyond her walls had stripped away any semblance of bravado from her bones, leaving behind only foolish desperation and wishes that wouldn't come true.

With only the smallest of fires in her hearth to warm her, the darkness allowed Aoife's mind to conjure the worst of magical beasts moving outside her window. They moved to music only they could hear—some graceful, some with two left feet, some dragging their bodies, others soaring through the skies like the dragons of tales long forgotten. She watched through the leaded windows as they moved in unnatural ways, with limps and missing limbs, hunched over or too tall to see their shoulders. They were the beasts of the dreams that had plagued her since she had been old enough to know what crept in the darkness. Her mortal father, not the creature who helped birth her, warned her from sharing her thoughts and dreams with the Lords and Ladies of Whitwick Gates for fear of being named a witch—an accusation that came with fire and stones. Halflings could never announce their happening, who they were or they'd be killed on sight, blamed for what their full-blooded brethren did—blame they so deserved, for they were the halflings that kept the Fae coming. Half-Fae blood kept the gates open. Fear of consequence kept Aoife from warning others, while the guilt of her knowledge kept her soul twisting. She could only watch and pray to the Gods that the Fae would spare her and her child. But she wasn't a fool. The Gods were not that generous nor that forgiving of wickedness.

Each moment passed slower than the last. Aoife stayed hidden within the darkness of her home, alone. Her father was gone, trampled by a horse ridden by a small child in a dreamlike state, not but three hours previous. Aoife had sent her daughter away, just moments after her birth, in preparation for the night the fog came. It was a sacrifice more significant than she had imagined. It ripped her soul in two. But to keep her daughter this close to the Gate of the Fae would undoubtedly be the death of Aoife's line in one fell swoop. If the Fae spared the child from their own hands, Aoife had seen a mother drown her baby, a father beat his children to death. Aoife didn't know what was worse, having the Fae kill the child or having the magick of Elphame force a parent to become the executioner. Aoife, like other halflings, was less susceptible to the pull of Elphame magick, but she still felt it, always heard the whispers and fought against the nudge to fall into madness. She felt guilty for saving her daughter and allowing every other child to face a fate reserved for devils and demons, but she couldn't protect them.

The night started with the death of the man who'd raised her, the death of her child's father, the longing to see her daughter one last time and the end of her lifelong friend, Abelia. Both Aoife and Abelia had been born on the same day, bound together until the end by friendship and sisterhood. Their souls were tied together by an unspoken truth. Their fathers were both Fae, the same man.

Aoife's pulse throbbed in her ears. She felt every beat as it radiated down her body and into the ground at her feet. The stillness of her home surrendered to the deathly screams of her neighbors. The fear in their voices and last cries had painted her body in a thin and cold chill. Aoife watched out of her front window as her community ripped each other apart. Violence erupted, man turned on man, animals rebelled and wives, mothers and sisters ran through the streets in fear. Crazed mothers drowned their babies, and horses carelessly tossed children from their backs. Watching the shadows with many legs, Aoife trembled at the sounds erupting from her village as it burned by their own hands. Chaos happened every time the Fae were near, when they came to collect their newest Crow.

From every corner of her house, Aoife could hear the creatures of the fog trying to get inside. Although she was scared, she knew not a single twisted finger could enter her home. She had spent years preparing, guarding against the strangers in the night. Her doorway, lined in cold iron, an expense she had carried by working on two farms and selling jams and cheeses at the weekend market, offered Aoife safety that no other in her village had. Each window held chimes made of old iron nails, decorated with herbs to ward against those who now sought to enter. Horseshoes covered every entrance and were fixed tightly to every corner. Around Aoife's neck was Abelia's necklace of blackberry stems, ivy and rowan. Built into the very foundation, walls and roofing were constructed of boxwood. The magick within her walls made her skin crawl, like tiny spiders dancing upon her flesh, but she was only half of what crawled through her village.

Aoife's ears twitched at the calling of her name. It was carried over the wind and pushed under her front door. Adrenaline flooded her system, forcing her muscles into a twitchy dance. She could taste saliva thickening on her tongue and feel beads of sweat trickle down her brow. Her heart pumped like a bird trying to escape the clutches of a cat. Aoife's eyes widened with horror, yet she forced herself to remain where she was. There was only one thing she had left to do, and that was pray she didn't die before sunrise, pray the outcome would not leave her body open for the birds. Every seven years, they taunted her. Every seven years, she thought it was her time.

"Aoifeeeeeeee..."

Her name drawn out, like an echo down the corridor of a cave, snaked down her spine. It slid under the door and crawled up her legs. With each step back she took, the anxiety in her stomach began to climb, and the voice deep within her gut started to panic. It told her to run, cower and hide from the monsters.

The air around her turned soupy, too thick to breathe. A glossy sheen glazed Aoife's eyes, but she dared not close them. Her thoughts scattered like a storm inside her head. All she could think of was failing and that not being an option. Her mind and soul were being torn in two. *Run, stay. Hide, fight. Live, die.*

"Aoifeeeeeeee..."

Again...her name on the wind. This time, it whipped against her body with force. The pain started as an unpleasant warmth, like standing a few inches too close to a fire—uncomfortable but tolerable for a moment. With the heat came nausea, just enough for her to move to the table for support. Whitwick Gates didn't produce cravens or cowards. In the harshest of conditions, whether frigid cold or missing more meals than healthy, Whitwick Gates allowed only the strongest to survive. Aoife had prized herself on her ability to ignore pain and muster, regardless of a limp or illness. But for the briefest of moments, Aoife clutched her table and breathed deeply, bending slightly to the pain. The tightness in her chest reminded her of being kicked by her father's horse. She ran her fingers over an engraving on her table, carved by her mother long before Aoife's birth—*Eagla aon rud, iontaobhas aon duine*. 'Fear nothing, trust no one.'

Aoife held a hand over her mouth and swallowed the vomit in her throat. She clamped her eyelids tightly against the bullish force of panic in her gut and steadied her nerves. Silent tears ran past her blistering hot cheeks and dropped to the floor with as much a sound as the silent agony she'd felt when she'd given her daughter away. She hadn't screamed. She'd known what she had to do. Two halflings together attracted far too much attention. She also knew that she could mourn when the sun came up again if she were blessed.

Aoife would be the first of her line to cleave the Gate's magick and start the closing. She would force the Fae back into their realm, force them to suffer their oaths as the mortals had. Abelia had given her life to the spell, a sacrifice surely worth the notice of the Gods and Goddesses. Like Abelia, Aoife was willing to die for the spell to protect the next generation, her daughter and daughter's daughter. Like Abelia, Aoife would give her life to ensure the gates would close.

As the door opposite her slowly creaked against a thunderous wind, a narrow stream of moonlight graciously wandered through the room. The door splintered at the lock and finally gave way and allowed the night a full view of Aoife, who stood clutching her cold iron knife. Aoife wasn't too proud to show her fear. She knew the sweat that clung to her body would have been a dead giveaway. It took her several blinks to remember to breathe and release her chest's dread. Her stand against the Fae would be for nothing had she passed out, starved of air.

Aoife listened to the many footsteps outside her home. Each second seemed to last a lifetime. The rocks crushing underfoot had muted the pounding of her heart in her ears. Against the backdrop of the night and burning of her village, he stood, the man who haunted her dreams. His many arms melted away before her eyes. One of the creatures of Elphame, one of the most terrifying of Elphame, stood in the doorway.

He stood tall, his skin the color of fresh milk, pale as the moon, like the creature he was. His eyes, ever vigilant, like a snake seeking its prey, buried into her soul. He blinked his black eyes, the long lashes, momentarily covering the glint in them. The air around him seemed to slither and ooze from one place to the next, as though his very soul was skulking in his black shadows. His unnaturally long tendril-like fingers clasped at his front, the tips looked like a parasitic plant, twitching and reaching. Each movement of his body was slow and expert, as if he had no bones at all. And in an instant, a slight movement in his shoulders had locked away the hell found in the pits of his eyes and brought out a charm Aoife feared more.

"Aoife," he finally spoke. "Good evening, Crow."

He held no knife that Aoife could see, but still, she felt the chill of metal against her throat, against the hammering of her pulse, a promise of what he could do if given a chance. Aoife could hear her breathing over the chaos outside. The salty sweat from her brow stung her eyes as it trickled down. She blinked away the saltiness and hoped that she'd wake and the day would be a dream, her father would be at the table with breakfast, her partner would be stoking the fire, her daughter on her lap and her friend would be waiting at the Gate with spells of fortification. But no number of blinks could remove the man at her door or the fear of ending up nothing more than mangled limbs and rotting flesh, one more failed attempt to rid this realm of horror.

Aoife cleared her throat. She had known it would be he who came for her. "Solas, I have been waiting for you. Have you stooped so low as to do the bidding for the king? Which are you today, light or dark, good or evil? You have far too many faces for me to keep track of."

"Good or evil? Who is to say the night is evil and the sun shines in goodness?" He smiled and, for a moment, laughed. Aoife would have thought him to be handsome when he smiled in any other situation. "You have no idea what good or evil truly is, halfling. Your small mind and shorter lifespan couldn't begin to comprehend either in their truest form. Some are born good and turn bad, and vice versa—as is said for you and your kind."

Aoife knew the Fae could tell no lies, but they were fluent in riddles and stories that talked circles around the truth. "You didn't answer my question."

"Little Aoife, you, yourself, do not understand the question you are asking. One cannot be completely good unless one possesses the ability to be fully evil. Good and bad are a choice one makes at the moment. But one must have free will to choose. And that is not something I have. Therefore, I am neither, for I've chosen neither," he answered as he leaned his shoulder into the doorframe, crossed his arms and propped an ankle over the other. His appearance shrank slightly, and his eyes brightened. He looked less frightening, like a rabid wolf would if he could smile before chowing down on your flock.

Solas tested the threshold and pulled his foot back. "My, my, for someone who ought not to know about our coming tonight, you are awfully prepared for me to be at your door. Which little birdie has given you the gift of knowing? I've always suspected little Abelia and her loose tongue."

Aoife smiled. He didn't know Abelia had taken her life yet. But he would know soon enough. "I've known about this moment my entire life, as you've so kindly pointed out my halfling blood. The villagers may never feel you're coming, but my line will never forget. I know how this day will unfold. I see your failures as well as I see the mist at your feet."

"We shall see what fate has in store for us all, for not even you can see what wicked plans she has."

"You may kill me eventually, but I will stain your world with my blood."

"Many support the killing of your kind, halfling, but I am not one of them. I've always been far too curious to vote on your deaths. I rather enjoy these little strolls." Solas' words did not sound kind. They felt like a warning. *One word and my line could end with his vote.*

His smile made her stomach roll. Aoife wasn't a fool any more than she was a coward. He would win no friends in her household, no matter how buttery his words were, for even the devil could be charming. As the man tried to win her affection, Aoife could feel her courage in the form of sweat drenching her skin. It danced down her spine and threatened to run out of the back door. Her village's screaming was eaten by the fog that pressed at the man's back. Aoife knew her fears were her greatest challenge and her devil to slay, for if she gave into them, those devils would come, too.

"Devil," Aoife whispered. "You are not welcome here."

His head tilted to the side, and he grinned. "The only difference between an angel and a devil is one's intentions. I can be both and neither, for the intentions, here this night, are not my own."

"You are no angel or God."

"I would not say those words any louder. You may bruise the egos of many. It wasn't that long ago that we roamed free to do as we pleased. And so many wish for those days once again." Solas sighed as if he had had this argument many times before me. "Lest you forget, you are closer to my kind than those of this community. Now, remove your wards, or I shall remove them for you. I have a great many things to finish before this night is over."

He said the words as casually as passing the salt. It was Aoife's turn to grin. "You will not. You will not touch me. If I am to become the next Crow, you cannot harm me. Your need for me only protects me. Without halflings, your realm has no one who can walk between worlds on a whim, no one to keep the Gate open. We witches provide you with the freedoms you've taken advantage of."

"Witches? Is that what you're calling yourselves now, halfling?" Solas mocked her.

"We have many names. This is true," she responded.

"No matter, it does little to protect you or your lands," he countered. "How many shall die for your bravery? How many children do we take for the sake of your own life? Shall I tell them why their fate is death and who holds the blame?"

"Do your worst, but you will not have me." Aoife threw the knife at his feet, and it plunged into the wood floor and wobbled. Like Aoife, the knife held firm. "And since you cannot take me unwillingly or the Gate will close the moment I step through, go back to where you came from, Fae. I am not a willing sacrifice."

"Foolish child, I can take what I please. It is your choice to die at the Gate or to step through. But the sacrifice will be made whether your heart still beats on the other side or not. The longer you wait, the more of your people will die. It is as simple as that. Their deaths are on your hands. It is up to you how many must die for your bravery." He took a shuddered breath. Aoife could feel it dance across her skin in excitement. He wanted her to take all the time in the world. He was Fae. Death was all he knew. "You cannot possibly know how this show ends, wee witch. If you believe nothing I say, believe this. You will go to Elphame one way or another. It is your fate. The only difference will be how many of your people you will sentence to death before you go. It is the oath forged so many moons ago, one Crow—and an oath I'd be delighted if you broke. Break the oath, and the Gate comes down."

"If you so wish for the oaths to be broken, why the force?" Aoife asked. Although she understood the treaty between the Sidhe and the mortals, she would stall for as long as possible.

Solas spread his arms and feigned a half bow, his eyes never leaving Aoife. "As the king commands, so shall it be."

"You should not have come. You have failed your people and squandered your favors on crossing the Gate." Aoife stared the man in the eyes and straightened her spine. "I am warning you, Solas, leave before your failure costs your people. Leave and never come back. You do not want me. I'll bring you damnation, I promise as much."

Solas grinned. "Aoife, there is nothing you could do that we haven't done to each other thousands of times before. There is no power greater than Fae."

"You will feel the burn for the seven years I am your Crow, Solas. Choose wisely." She stepped back into her salt circle, lined with pieces of her life, a leaf found on her grandmother's headstone, twigs gathered after a storm, one stone from the foundation of her church and a crystal owed by her mother. The next sacrifice would be great, but Abelia had paid the dues to the Goddesses but hours ago. A blood sacrifice so great, it cost Abelia her life. She kept Solas talking, waiting out the time it would take for the spell to fall into place. She could feel the moon at its highest point in the night's sky.

"Time is but a blink to me. It means nothing," he replied. Even though he held little emotion on his face, Aoife could see the turmoil festering in the black pools of his eyes. Seven years as their Crow may go by in a blink for the Fae, but his failure would make each hour she felt count for something. The cursed creatures of Elphame would pay as dearly as she had.

"Mother, send your power strong and white and weave a web of blooming light. Grandmother, send your power strong and red and weave into my strand of a simple thread. Goddesses cast the circle around me black and weave it into the wisdom that I lack. Elements, I call on you to protect this nook from wandering eyes and their prying look." Aoife held a red thread, knotted and woven with her hair and twigs. A witch's ladder started nine days before the fog. Each night, Aoife tied a new knot and prayed hard enough to bruise her knees.

"You will force an outcome you do not desire, nor do I," Solas spoke over the wind. His words clung in the air, coming to a coiled rest inside Aoife's stomach, tasting of vomit.

"You, Solas, have forced this outcome."

He nodded once. "I will see you before the sun rises, and you will come willingly. You forget, little witch, you are not the only halfling on this side of the Gate. We do not need you alive to maintain it. You will mark yourself for all times as an oath breaker."

From deep within, a storm raged, charged by her words and her truth, her rage and destiny coming full circle. From every pore, she burst with the wind of her anger. It was a madness that destroyed ships and reduced men to ash. It came hard and fast and burst through her home with a demolishing effect. It smashed her books and paintings and dishes. It hit the creature at her door and pushed him to his back. Her front door slammed shut and sealed Aoife inside. Her ears rang in the sudden silence. A high-pitched hum told her magick was in the air and charged by her words. It would move through Whitwick Gates until every creature had been marked by it.

Aoife waited out the hours until just before the sun rose from the safety of her home. She could not risk opening her door to those begging for protection, scratching at her door. They were dragged away as they prayed for shelter. To let them in meant to let in the threat of death at the hands of her neighbors. She sat on her floor and wrote out the happenings in Whitwick Gates—what is yet to come, what must come next. She sat and waited for fate to provide the seal against the destiny she knew she could not escape with the rising of a new sun. She waited for the spell to sit firmly against the marrow in her bones. Many died while she waited, but the sacrifice of 'now' was needed or there would not be a 'later' to protect. She calmed herself, knowing that she had done everything she could do. She sacrificed all that was hers to give. With tears in her eyes, she weaved a curse. No Crow would ever return from Elphame. No Crow would return and birth future halflings. The spell would curse Elphame and their ability to come and go as they pleased. As the halfling line died out, the Fae magick on this side of the Gate would fade in years to come, weakening the link to the human realm.

Once she left the human realm, Aoife knew she'd never see her daughter again. She'd never see her grow and would not be able to protect her from becoming a Crow. But she also knew that only a spell strong enough would frighten the Fae and make her line, the Darkmore line, less desirable for the Taking. Creating fear of the Darkmore bloodline was the only way to protect generations not yet born. And so she penned her final goodbye, a warning to those who have not yet come.

My dearest children and grandchild and greats,

We are the Crows, the halflings, the sacrifices for mankind.

The Seven-Year Crow, a Taking of one halfling for seven years, is our payment for peace.

We are the Teind for the mortal world.

This night, I will have changed the course of destiny, our oath to Elphame. No Crow will place a halfling within the human realm upon their return, for no Crow shall ever return. When there are no halflings left, the Gate shall close for all times, for the Fae realm cannot sacrifice a full-blooded human.

Aoife placed her witch's ladder inside the envelope and added the prayer, hoping it would help the next generation or generations to come who would need to seal the Gate. She chanted the words as she scrawled them on her parchment.

With knot one, the spell has begun.
With knot two, my heart is true.
With knot three, so mote it be.
With knot four, the Gate is restored.
With knot five, our people shall thrive.
With knot six, the Gate spell is fixed.
With knot seven, their powers will not lessen.
With knot eight, this spell is our fate.

Before the sun touched the self-inflicted war in Whitwick Gates, Solas stood at her door. Aoife knew her end had come. She had seen it as clearly as she could see the tears puddle on the floor at her knees. Aoife stood, grabbed her sack and opened the door. Solas held Aoife's newly born daughter. She was not surprised and knew the child would be unharmed. They wanted her, not the baby. A baby was of no use to them, for they could not endure torture long enough for the Fae not to feel cheated. However, if Aoife did not step outside, the child would be dead before hitting the ground, as would everyone within Whitwick Gates. Aoife's reluctance to leave was posturing, buying time. Even if the spell didn't work, she'd have gone with the Fae, if only to save her community and child.

"End this now," Aoife spoke. Her words were as firm as her resolve.

"Your word, you will uphold the oath?" Solas asked, and Aoife nodded.

She knew she didn't have to say the words out loud to be held to the agreement. Solas snapped his fingers, and the fog and everything that lingered within it was gone as if pulled back into Elphame with force. Solas handed the child to Aoife, and Aoife placed the child on the doorstep and grabbed onto the hand of fate…Solas. In as much time as it takes to form a regret, Aoife was gone from Whitwick Gates, wrapped in darkness, to take up the position of Crow among her full-blooded brethren.

As Aoife moved through the Gate, she caught a glimpse of a young girl who stood opposite her. The girl had the hair of Aoife's mother and the eyes of Aoife's grandmother. She was like looking in the mirror—if the mirror had added years of terror to her eyes and a wariness that only war could bring. Her sadness added a hint of salt to the air and rolled across Aoife's lips.

"Who are you?" the girl asked, a voice as familiar as Aoife's own.

"Aoife," she answered. She reached out to the girl. "Trust no one."

The girl smiled. "You can trust Solas."

Aoife nodded. She trusted the girl she'd known for mere moments. She'd carry the girl with her until the end of her days. It felt like Aoife had all the time known to man to stand and watch the young girl but was ripped away long before she was ready. With a soured stomach, Aoife stepped through the Gate into Elphame. Never would she see her home again. With the breath ripped from her lungs, Solas whisked her from the Gates, wrapped painfully in his darkness.

"We will always find a way around the magick of man. You've done nothing more than make your stay in Elphame a little less comfortable. You will live a very long life here. Seven Elphame years is a long time, Crow," Solas said before pushing Aoife to her knees in front of the king. As Aoife crumpled, her knife sliced the hand of Solas and washed over Aoife's skin. The final spell snapped into place. A sacrifice from both worlds.

"With the knot of nine, the cost is mine. So mote it be." Aoife's words seeped from her lips as the Gate slammed shut and echoed their fates through the golden chambers of Elphame. It clanged like a bell for all to hear. No Crow shall ever return to the human realm. With each new Taking, the Fae would eat away at the halflings until there were no lines left to take from. Eventually, the halfling blood would dwindle. Her hope was to end the Taking, and her sacrifice was that she'd give her life and the future of her line, to ensure it would end.

The cost of the curse was Aoife's life, forever trapped inside Elphame. She looked into Solas' eyes as he realized what she had done. "I've seen your future. I truly hope time is but a blink to you, because fate has other plans for us."

Solas looked down at Aoife. "Aoife, time means nothing to me. I am as much a part of your fate as you are of mine."

"You have no idea." Aoife closed her eyes and thought of the child in the fog. "It may take centuries, but I have loosed the very darkness of all Elphame, and together, they will eat your cursed world."

Solas grinned. His words whispered over her soul for only her to hear. "I'm counting on it."

Chapter One

Whitwick Gates was nothing more than a skeleton of what it once had been. Its bones were stripped of flesh long ago by battles fought and lost, and the dead long buried and forgotten. It was a war that never ended but was fed often enough for it to quiet and allow the town to rebuild once again.

In a place that never changed, nothing ever felt the same. Death did that to places where it strangled their children more often than not. It had hung its hat in Whitwick many years before and waited, comfortable in the respite we rarely gave it. It was always there, always plotting, and was always sated in the end. You couldn't starve Death. He ate his fill no matter how hard you prayed or bargained. Our demise went cheek by jowl with the coming of the Fae. It always had and always would. The mortal realm's fate was to pay tithe to Gods who never cared much for mankind. Our God had left so long ago that none of us could remember His name. I didn't blame Him. Most of us didn't. We'd have left this hellhole if given half the chance, too.

Instead, we tried to forget. But it was hard to ignore when each time the fog came, it reminded us we could never really disregard the fate of our little town and its young, those the Fae would pick and choose from. But halflings, half of this world and half of theirs, were cursed with the knowing. We were always aware of when our time was coming for the Taking, but none spoke it aloud. Saying the words felt too close to blasphemy, offering ourselves, guaranteeing we would be next. It was tantamount to cursing the God who wasn't here, to begin with. Whether we said the words or not, the Fae always came to collect their Crow, and when they did, the town filled the hat of death to the brim with souls who died in vain.

The fog came that Sunday morning when Mr. Grant, the local priest, cut an entire cord of firewood, as he did every Sunday before church—the wood he often donated to the widows of Whitwick every winter. Warm widows meant a packed church. That was the only reason people still went into the House of God. It had nothing to do with being saved by the All-Mighty. No one could protect us in Whitwick, not even our God.

Today, Father Grant started with his dog, Harold. When Mrs. Grant woke to the noise and went outside to see the commotion, she, too, kissed the ax wielded by Father Grant and became part of row number four. Her purple hair curlers hooked on the wood in row five. The firewood, stacked in its ramshackle way, had become damp and red from the hound and Mrs. Grant. As I learned of the events at the farm, I remember thinking it would stink to high heaven once flame touched the hair this winter. Never would I say out loud the cause. I would ignore the heavy haze resting over our town, just like everyone else.

The backyard frenzy had attracted the neighbors from across the field. But by the time they had gotten to the Grant Farm, Mr. Grant was pouring himself a drink, not a drop of blood in sight. Mr. Grant, the God-fearing man he was, never drank, but this morning was different. The air on the farm faintly smelled of drink, sugarcane, clover and a butcher's block. Father Grant was kind enough to offer the Thompson boys a glass of their own. Reaching for a drink, Mr. Thompson saw what the morning fog had brought in. All farms smelled of meat and death, but firewood didn't wear purple hair curlers, nor did they wear a dog collar with fur still attached. I was told it was the curlers that tipped off Mr. Thompson and not the intestines holding the cord of wood in place. It's weird, the things we notice when our little piece of the world is off kilter, when we choose not to believe one of the town's children would suffer a fate worse than Mrs. Grant, like the color of hair curlers or the number of times intestines can wrap around a cord of wood.

I had heard about the Grant Farm from Mary Jane Hilliard, the local gossip, the promised one. She was the one we never thought would ever go to the Fae. Each time the Fae came, she always received a free pass, as her father was Captain of the Guardians, the Gate guards. The Fae, however horrible they may be, were selective in what wars they were willing to pick. Mary hadn't once felt the terror of their coming. I couldn't bring myself to hate her, though. Most of the town would give anything to have the same freedom as she had, and we'd trade the neighbor's children for it. Mary rang up my purchase at the local shop, telling the farm's gory tale as if she weren't speaking of people who had always baked cookies and sweets for us children. She was more interested in being the first to know than being the first to sympathize.

While it made my gut twist, I didn't connect it to the curse of Whitwick, of being a halfling—not then, anyway. Ignorance is bliss, and we in Whitwick tried to remain oblivious for as long as possible. It kept us sane. It allowed us to pretend we didn't know the next child who would be Taken, and that child wouldn't be from our line. It allowed us to live when our time could be up at any moment. After every Taking, we ignored their absence, save one day each year, marking their anniversary when they entered the Sidhe. We said it was to celebrate that they were still alive in Elphame, since the Fae hadn't come for another. But deep down, we celebrated another year a new child hadn't become a Crow. We were a morbid bunch to the core.

In my seventeen years, I had learned a number of truths in Whitwick Gates. One, people are rarely as sorry as they should be, and many of us here had a lot to be sorry about after the fog came and went. And second, the Fae made you realize number one in the most creative of ways. And three, as a Darkmore Witch, I was sure the town was going to hell in a handbasket, weighed down by a fog I knew was coming. I could try to ignore it all I wanted, but I could feel it in my bones. Hell would be loosed upon our town. The Fae would see to it. They always did. They always would.

I had read all the Darkmore journals and had believed enough of the Whitwick folklores to know that no one had ever survived a Taking, the becoming of a Seven-Year Crow, since my greatest of grans had woven the curse that made the Gate to Elphame a one-way street for Crows. Only stories passed down through the halfling lines survived intact, and there weren't many halfling lines left. Soon, the stories would fade, with no one left to tell them.

Long ago, Crows who returned were never whole again, not entirely. Their minds were broken. They birthed halflings upon their return, against their will, and faded into a bottle of hysteria. Drink was the only sanity they could find. They needed constant supervision so they didn't end their lives. I thought it would have been merciful to allow them an end, but my vote didn't count. I was just a child, old enough to die but too young to speak of death. But since Crows could no longer return and didn't live out their seven years, the Fae came every year. Their coming more frequent was a punishment for a curse made to protect the rest of us.

We had Guardians to send back the stranglers—Fae, who managed to get across the Gate between the Taking. And there were plenty who tried. Whitwick was home to many Fae who had escaped the clutches of Elphame. That should have told us all we needed to know about where the Crows were sent, if their own people were too scared to stay there. But no one spoke of it. It was easier to pretend than it was to know the fates of our children. It was easier to ignore than imagine.

I had dreamed of this day, every moment of it, from waking this morning, to the reaction I'd have when learning of our priest hacking his family to bits. While Harold and Mrs. Grant were becoming a ghost story to tell every time you lit a fire or burned your hair, a small yappy terrier was mauled by an orange feral cat. The terrier was scattered across the lawn at the school. Today was not the first day that cat had attacked another being, and I was sure it wouldn't be the last. But with two happenings in one day, I started to pay attention, however unwilling I had been to think of it. It was like a hangnail you tried to ignore but kept snagging it just the same. With enough force, you'd tear down to the bone.

This would only be the beginning. The knowledge of what the rest of the day had in store for us tickled the back of my brain like an aneurism about to blow. But even then, with a dog scattered across a once-pristine lawn, I tried to ignore the horror coming to our fair town. It was how things were done here. We pretended like everything is fine, even when staring death in the eyes, which we did every day. But today, it was harder to ignore, given the sun rose to the fog and its devilish delights. No matter how hard I held my breath, I could smell it coming.

The fog was the telltale sign the Sidhe had opened, and the Fae would be close on its heels. They had one day to do their worst, and they did. And if the Crow died before the Fae could collect, they'd simply select a different one. There was never any winning or circumventing an oath with the Fae. We wouldn't be free of the Taking until the Taking took place. The Guardians could do very little during this time to protect us. The agreement between our kind and theirs had limited what we could. So, each time the Gate opened, it was business as usual, and we were all up for grabs. Life is a bitch when it has no value.

Before I was halfway home, the town's only twin sisters jumped from the roof of their house, both smiling and flapping their arms as though they could master their plummet to the ground. The teacher's pigeons escaped and were now nothing more than glossy red pillow fill. In unison, they flew into the front of two big windows. Just before their untimely death, they were seen flying with the sisters, right up until they landed headfirst onto a freshly red-bricked pathway. Up until that moment, I thought the red brick looked a little too macabre, but now I'd agree with the color choice. When the sun rose tomorrow, the stain on the brick wouldn't be as noticeable.

Whitwick had been built on legends, stories that were passed down from generation to generation. The hills crawled, the fog killed, creatures hunted, magick was real, and at any moment, you could die—or worse, be Taken. Most were stories to tell children to get them into bed on time. But the terrible ones, the ones that scared children the most, were as true as the bird flies. The stories that I hung onto from my childhood, spoke of the day we'd be free of the Taking. But those were fairytales, stories from old women long forgotten, nothing more. Still, I had always hoped we'd skip a Taking, that somehow they'd forget and stop coming altogether. But they never did...and never would. The Fae never forgot, even when we tried to. For three hundred and fifty-four days a year, we could pretend. And if that's all you've got, then that's what you did.

The thought that I could be next sent a shiver skittering down my spine. I was so close to being free. In almost one month, I would turn eighteen and no longer be at risk of being pulled into Elphame. The Fae never took adults. They would only take what was of most value to man, their children. In weeks, I would leave Whitwick, leave the Gate. When I returned, I'd be a Guardian and would protect the next generation of potential Crows.

Halflings always returned to Whitwick. The Gate, Elphame, called to us as fish to water and birds to the air. Elphame, to halflings, could be felt in the soul and very marrow of our bones. It promised freedoms and life forever. If you were quiet enough, you could hear it sing softly, pulling you toward it. None of us listened, and none of us were stupid enough to answer the calling. There were no promises in Elphame that a human or halfling could endure. Nothing from the mortal realm could withstand the Fae or their delights. But every now and again, a halfling would go off the dead-end and claw out their eyes and ears, trying to make it stop. They'd be found delirious by the Guardians at the border to the Gate, caked in dried blood, finally given in to the call. Those souls were usually locked up shortly after, too crazed to be left on their own.

As I walked down the sidewalk, the same route I had taken for years, in a town that had always felt the same, I passed the same haunted houses with their tenth coat of paint. I chewed the candy my father said smelled of times he'd rather forget. He never liked sugar or the smell of it. As typical the day was, save the carnage that was just as characteristic for Whitwick as the rain or the fear lining the eyes of the elders, I couldn't keep my mind adrift. It kept pulling back to the corner store and the fear held back by Mary Jane Hilliard's casual smile and perpetually cheerful voice. Hearing her voice tipping on the edge of fear had sent a shiver up my spine. I knew the Fae were close when I could see the careful lie of Whitwick melt from Mary's eyes, replaced with knowing it was almost time. When we stopped pretending, the façade was over. None of us wanted the curtains to fall on our second-rate show.

With each step, paranoia started to coat my skin with sweat. I watched the smaller Fae, who were always here, scurry through the yards, seeking shelter. Fae glamour didn't work on me as it did the others, leaving me the only one to see the warning. I glanced over my shoulder, unable to shake the feeling of being watched. The pit of my stomach twisted into a knot. The hairs on my arms stood ready for a pending assault. I didn't need the Guardian's bells to sound for me to know the Fae were about to cross the Gate. I felt it as my heart palpitated, like a tiny marching army across my ribcage.

The town looked as it always had, as it ever would—just trying to get by, knowing their young could be Taken at any moment. But out of the corner of my eye, I could see a thin veil of fog. Each time I focused my eyes directly on it, it was gone as though it had never been. I could feel the haze tickle the hairs on the back of my neck. Its coolness stuck to my skin like I had already run from it and failed. My stomach clenched, knotted in a burning warning. My muscles twitched in anticipation. My body knew, my heart knew, but my soul begged for another day.

Standing not thirty feet to my left was a man from Elphame. Faolan stood with his hands on his hips. He was powerful enough to cross between our realms, with or without the Gate opening. He wasn't like the other Fae. Although my father would say different, he didn't want the Gate between Elphame and the mortal world to remain open. Faolan's father had helped the first Darkmore Witch escape Elphame to Whitwick Gates before the oaths between our worlds had been forged. I had kept my friendship with Faolan a secret for fear the town would hang me, for fear of my father's anger. The Guardians hanged Fae sympathizers, and those who befriended a Fae were as good as dead. Oddly enough, there were many followers of Fae, a surplus of fools with misplaced trust. And so, there were also regular hangings. I didn't attend, not because I was still a child, but because I couldn't stomach pointless death. Whitwick suffered enough at the hands of Fae. Why we were driven to kill our own, I didn't understand and didn't care to.

Faolan only showed up in the open like this when something was wrong. As I turned to walk toward him, he shook his head and pointed toward my house. I glanced down the road, saw nothing and turned back to him. I frowned in confusion.

"Run!" His word carried over the still air and pushed my shoulders.

The bells finally chimed. Their ring carried over the hills and into the valley of Whitwick Gates. The Guardians, Gate watchers, the mortal army, sounded the alarms to warn the people of Whitwick that Fae had crossed the Gate. But I didn't need the bells to know. I had felt them coming. When the chimes echoed, I ran like everyone else. But unlike everyone else, I knew there would be no place I could hide. There never was.

Whether I could hide or not, outside was not where I wanted to be when the full force of the fog came. I learned this the hard way years ago when I spent four hours in a corn maze chased by leprechauns. Up until that moment, I hadn't known just how utterly terrifying a leprechaun could be. If it weren't for the small gifts of magick I had and Faolan, I'd have never made it home. When the spell came back threefold, I puked for hours. Nothing is free, not even my blood right. The cost of magick, if too great, would take my life in return. I didn't use it unless I absolutely had to.

I sped my legs up before my brain registered the run I had sprung into. My bowels quaked in fear. I had learned to trust Faolan over the years. He was righter than rain and never led me down a dark and twisted path that ended with me dead—not yet, but the day was young, and there was always a first time. Which, consequently, would be the last time. I wouldn't care, though, because I'd be dead, and the dead don't care about much and can't complain, even if they did.

More than the warnings from Faolan, my gut told me to run. I trusted my instincts more than anything, given the number of times I hadn't given them a second thought and had come close to death at the hands of the Fae. Faolan had kept me from death, the times I thought I was braver or smarter. Mortals never were, not when it came to what Elphame could deliver onto us.

I had felt the very moment the Gate opened and Elphame called out. As the Gate slid across the earth, it filled the air with its magick, like talons dragged along my bones. I sensed the Fae right down to my marrow. Hell was coming fast and nipping at my heels. The town was about to twist and turn into something grotesque and unrecognizable. Before the fog would end, I knew, at exactly six in the morning, which is when Mr. Grant had started on his woodpile, I would see my town burn once again. When the Fae came to play their games, it was nothing short of a nightmare of bodies and screaming, where none of us knew the rules or how to play. Even if we did, we never won.

For me, this would not end in the morning. It would never end for me. I would always be a witch, a halfling, and would feel them coming. If I were spared the Taking, I would spend the rest of my life fighting off the power of Elphame whenever they came. I would watch my neighbors kill each other, drunk on Fae, and I would struggle not to join in. None of us were truly safe—not me, not my neighbors, not the babes in their mothers' bellies.

Through the fog, over the screaming, I could hear the laughter, the contemptuous shrill of enjoyment at our demise. The stench of sugar cane came on the wind, along with my name. We always heard our names.

Sometimes for a game, and other times, you were named the Crow. The smell of sugar told me why my dad hated it and why I'd grow to dislike it as well. No adults ever ate sweets. After a lifetime of this, I understood why.

I bolted the doors, deceptively safe inside my home. I watched out of my window as the fog I had seen every time the Gate opened, thickened. As it grew, it bred violence with every minute that passed. The streets darkened, growing to pitch, as nightmares flooded our town and death woke from his respite. Neighbors fought neighbors, leaving bloodied messes we'd clean once the Gate closed again. Graves would be dug, and the shattered would be laid to rest. Markers would line the ground, reminding us of the horrible power of Fae, who broke us each time they came.

The bells didn't stop chiming. The Fae had come for their sacrifice. And they always got their Crow, no matter how many of us died beforehand.

Chapter Two

"Perdita..." My name carried to my door. His voice taunted me and bargained my life for the town's safety. Sweet promises I could feel in every nerve as they came alive.

My heart plummeted into my stomach. There was no fear greater than hearing your name in the fog. I fought against the pull of the Fae. As much as I wanted to, down to my very soul, I did not go outside. As urgent as it felt to open my door, I didn't move. Like telling myself to stop breathing, it was impossible. Standing still edged on painful, I waited.

"Nix, are you here?" I called out to an empty house. My father would be at his station with the Guardians.

Nix, a once-stray gnome who now lived in my garden, climbed out from under the couch. He had lived with me for a dozen years and counting, since the day I'd trampled his mound. Once a member of the Royal Fae, he was banished to the Court of Less—the courtless folk, outcasts, unwanted. During a fog, he had walked through the Gate and didn't return with the others. As a gnome, too small to feel the pull of Elphame, he could walk between worlds and return on a whim. He chose the Iron World, a world where he could be free. There weren't many around who could see him if even the chance arose. Only a halfling could not be glamoured fully by the Fae and forget that they had been walking beside you. There weren't many halflings left in the human realm to his benefit. We were a dying breed.

"I can smell Royal blood." He climbed my leg, no heavier than a ladybug, and perched on my shoulder. "He's early."

"Royal blood? So soon? I thought the negotiations between the Guardians and Elphame weren't happening for another two years?" I asked.

"Two years and twenty-six days," Nix answered. "That they're early is unsettling. Kings do not collect Crows."

When Elphame and the human realm negotiated their oaths, the Guardians would ask for the Taking to end, and Elphame, as usual, wanted more of what we couldn't give. They grew less and less picky as to how pure the Crow's bloodline was. The Royals feared running out of Crows, and mortals feared what would happen if they did. If it weren't for the Gate, there'd be a war.

"I hate to point out the obvious, but I think your math is off," I replied. My eyes darted from window to window, and each shadow pulled my attention. "Didn't you feel something was off?"

"Everything feels off in the mortal world, Perdi. It always has," he replied. I turned my sweater around and tucked him into the hood. I could feel him shaking against my chest. Nix would fight to his death for me, but that didn't mean either of us was looking forward to it.

Faolan appeared in my living room, as he had every day for a decade, in a mist of cold wind. He always smelled of fresh snow when he came. "I don't like this. You need to go. Something doesn't feel right. It feels…off, wrong. I feel it in my bones."

"Oh, something doesn't feel right? I don't know what you mean, Fao." My sarcasm was not lost in my voice. "Everything feels off today. Mr. Grant chopped up his dog and wife. That orange cat Nix rides around on ate a bloody dog. I watched two girls jump off their house and hit the stone ground. So, Faolan, what part sounded off to you?"

"That, unfortunately, is pretty normal for today. The Fae do this to humans, you know this. When too many of us powerful gather together, it makes you all a little crazy. It's what we do for fun." Faolan answered as if he hadn't just said torture was ordinary and fun.

"I don't think anyone was having fun—certainly not the Pryor twin's father, who has to scoop them off the ground with a shovel," I countered.

Faolan shrugged a very human shrug. "The Fae don't care for mortals. I'm sorry, but it's true."

"You care, don't you?" I asked.

"Not for all of you. Some of you deserve this fate for crimes committed and never paid for. But for you, Perdi, I do." He smiled and gave me a wink. "It'll be okay. Just stay inside. Don't open the door, and it'll be okay."

I raised my brow in question. "You sound about as confident as I feel."

"Perdita…" A taunting voice, which came from someone just inches on the other side of our front door, pulled my full attention. A single knock, barely audible, jolted my heart. It registered more in the pit of my stomach than in my ears. "Perdita Darkmore. Open the door, little Crow."

"Crow?" I whispered. The word hung in the air like a noose. The word slapped me across the face and knocked the wind from my lungs. "No," I called again, my voice lost to the grip of fate.

"Open the door, little Crow, or I will open it for you."

I stepped forward. The very oath between our worlds was tethered to my soul and compelled me to do as asked. Faolan pulled my arm back hard enough to stop me from shuffling farther. I knew there would be no way he, the man at the door, could enter. I had placed wards on every access point—cold iron, rare woods, chimes and spells, guided by the Darkmore journals. But that knowledge didn't stop my stomach from knotting. The only way he'd get in here was for me to open the door and invite him in. It's how Faolan could stand to be inside without suffering pain.

"Perdi, hold on," Faolan shouted in my ear. His high-pitched voice pierced my brain and chased away the compulsion to open my home to the horrors that danced on the streets.

Before I could ask what was happening, why they were at my door, my house shook down to the foundation. The wind hit me from every angle. It pushed me forward, only to slam me into a wall of frosted air. A whirlwind of debris circled me, ripping books and pictures, twisting my living room in every direction.

"Hold on!" Faolan screamed again. This time it was followed by shattering glass.

I pulled a witch's ladder from my pocket, crusted and old, created decades ago. I rubbed Darkmore blood over each knot with already bleeding hands from the glass and chanted into the storm. Each knot brought thunder and lightning, waves of frigid cold and heat, every element crashed down upon me. My front door, carved of hardwood and cold iron detail, burst off its hinges and sored over my head, embedding into the wall behind me. I was caught between a winter's storm, a fire and hell on earth.

"Solas." Faolan's voice carried over the hurricane, which was now my living room. "Perdi, run!"

Solas, the man who'd named me as Crow, dressed in black, with skin creamier than milk, placed a foot across the threshold and smiled. His shadow played around him like black steam, twisting and turning like eels in a hot frying pan. His pitch-black hair swirled in the wind that was him. He was larger than life. While he looked as human as any other, I knew, beneath all his magick, he was more and less at once. His eyes were empty of soul and life worth living. Everything about him told me why we feared the dark. He was why we never ventured off the beaten path, why death was a better option than he was. As brave as I was, had I been alone when he found me, I'd undoubtedly have died of fear. They'd have dragged a broken Crow back to their lands.

His movements were slow but deliberate. I could feel his push to get inside. As each ward broke, I felt its force against my bones. A Darkmore Witch had died for him to wield that power, to walk amongst it without suffering its burn. There were two Fae who could gain access to my home, and the Taker of Crows was not one of them. To break the spell, the spellcaster needed to remove it through death or purpose, or those who tried would need to be more powerful than they were. Solas was a lot of things my mind couldn't begin to imagine, but a powerful witch he was not. Aoife, the last of the Darkmore line to enter Elphame, my greatest of grandmothers, the maker of the protection spell, was dead. She'd have died before removing the spell. Hundreds of years at the hands of Fae, and now she was granted the sweet mercy of death. A flash of grief mixed with being thankful that her misery was over had washed over me. That was what was 'off'. I felt her warning in my bones and didn't heed it.

"Don't run, little Crow..." Solas' words slithered across my brain like heat stroke, and I staggered. When Solas stood inside my family home, his eyes were only for me. He wasn't showy like the rest of Fae, but he was as grand as any owner of a corner in hell could be.

"Run!" Nix popped up from my hood and grabbed my face. He pulled my attention away from the collector of Crows. "Run, Perdi! Please!"

"This is going to hurt. It's your choice how badly and who suffers with you," Solas whispered. He glanced down at my shuffling feet. "Don't run. You'll never run fast enough or far enough."

I snapped back from the far-off place within my mind. I turned on foot and moved toward the back of the house. I ran, knowing full well there was no place I could go. Fae would be everywhere, and I was heading straight for them. They'd cover every meter of Whitwick. I might as well have gift-wrapped myself. I ran through my back door with enough force to land on my knees when I came to a stop in the garden.

The stench of fermented graveyard flowers was thick enough to chew. I gagged on it as it burned my nose and watered my eyes. The scent coated every breath I took. Under the flowers, the smell of cakes and cookies and all things sweet, pushed into my lungs like kicking down a door. I didn't know what smelled worse, the flowers or the cakes. Without looking up, I knew who was waiting.

In the middle of the yard, in the gazebo built by my father, sitting at the table my mother repainted before she was hanged for being a witch, three Fae sat with my father. Behind, with his hands on my father's shoulders, stood the Golden King, himself, King Aelfdene. Aelfdene stood as all Fae did—bold, cocksure and larger than life. At just over six feet tall, with white hair that fell in a lush bounce, his blue eyes felt like weights on my shoulders. I didn't know him, but my soul recognized him as someone to hate. The magick I held within focused her attention on only him and tempted me to try. Even if I didn't kill him, I'd be dead and wouldn't care what happened next. The dead don't care about such things.

A blast of icy wind hit me with the same force as a frozen fist. The king would have me bow one way or another. It took longer than I'd have liked, but I mustered a small curse of protection and stood straight. If he wanted me to kneel at his feet, he'd have to break my legs. Heat oozed from my pores and chased the cold away. To pay for the curse, I'd probably get hot and cold flashes later…or my fingers would turn blue. If I were Taken, I didn't care if the payment for my curse was the loss of my entire hand. That was just one less hand for them to cut off later.

Faolan burst through the back door and moved to my side. He pulled the cold magick from the air and settled it into his bones. He gripped my shoulder with his hand and helped me stay standing. He held my feet in place with his firm hold. If anyone knew what the king was capable of, it was Faolan. I was surprised that not the king, my father or the Seelie guards were shocked to see Faolan with me. My ten-year secret wasn't as secret as I thought it was. But what had perplexed me most was how the Fae had gotten into our home and into my yard through my wards to begin with. Now I knew, without a doubt, that Faolan was a traitor, a thief of trust, a stealer of my faith. Only he could have allowed them entry into my home, my safety, my sanctuary. It wouldn't have been Nix. He was as scared as I was. I could feel him shaking in the hood of my jacket, praying to Gods who'd obviously stopped listening to our pleas. My stomach was a riot of anger and vomit that tried desperately to introduce itself to our guests. I wanted to be brave, but I also wanted to sully the king's golden garbs with my pure sugar puke.

I pulled the small witch's ladder back out from my pocket, crusted and old, created decades ago. I pricked my thumb on a small needle stitched into the rope, rubbed more Darkmore blood over each knot, and chanted quietly, led only by instinct to protect myself. I channeled the darkness held deep within me, the dark arts learned from my mother and her mother and hers. We, the Darkmore line, carried Malice, magick that touched the soul of another. The Darkmores who had come before me, held but a hint of it, the ability to feel the intentions of others, their heart's desires. For me, I was all Malice. Pure Malice was a rarity among witches and came at the cost of soul, mine or theirs. Today, however, I'd give my life, willingly, to kill them all. The dark thoughts of death swirled in my mind and pushed me, little by little, to that edge of dark magic.

From the bottom of my soul, where my Malice lived, I could hear her coax me into opening all I was and eating the souls of those around me. It would be so simple. I'd die in the end, tarnished and rotten to the core. But I was going to die anyway, the moment they stole me into the cursed lands of the Fae. I had nothing to lose and enough to gain for it to be worth it.

At the second knot, the cuckoo clock in our kitchen chimed six, and the chaos outside ended. The screams came to such an abrupt end that I staggered. It was time for the Crow to leave Whitwick, but not a soul stirred in the yard.

They had selected their Crow.

The only thing left was for them to collect.

"Perdi the witch… I've heard so much about you." The king's taunting voice was smooth like butter, but each word forced down my throat tasted like milk sat in the sun to spoil. "So quick to break your vows? It is a slippery slope, those selfish spells. To work one in only your favor would be perilously close to dark magick, no?"

I stared straight into his eyes but said nothing.

"I wonder what the payment would be? Your life? The life of your father? You protect yourself but leave the little girl across the street vulnerable. I would think, surely a Darkmore of your pedigree would gladly sacrifice herself to save her community, to save a seven-year-old neighbor child?"

"Perdita." All it took was one word for my father to cut my attention down from the king. My eyes moved to my father, who was still dressed in his weapons. Guardians were always there during the Taking. My father walked a dangerous line between the love for his child and the safety of the mortal realm, and I envied him not.

I wanted to finish my spell, but his words halted my hands. If I struck, I jeopardized the oaths and the lives of us all. Was it selfish to kill them all for threatening my home? Was I truly willing to pay the cost of a spell this grand? If I lived through the thrice rule, could I stand against all Elphame for killing a Seelie king? If I wasn't supposed to use these spells, why would I have been taught them? Was this the balance my parents had spoken of—the same one that had claimed my mother's life when she was hanged for being a dark witch? To know how to be evil, to be tempted, but not act upon it, was that my curse? As it was my mother's? I, like my mother, held a hunger inside of me for war and justice. And if I acted upon the starvation for justice, would all die for it?

I put away my witch's ladder and nodded. I could live with the cost, but I knew my father never could, and neither would those in Whitwick, who would die in my place. As a Guardian, he had to protect the community and the oaths made hundreds of years prior. Guardians lived and died by those oaths, and so must the rest of us. I didn't have to like it, but I had to live it. And, as fate would have it, die for those oaths, as well.

"What are you doing here?" I finally spoke. I was proud that my voice wasn't a shrill of fear.

"Rest assured, little witch, I was just leaving." The King snapped his fingers, and his men moved away from my father. "I came to inform the Darkmore family of the devastating news, the death of our sweet Aoife Darkmore."

"She is *ours*, not yours," I snapped back.

"As it seems, time does drag on. Crafty little thing, she was." Solas' laughter burned inside my head. He walked into the garden, chewing on an apple from my kitchen table—made from an apple tree Nix had tended to with his bare hands. I hated the man for sullying mine and Nix's home.

Beginning today, I'd finally pray. I'd pray for the death of the man with our apple. I wondered if my God would show up for Solas' death. He hadn't come for ours, but I could hope he'd come for someone more deserving of a hole in the ground. And I didn't care how selfish that was. It's not like I could be damned any more than I already was.

Faolan stepped forward. "Enough."

Solas bowed. "As the Unseelie Master commands."

"Unseelie?" I whispered, caught off guard. I felt my temperature rise. My constant companion, anger, threatened to spill over. It came with hating half of who I was. Faolan was dark Fae, Unseelie Fae?

"That's not the best part, little Crow. Ask the Winter King, Faolan, why he is here," Solas added, stirring up an already blazing fire within.

"Stop it, Solas," Faolan commanded. Solas backed away with his hands up, taunting him.

"*King*? What? What's going on?" I asked and pulled back from Faolan, a friend I thought I knew. I shouldn't have been so stupid. Trusting a Fae was digging your own grave. Trusting a Fae always led to pain and suffering. It's what my father had made sure I knew. And to my ruin, I hadn't listened to him. I had invited him into my life, and with him, all the agony I would soon feel. I had a brief moment to think back to my previous thoughts about the fools who trusted Fae. I was one of those fools now.

"Enough." My father raised his hand and slammed it on the table. "That's *enough*."

"Not quite, Guardian." Solas turned to me when Faolan wouldn't answer me. "Your Unseelie King here has come to collect a Crow. As I recall, he wanted his very own Darkmore Witch and marked you for the Taking the day of your birth. Why do you think no one has Taken you? When a king marks a Crow, they are off-limits to all but him."

I stepped back. "Faolan, answer me."

"Perdita." Aelfdene said my name as an order. "You can come willingly or I can force you."

"Me? You haven't Taken a Darkmore since Aoife," I countered.

Solas grinned. "I do miss her. She was feisty. Sadly, you would be going to Faolan's court."

I stepped farther from Faolan. "I'd rather die."

"No." King Aelfdene's words cut the air with a hot knife. "She is mine."

"No, she belongs to the Unseelie Courts." Faolan's voice shook the very ground.

King Aelfdene smirked. There was a challenge held in the grin on his face. "Young one, the Darkmore line is mine. It always has been and always will be. Her line belongs to us. It has been written."

"I have marked her for the Unseelie Court." Faolan stepped forward.

"A war, for a Crow? And here I thought this day could not get any better." Solas leaned against my apple tree, enjoying the show. "Who thought kingdoms would fall for a little Crow?"

"What will it be, Faolan? War?" Aelfdene asked. He looked like he hoped Faolan would choose war.

"*Eagla aon rud, iontaobhas aon duine*." Solas stared into my very soul as his words flowed across my skin for only me to hear.

"Fear nothing, trust no one," I frowned and whispered back. Those were the exact words my mother had carved into the very table my father sat at, penned into the Darkmore journals on page one.

I stepped back. I shook my head slowly, side to side, as the world tilted just enough for me to stagger slightly. I looked from Solas to my father's wet eyes, and my heart broke. I felt the hairs on my arms stand at attention. The air grew icy and coated every inch of me. I felt naked in a snowstorm. Faolan grabbed my shoulders, yanked me backward and turned me to face him. He twirled on the now-frosted ground and put himself between the king and me. "Close your eyes."

"Let me go…" I barely got the words out before the blast of frost hit Faolan's back and chewed at my bones. My knees buckled. If it weren't for Faolan holding me, I'd have hit the ground, frozen. I would never have survived the full force of the king's ice.

"Now!" my father screamed, and Guardians poured into the yard. The Fae had never taken a Guardian's child…until now.

"Nix," I screamed until my voice cracked.

Faolan pushed me backward into the arms of Solas. "I'm sorry, Perdi."

"Traitor," I screamed at Faolan as the air was sucked from my chest.

"It is this or death. If King Aelfdene cannot have you, no one will." Solas' words cut the air in the yard to mist.

"Death!" I screamed.

"Fear nothing," he whispered in the darkness that consumed me.

"Trust no one," I answered. I didn't fight. I didn't exist. Everything solid, my home, my life, was gone.

* * * *

Smoke filled my lungs and stung my eyes until even my tears burned as they dropped. Screams and shouts blended together in the darkness that engulfed my body and dragged me from the mortal world. The land Faolan had spoken about, sang praises about, read me the history of, became the only thought I could muster.

The pain of the Taking had shut out the life I had in a world full of iron and dreams and the promise of what wonderment my future held and pulled me to a place no one lived to talk about. It dragged me over hot glass I felt on my soul, somewhere unknown and terrifying. It drew me toward a horrifying new life. It burned away my past, charred the life I knew and begged to keep. It hurt more than words could say, a pain so deep and sharp that I couldn't scream.

The mist pressed against my chest, suffocating me, stealing every drop from my lungs. Static prickled against my flesh as I starved for air. I knew I had to step forward. I had to cross the threshold of my own volition. Without hearing the words, I knew that if I stayed in the in-between, I would die, and the Taking would begin again. As tempting as it was to take their Crow, me, away from them, I couldn't curse another with this fate. I took a hesitant step forward. My legs screamed in protest. Painstakingly slow, I inched my way through the darkness that was the Gate, farther away from my childhood, closer to a life I knew nothing about and wanted nothing of.

The void I moved in tugged at my subconscious, whispering warnings for only my ears to hear. It, the darkness, was surprised I would come willingly. For the briefest of moments, I wondered how many Crows had died in the in-between. Its whispers of shock were felt down my spine. I fought against its kindness, its offer to sit down and rest awhile—the empty vow of taking away the pain. I pulled against the pressing blackness until I didn't know if I had shut my eyes or if the darkness had eaten my vision completely. Once the power of the Gate touched me, it was no longer curious. Where it had whispered kindness, it now yelled of anger and mistrust. It didn't want me there any more than I had wanted for it.

You shouldn't be here.

The voice hissed around me from all directions.

Go back.

I felt its fear snake down my spine.

You're not welcome here.

When the magick of the Gate snaked its power along my skin, it pulled back as if I had burned it. It no longer desired me to curl in its arms and die. Gone were the empty words. It didn't want me at all. Where there had been anger was now fear.

No. Turn back.

The Gate was everything and nothing at all. It was living and breathing, but not life as I knew it. It was all the lives before, the lives it ate and the promises of life not yet consumed. And it was terrified, of me, more than I was of it. It sent tendrils of magick to my feet, dark and oily. I felt it crawl across the ground toward me. The magick curled around my legs and pulled at me, tasting the power that was Darkmore. It twisted and snapped against my skin.

Go back!

I shook my head. I couldn't go back, not without damning my people. The mist pulsed like a heartbeat, faster and faster, tightening around me. The Gate clawed along my legs, pulled at my arms, desperate to send me home. I pushed at it and pulled it from me, but it clawed at me frantically with each step I took forward.

Starved of air, I lashed out at the Gate in return. I pulled on the knowledge I was not meant to have or ever to use, from a time when dark-art writers were hanged, when the spoken word was the only way that we passed along our darkest knowledge. The

Darkmore line was the wisest of women, the crafters of spells used to protect the mortal world, the only defense between our world and the Fae world. They wove their words in every act, every song and every story. These words were as much a part of me as my mother, a Master of Crafts, and I was the last holder of words.

I opened my hands and reached into the darkness that was the Gate and drank the power it unwillingly offered. I greedily ate it until the Gate pulled away, its power resting in my bones, its fear thick enough to chew as I walked through the mist. Its power coiled inside me, and a part of me clicked into place. The part of me that knew, if I was going to hurt because of this hellhole, so would it, so would they…all of them.

You shouldn't have done that.

"You should have allowed me to pass."

You will die here.

"You all will die with me."

The Gate echoed behind, as familiar hands pulled on me. I chanced one look back. An older woman and…me…stood mere feet from the Gate, which rested between two trees. But it was not me. It was a version of me—hardened, tired, sad. She spoke to the older woman, but I couldn't make out what was said. The older woman felt familiar, like looking at the same photographs year after year. I heard Solas' name dance across the mist before my ears popped. The ringing in my head was far too loud for me to hear much more, as my lungs starved. Solas gripped me tighter and pulled me through to the other side.

Bright light, white and sharp, prisms of blistering color, played out before me. A cloudless sky, full of every hue, filled my vision. Under the sunshine, every hue was a flash of painful beauty. It looked like a rare painting for only the eyes of Fae to see. Each color shone under the warm sky as if, like the Fae, they had evolved over eons. I stepped away from the darkness of the Gate and immediately doubled over. I braced my hands on my thighs and willed myself to calm. Breathing the air of Elphame made me dizzy at first, the new scents and purity of it. It twisted and settled around the fear, forcing it to become something vile and horrific. Vomit crawled up my throat as my gut knotted.

Solas stood in front of me. His body casted a shadow around me, blotting out the brilliance of this new and horrible world. "Breathe, little Crow. I don't think you want to pass out here, of all places. Elphame is no place for a defenseless Crow."

"I hate you." I groaned and clutched my stomach. The words spilled out as nothing more than moans around gurgles.

"Good. Your hate for me will keep you alive. Let it grow and fester, give your rage a target," he answered. "I'm the only one here you can afford to hate, as I'm the only one who won't hate you back. Be thankful for that."

"Screw you," I muttered.

"I would not offer that so openly in Elphame. Unlike those you'll meet, I'm the only one who doesn't have a taste for broken Crows."

When Solas stepped away with a smirk, he took with him his shadows and the cool breeze that stilled the fire in my stomach. I fell and curled onto my side with the force of this new land. Sweat and blood filled my nose, mixed with honey and sugar and a smell that the back of my mind told me to run from. My eyes slowly adapted to the shining sun. My senses took a few moments to catch up, as though they had taken a wrong turn and gotten lost at the Gate to Elphame. The sounds hit me at once, ripping my attention away from the beauty of the land—whispers, laughter, growls, the flapping of wings and the stench of death. Panic wretched at me, and I waited for a scream to rip from within me, but it never came. Only darkness. I fought against it, the fear of not being awake and aware and able to protect myself. But it wouldn't matter. I'd never be able to defend myself here, regardless of my conscious state.

Chapter Three

Everything hurt in a frostbitten and fire burned sort of way. The air around me smelled of seared flesh, scorched with flame and left rotting in the sun. Gone was the sweet smell of a candy store. My bones were frozen, yet heat pressed down on me and coated my body with sticky sweat. My skin was bare, and my limbs felt too powerless to cover myself. My stomach cramped, and I felt nothing but that agony. I faded in and out, from excruciating pain to utter relief of nothingness. Wave after wave of illness and pain and relief pulsed against my body. It was what happened when a mortal came to Fae lands. Our bodies revolted against being pulled into a land we knew would kill us. The deepest of all instincts, survival, twisted inside our bones as a warning. But there was nothing I could do to help myself.

Had it not been for my halfling blood, I would be in even worse condition. Before the oath, there had been stories of mortals who had come to Elphame, only to be returned a hobbled mess, retching and writhing from the pain the cursed lands had left them in. It was rare for a human to survive once they were released from Elphame. We simply lacked the medicine they needed, and none were brave enough to enter Elphame to get it. Those who bargained with the Fae to save a loved one suffered a horrible fate. 'Fae sickness', it was called. But it was more of a curse or an illness. Halflings were built for both worlds, but it hurt just the same for me to be here.

I could hear voices in the background, like listening to a voice from underwater. "What have you done, Solas?"

"I had no choice." Solas' voice scratched along the inside of my skull. I cringed to know I was still with him. "It was this, or Faolan would have Taken her. Would you have preferred that? Say the words, Nix, and I'll dump her on his border and he can deal with her. I'd like nothing more than to go home and not have to do this shit again."

"No."

The thought of opening my eyes felt like a choice between remaining in ignorance and the stark reality of where my curled body landed. The pain in my heart burned, the leftover fire from my Taking rolled my stomach. It owned every breath I took and controlled my desire to take another. It stole who I was, the part of me that pushed on, no matter what. Each groan that escaped my swollen lips snuffed out my inner light, little by little. I wanted the darkness to come. I yearned for the ice of hate to cool the pain of hurt. I knew my need for anger was a mask for the alarms going off in my brain. Fear. Terror. Dread. Betrayal. Anger would be easier to deal with over acknowledging I would die soon.

With my eyes closed, I pushed a little of my magick into the air around me. It was heavy, staticky, wet and tasted of sugar. But I couldn't focus it. It blew around me like dust in a storm. My mind was scattered, fractured into a million little thoughts I couldn't control. I picked up the pieces my magick brought back and understood none of them.

"Don't, Perdi. Magick is wild here, and you have too little control," Nix whispered.

Relief flooded my veins with the sound of his voice. I pulled my magick back in and slowly opened my eyes. The world swam with explosions of color. Nix stood behind me and held my hair back while I emptied my stomach onto a slim-covered wooden deck. Each sudden movement made me heave harder than the last as I rocked with the boat. My dread burned my throat. Fear gripped my stomach as I played back the Taking. It wasn't the fear of death that grabbed me. It was the fear of still being alive, of being a Crow.

"Where… Where are we?" I asked, my throat raw and my voice jittered with a frost that still lived deep in my bones.

"A boat," he answered.

"Where?" We were not in Whitwick Gates. I could feel it in my bones as if something were missing and something unknown was added. I had to make sure it wasn't a dream, that I really was in Elphame. In the pit of my stomach, I knew that no amount of wishing would work. I would not wake, and this would not be a horrible nightmare.

"We're not in the mortal realm anymore," Solas answered, his voice too close for comfort.

"Elphame?" I groaned at the thought of where I was and who I was with. I vomited once again. I heaved until nothing but angry screams came up. I had a good reason for the fear. Solas. Elphame was a nightmare, and Solas is what haunted the Fae in their dreams. Solas terrorized both my world and his. He was the Taker of Crows. But what churned my stomach was not fear, it was anger, and it was all for Faolan.

"Where else would you be, little Crow?" he asked, sarcasm thick on his tongue.

"Don't call me that," I muttered.

The sky, once blues and oranges, was now black. I was in and out of consciousness. I woke to Nix and five other small creatures cleaning the vomit from my hair and face, dressing me and trying to nurse my wounds and empty stomach. Solas leaned against the side of the wooden boat and watched me. His gaze felt like spiders on the skin. Without a smile or frown, he looked utterly bored. I was an inconvenience, something to check off his list for the day.

"Why am I on a boat, Nix?" I tucked myself into the corner, as far from Solas as I could get, without being in the water.

"It's the barge of the dead," he answered.

"Am I…dead?" I asked.

He smiled and shook his head. "No, Perdi. The barge is how those banished, those who are seen as dead to the rest of Elphame, are brought to the courtless lands, to the Court of Less."

"Why?"

"It's no-man's land. The courtless Fae reside there. It's where the Crow always lands. The Gate rests on the courtless lands. They are then brought to whatever court they will reside in. There, in their honor, a celebration is held where they are crowned the Crow."

"I doubt very much I'll enjoy the celebration of being dragged to Elphame," I countered.

"Probably not," he answered. "But you are required to attend the celebration of The Seven-Year Crow."

"Why are we called Crows?" It had never dawned on me to ask.

"Halflings are seen as scavengers, scroungers, pests—those undeserving, like crows," he replied and winced at his comment, as if he knew how rude it would have felt to hear.

"Aren't crows a symbol of bad luck?" I asked.

"Bad luck? You've no idea how bad it can be." Solas laughed, but he seemingly meant it as a sneer. "You truly know nothing about becoming a Crow, do you?"

I shrugged but didn't look at him. "How would I know anything? No one ever returns. Those who once did, didn't come back whole. Nothing they said made any sense. You broke them beyond repair. You took everything they were and twisted them inside out until the only thing we could figure out is how horrid being a Crow is."

"Trust when I tell you, those we twisted inside out never went home."

I shuddered at the thought. "Thanks for the visual."

"Your Little King didn't fill you in on what you could expect?" he asked and picked lint from his white cotton top, apparently bored of me. He leaned casually against the boat, one ankle over the other, smug in his freedom. "He knew you would be Taken, and he didn't tell you?"

"He's not *my* king," I answered, bitterness thick on my tongue. I said nothing more. My silence told him everything he needed to know. Faolan hadn't liked talking about it, and neither did I, so we hadn't. I had always thought I was safe because I was a Darkmore.

Solas didn't react to my anger. He didn't look like much got under his skin at all. "He is not *my* king, either, but he is still a king, nonetheless. For better or worse, you'd be smart to remember that."

Finally, I glanced back to him with a pitiful shrug. "Faolan didn't tell me any of it."

"But you know why you're a Crow?" he asked.

"I know the story, about paying tithe to your Gods and Goddesses."

"Once, before the time of the Crow, every seven years, we sacrificed one member of our courts to the Gods, priests and priestesses, only the most deserving of an offer. Before they were sacrificed, they were king for seven years. From the day they were chosen to the day they gave themselves to the Gods, they wanted for not. That very tithe gave us the magick we use, the crops we eat, the very air we breathe. But the mortal realm would not offer sacrifice. Because of the oaths between our realm and yours, there was no sacrifice from man. Fae died every seven years for your realm to prosper," Solas explained, as though he's had to tell the story more times than he'd like and grew tired of it. "Soon, we did not sacrifice for the mortals. When your people finally began to die of starvation and disease, the mortals agreed to give sacrifice, but only of a halfling bloodline. Since halflings can never rule in Elphame, you are not called kings. You're Crows, scavenging on the powers and rewards of Elphame, eating the scraps of what we throw away. It is by our mercy that you live—and at our whim that you die. The court from which the Crow's line originates is the court which holds the Crow for seven years, where they remain for seven years, as a sacrifice from the mortal lands."

"Does Elphame still sacrifice or is it just children from Whitwick who die for your Gods?"

"Every single day in Elphame is a sacrifice for us—some, more than others."

That was answer enough. Crows were the only ones to die for Gods who didn't care. "What line am I from?"

"Your line has always been Wildfey—witches, as you call them, of many types and flavors. But you, little Crow, are the last of your line. There are no Wildfey left, as there are no Darkmores left," he answered with a grin. "After you, there will be none. You are the last. I do hope you make it count."

"What happens to the Crow at the end of seven years?" I asked.

Solas shrugged this time. "Only one has ever lasted beyond the entire seven years, which was Aoife." His eyes blazed when he said her name. The emotion burned its way out and flushed his cheeks. "Seven years in Elphame is a sacrifice greater than death. If you survive, and that is a very big *if*, you're then free."

"Why didn't Aoife return?"

"I don't think she could, not after she cursed the Gate. I don't think she would have, though, even if she'd wanted to. Seven years here is not the same as seven years in your realm. Time moves differently in Elphame, but not in the way of a clock. This place ages and changes your soul. After so many years here, you lose your mortal side," Solas answered and shrugged off his history lesson. "She left the Golden Court the moment her time was up, and no one saw her again, but she never left Elphame. We would have known if she crossed the Gate. Even if you could return to your mortal world, you will go mad, just like the rest did—and would need to be put down, just like the rest did. Again, that all rests on whether you can survive seven very long years with us."

"Great, so if I survive, I'm free, but forever a prisoner?" I asked.

"That's a pretty big *if.* And *if* you do, what you do next is up to you. Stay or try to leave. I really don't care."

"And if I escape?" I asked.

"Escape?" His laughter rented the air, both amusement and disbelief. "That's rich. Like those who have run before, you'll die in our ditches, just like the hordes before you did. You will be a waste to this realm and your own," he replied and stared at me. I felt his judgment without him needing to say the words. I was beneath him. I was a Crow.

"You didn't answer my question."

"Very well. Your choices are the same as every other Crow who has been stolen into our lands. If you try to run, you'll be hunted and killed outright, and that, if you can believe, will be a mercy. You won't escape. There has never been a Crow who has. If you survive your years, you can leave the court that caged you, but you'll always be hunted for being a Crow. Or, you can return to the mortal world if you can pass a cursed Gate, and go mad. The costs for the Crow are never-ending and never paid in full. It is what makes becoming a Crow the truest form of sacrifice. You are Crow and always will be that. Nothing will ever change it—not leaving, not staying, not death. You were born a Crow, and you will die a Crow. But I suspect you won't need to worry about your future here. Like I said, *if* you survive."

"Anyone ever tell you that you're a ray of fucking sunshine?" My glare turned to a smile. "I'll burn your world to the ground on my way out. I sincerely hope the flames find you first."

"I'm sure you'll try. They all do."

I'd deal with that, if and when I survived. I turned away from Solas' attention, back to Nix. I trusted Nix, and in a place like this, friends were as important as air. "What does it mean, that Faolan marked me?"

He sighed. He looked how I felt—like he had aged a dozen years in a split second. "Until now, he has always forfeited his turn for the Taking. Most of Elphame forfeits until they have no choice but to pick. You'd be surprised how few of us actually enjoy Taking of Crows. It's barbaric, even for Fae. When Faolan was not allowed to forfeit again, he claimed you as his own. He was going to select you once you were old enough. It bought him almost eighteen more years of not selecting a Crow."

"Why was he stopped?"

"There are two main courts—Seelie and Unseelie—and each one hosts smaller courts. You are from Wildfey. The land your line comes from rests on the edge of the Seelie Court. In turn, that means the Darkmore line belongs to the Seelie Court. It is part of the original oath, where Crows go. Only a Royal Seelie could select from your bloodline, and no Seelie Court is stronger than King Aelfdene. But since Aoife, no one has tried to take another Darkmore for fear of another curse."

"Then why now?" I asked.

"I don't know, Perdi. I think it is because soon, you will be too old to be Taken and are the very last of your kind. This was the last chance they'd have to Take you."

I nudged my head to Solas. "Why are you here? You don't feel like…" I searched for the word, "a flunky."

"A flunky?" He smirked. "That, I am not. Alas, I do as I am commanded. You are to be brought to the Seelie Court."

"When you took me, you said the choice was this or death. I chose death and still do."

"They always do. Rest easy in knowing you'll still get the death you desire, but on our terms, not yours." Solas walked to the front of the boat, no longer interested in me. I didn't mind. I wasn't interested in him, either. The farther he got from me, the better I felt. He turned once, and I swore I saw a sadness in his eyes for the briefest of moments. I don't know what I hated more, his pity or his hate.

I swallowed my burning tears each time my mind drifted to Faolan. It turned out he was a lie. But at least, for a short while, it was a beautiful one—deadly but beautiful, just like the rest of his people. There'd be no more beauty in lies, not here, not on this side of the Gate. Now, the only thing that remained was the truth of Elphame, the sad certainty for a mortal in places she doesn't belong. Here, the lies I feared most are the ones so close to the truth that I'd be their victim until my last breath, believing I'd be free. I would see the truth in pain. It is what the Fae did best, hurt the mortal realm in ways that became our greatest fears.

Nix pulled on my arm. "You smell different, Perdi. You smell like the Gate."

"I was just there."

"No. You smell like you're still there. What did you take from it?" he asked.

I shrugged then paused, remembering my walk from home to hell. "I took power."

"It'll want it back."

"It can have it back when I'm cold and dead," I answered.

"You shouldn't meddle in things you don't understand," he groaned.

"Nor should Fae. If the Gate is going to take our lives, it can hurt along with us. If I suffer, so does the rest of this cursed place."

"I wouldn't say those words any louder," Solas called from the front of the boat.

"Fuck you," I called back, as loud as I could, to his entertainment.

"Fuck me? I don't think we'll have time for that this afternoon."

I sat on the cold wood of the boat and took in Elphame and all the glory I'd never see the same again. To say it was merely beautiful was an understatement. It was more than I had imagined. I knew it was beautiful from the stories both Nix and Faolan had told me. They spoke of the good parts of the Sidhe in hopes I'd never see the gory bits—little pieces of this land had reminded me of my home as if Elphame had spilled out into the mortal realm, and we hadn't noticed.

The boat followed a path along banks of lush greenery. I could feel thousands of eyes but saw not a single Fae outside of those on the barge. It was puzzling, not a soul in sight. For a place this vast, I would expect to see life, Fae, someone who came to see who floated down their river, but I saw no one.

"Where did everyone go? Is it not odd, that there is no life around?"

"They're all terrified of Solas," Nix answered in a hushed voice. "He's not known for his charming personality."

"I couldn't imagine why," I replied. I didn't like Solas either, and I didn't even know him. "What is he known for?"

"Death, war, nightmares…the usual."

"Why did you come back here? You should have stayed in the garden where it was safe."

He climbed up my legs and sat on my knees. "I'd never abandon you, Perdi. You saved me at great cost to yourself. You protected me, knowing I'd attract Fae during each Taking. Every time the fog came, you kept me close and never let them take me back. You fed me, warded against all who came for my life and never treated me like the Fae. Even when Faolan found me and tried to rid your garden of me, you threatened him to protect me. No one has ever threatened a king for me. I owe you a debt."

"Well, to be fair, I didn't know he was a king at the time." I smiled and huffed a small laugh. "Yeah, I'd still have threatened him, even if I had known. You are my friend. There is no debt for you to repay. You've tended my gardens, grown my food and fought any who entered my yard. If ever you feel you owe me, the debt is paid. You owe me nothing. Go home. Why should we both suffer this fate?"

He tucked himself under my blanket. "Perhaps there is no debt, but I am here just the same and will remain at your side. Plus, how would you ever survive in Elphame without me? You can't even take a simple boat ride without poking the beast."

"What happened to my dad?"

Nix shook his head. "I'm sorry, Perdi, but I don't know. When I felt you being pulled to Elphame, I jumped with you. The last I saw, before we came here, was of the Guardians coming into the yard. I suspect the Fae left with their Crow and nothing more happened. They always leave after they Take their Crow."

"What's going to happen to me?" I finally asked, both wanting to know and fearing the knowledge. It was always worse when you waited for a bad thing to happen. To not know, made it somehow worse.

"I don't know. I've never been part of a Taking of a Crow, but I've heard the stories," he answered, followed by a shiver. "If it's anything like being in courts that I know, it won't be pleasant...not even a little. When we get there, you need to swallow your anger or die because of it. It won't be a quick death, either. They'll take long enough for you to regret your anger. They'll wait until the day before your freedom to take your life. Whatever they say or do, you need to remember your place, and your place is to keep your head down and pray you make it another day."

"Seven years is a long time not to be angry about this," I countered.

"Seven years is even longer if you're tortured for it the entire time. Even if you lived out your oath, your soul would be long dead."

"Well, there's that." I smiled on the outside and shook on the inside. At least, if they killed my soul, the rest wouldn't hurt as bad.

We sat in complete silence the rest of the way. My ears twitched at footsteps here and there, snapped twigs, crunched leaves. But as I watched the banks and tree line for signs of life, I saw nothing. No one was brave enough to look out from their cover. Every now and again, Nix would nudge me and point to the sky. Black creatures dipped in and out of the clouds. Their eyes were heavy on my shoulders. They felt like pins and needles dancing across my flesh in a warning, almost as if they dared me to run away. Alongside the boat, gliding in the water, eyes surfaced every now and again. When I wanted to take a closer look, Nix pulled me back and shook his head.

"No one goes in the water of Elphame. Those who have, have never come out. The water is a kingdom all its own and is aligned with no one. They care for no king, no oath, no sovereign outside of the drink they swim in."

Nix answered the questions I had on the tip of my tongue before I could ask. Whatever was in the water, I obviously didn't want to find out. If they weren't scared of Solas, I didn't think I'd like to meet them. Although, making friends with the enemies of Elphame was appealing. The enemy of my enemy…

Chapter Four

The boat skidded against rocks, and dread began swirling in my gut once again. Solas jumped from the front of the boat and started walking. He didn't bother to wait for me. I inched my way off the boat, nervous about stepping foot on the ground. When my feet hit the earth and I was standing on Elphame land, it was like pouring gasoline on the spark of fear in my stomach. The realization hit me that I would live out my short life in Elphame. I wondered how long I would last before my body finally gave in and I died. My stomach twisted into a knot so tight that I struggled to breathe. My eyes watered. I begged myself not to cry, not to show them I was scared, not to be so weak. I couldn't afford it—not now and not here. But I wasn't brave. I cooked off all my bravery on my way into Elphame. Every drop of who I thought I was, I'd left at the Gate.

I shook my head, jerking it side to side, panicked. I couldn't do this. I couldn't face the path that sat before me, a destiny I hadn't prepared for, one a mortal could never fully be ready for. I couldn't take another step forward. The once-smoldering fire deep within was threatening to engulf me, to burn me alive. The once-fresh air, salty from the water, was replaced with flowers carried on a breeze from the trees ahead. The smell reminded me of a funeral, the cemeteries from Whitwick, and I froze. I was marching to an already-dug hole with my name on it, led by Death himself, Solas. Although the sun shone down like the perfect summer's day, I couldn't shake the feeling of darkness creeping in from the horizon. I couldn't get enough air. This time, I didn't want to fight for a single breath. If I were to die on these lands, I'd sooner I did it on my own terms.

I clawed at every ounce of bravery held within my soul and tried to take another step forward. I trembled, and my eyes prickled with unshed tears. With every move I made, my future unfolded before me, and it was horrifying. I was terrified to my very marrow. My heart pounded in my ears and blocked out the sound of everything else. Adrenaline flooded my system, and I almost vomited again. I could feel saliva thickening in my throat. At some point, I knew I'd have to move again, but I couldn't bring myself to do it. It wasn't the predictable torture or the pain that made things worse. It was the unknowns. The Fae were too erratic and impulsive for me to be ready for what they had in store for me. My entire life revolved around the Fae wreaking havoc on my small community, and nothing could prepare a soul for how bad it could get with them. I could withstand physical pain, but nothing would prepare me for the emotional pain I knew I'd feel. I had seen what they did to my people in a place where the oath protects us. But here, now, there would be no rules, no one and nothing to save me.

"No," I whispered. "I can't go willingly. Nix, I can't do this."

Nix stopped walking and turned to face me. "Don't, Perdi. Don't run. Please, don't do it. Running will make this worse. You'll never get away from him. There is no place in Elphame where you can hide from Solas."

Up ahead, the named man waited. His once-emotionless face looked excited. He hoped I would run. It was written all over him, from his grin, to his eyes, to how he prepared his body to run after me. The muscles in his arms flexed as if readying for the hunt. Two simple words carried over the air, daring me. *Do it.*

"*Please*. The sky is filled with Sluagh. They will hunt you down." Nix slowly stepped to my front. "Do not tempt them. They answer only to Solas. Not even the kings can command them."

"I'd rather them kill me," I replied. "I won't go. I can't. I am not the person who goes willingly to their death for the amusement of Fae. I may be a Crow, but I will never be the Crow they want me to be. I'll never be *their* Crow. No one gets to own me. I would sooner suffer for seven years than give myself willingly to them."

I backed up to the edge of the trees and looked out at the sky. The clouds were peppered with flying creatures—legs, arms and wings, too many to count. I scanned the trees. There was nowhere to go, but I still bolted. Solas ran behind me. His movements were slower than I knew he could move. I weaved through the trees, stumbling, branches slashing at me. Twice I fell, and twice Solas helped me stand, brushed me off, only to chase me again. He was enjoying the cat and mouse game. Screeches above told me that I could get as far away from Solas as possible, but they'd find me. I'd go nowhere without them. I'd never get away if I was out in the open. I shot off the trail to the right and plunged into the trees, out of view from the creatures above.

If I was going to be dragged through Elphame, Solas could limp his way there, too. It was time to bell the cat. My most favored fable crept through my mind as I skulked through the trees. In this tale, the mice held a general meeting to discuss how they could outwit the house cat, their common enemy. One of the mice suggested a bell be placed around the cat's neck to warn them when the cat was nearby. Although all the mice agreed, no volunteer stepped forward. The moral of the story was, don't only consider an outcome when making plans. The plan itself is useless unless achievable. And like any mouse who volunteered to bell the cat, I was putting myself in a perilous position. I'd volunteered to not only bell this cat, but also be eaten by it.

I picked my position and stood, ready to fight. It was explicitly selected for space. It was large enough for me to fight in and small enough that Solas would feel cramped and would lack maneuverability. In this one instance, his muscular size would hinder him, as my slender build would benefit me. Sure, he could kill me with one blow, but a dead Crow was useless to the Fae, and I was perfectly fine with him ringing my neck and ending this before it could even begin.

"Really?" Solas asked as he strolled under a large branch and stared at me. "You want to fight me? Fist to fist? Did you starve your brain of too much oxygen while in the Gate?"

"I'm not going willingly, Solas." I pronounced his name 'Soulless', dragging out each letter. I lifted my fists and readied myself. "So yes, I want to fight you."

"And if you win, you think it'll grant you freedom?" He laughed. "*If.* If you win."

"No, but it'll give me time to get away," I answered. "I'd rather spend the rest of my life running and fighting than spend a single day owned by Fae."

"And where would you go, with all of Elphame looking for you? Where would you hide? Would you seek refuge with a family who would all certainly die if you were found with them? Who will you sentence to punishment and death in your place?"

"As long as I'm not the one doing the dying, I don't care which of your people has to go in my place."

"Here I thought you wanted death?" he asked.

"I said I'd rather die, not that I'd like it to be anytime soon."

"I suppose this is as good of a place as any for you to learn what it means to be a Crow." He glanced around the small clearing I had selected and tilted his head. A blast of pitch-black wind pulsed from his body and uprooted the trees around us. The clearing now gave him space. He grinned and lifted his fists. His wind didn't budge me. I pulled the magick from the air and settled it into my stomach. I ate it down like a starved animal.

"No magick," I countered.

He smirked. "As you wish. But pound for pound, you cannot stand against me and hope to win. You are too weak to win."

"I didn't take you for a stupid man, Solas. Whether you win here or not, you all lost the moment you brought me here. You may be my beginning in Elphame, but I will be your end."

He raised an eyebrow. "I've heard the same song sung by Aoife, yet, here we are with her buried and us with another Crow—another to feed our lands."

"I hope I poison your fields and rot your crops."

My focus darted over his left shoulder. I let my lips part and eyes grow wider. I took a step back. Solas frowned and glanced back at nothing more than my lies. It was his first and only mistake. I knew he wouldn't make another. But violence was uncertain, unpredictable. Even the most accomplished of fighters could be taken down by a chance blow. I was not skilled, and Solas was, but Solas was not as desperate as I was. It was life or death for only one person in this fight, and I'd use the only opportunity I had created.

I pushed the power I had taken from him into the earth, sending the dirt and rocks and tree limbs into him. It wasn't enough for me to hurt him, but it was enough to blind him momentarily. I ran at him and swung a tree branch. I connected with the back of his head. The sound of a blunt object connecting with skull bone is unmistakable. It tricked your ears into not knowing if it was the object you used that shattered or the skull. The vibrations of the blow crawled through my hand, up my arm and threatened to drop the branch, but I held on. I swung again and connected against his jaw.

Solas went wide-eyed. The surprise would be my advantage. His legs crumpled, and I came down on his ribs with my knees and punched his now-broken jaw. I held his hair with one hand and lifted his head to my waiting fist. I swallowed the bile that was climbing my throat. I had never brought violence to the doorstep of a single being. I had never beaten a person to death. I had trained for personal protection but hadn't ever used it on another person. He didn't count. He wasn't a person, was he?

With his head in my hand, I pushed against his soul with my tendrils of magick, the very power that fueled my hate and anger. I snaked through his body, willing him to let me go. Just as my Malice touched the edges of intense rage, Solas grabbed my wrists and tossed me from him like weightless trash. The fight was over within seconds and ended with me on the ground, face down in the dirt and rocks. He had thrown me twenty feet through the air as if I were nothing. But I suppose I really was nothing to him.

"No magick?" He stood over me as I struggled, the wind knocked out of my chest.

"I lied. Are you actually surprised?" I finally said. I rolled my head to the side, away from his view. I didn't want him to see me cry. I knew it was pointless. Before the day was over, he'd likely see me do more than just cry.

"For future reference, like Aoife's magick, your Malice doesn't work on me, little Crow. You're not nearly powerful enough for someone like me. And I wouldn't try it on Royal blood or any Higher Fae if I were you." He scowled. "Hide it or be used because of it. You do not want to ever find yourself to be useful to the Fae."

"Malice? I don't know what you're talking about," I answered, faking ignorance. I knew my magick better than anyone. I may not be powerful enough today, but I touched something deep inside his mind. Today I felt a hint of guilt, but given time and practice, I knew I could tear his mind apart. I grinned at the thought—*if* I lived long enough, that is.

"Your magick will only bring you pain here," he replied. "At least Aoife was smart enough to hide it better, and you are much stronger than she had been."

"Good to know," I answered. "I'll try harder next time." I made it a threat.

"Are we done yet?" Solas asked, crouched beside me. "Or do you want to do this again?"

I shook my head.

"No, we're not done? Or no, you don't want another round?" he asked.

"Another round, we're not done," I answered. If I couldn't kill him, I'd force him to kill me.

"Get up, then," he said and stepped back. "I can do this all day. I fear you cannot, little Crow."

"Stop calling me that." I pushed myself to my knees but failed each time I tried to get to my feet. My ribs were screaming in protest. I groaned out my frustration. The landing had bruised parts of me I didn't know existed. Whatever the Gate hadn't singed off me was begging for respite.

"Just get it over with," I mumbled. "I'd much prefer death at your hands, right now, than march to my certain death later."

"Nothing is certain."

"I don't want to go." I struggled not to cry, but felt it building in the back of my throat like a sharp rock. "I can't do this."

"You have very few choices. You either walk into the halls of the Golden Court on your own accord, or I drag you there, kicking and screaming. How you get there is your choice, but you will get there nonetheless, alive. It is up to you whether you want to stand tall or cower."

I stared through the tree canopy. "How many Crows have you dragged to Elphame? How many souls have you sentenced to death?"

"Enough of them to lose count," he replied. There was a hint of regret in his voice.

"How does it feel to be the lapdog of the Seelie Court?"

"Everyone needs a hobby. Now get up, or I'm picking you up. Would you prefer me to carry you like a sack of potatoes or walk on your own?"

"Before this is over, you will hurt for this," I said through gritted teeth.

Solas stood me up and walked ahead of me. "You have no idea what hurt is. But you'll find out soon enough. I promise you."

The forest was calm around us. Whatever monsters lurked in the shadows weren't nearly as terrifying as Solas, for them to be silent and fear his hearing them. A shiver rolled down my spine at the thought of walking with the wickedest monster around. We walked for what felt like hours, finally stopping when I fell, winded and tired. My stomach growled. I hadn't eaten since the bag of candy, which I'd puked up on the boat.

"Sit. Eat. You have thirty minutes." Solas barked his words, irritated. The air around his hand turned black. The mist left behind a small white bag. "Here."

"How's your jaw?" I grinned and grabbed the bag. When I opened it, I half expected some sort of monster to climb out and eat my face off as punishment for what I had done to him. "Lunch?"

"Would you rather starve?" he asked, only to walk away before I could answer that, in fact, I'd rather starve and die long before reaching the Seelie Court.

"Yes, actually, I would," I called out to him, but he didn't turn back.

I sat on the ground with Nix and spread out lunch for us both. Nix was worried Solas would find a way to punish me for my assault. He was probably right. Although I wasn't hungry, I knew I'd need food if I wanted to keep my strength up. I nibbled while Nix told me stories about Elphame and what he thought I could expect. He knew of stories but had never been there himself. There were groups of Fae who disagreed with the Taking of a Crow. But those who didn't agree weren't powerful enough to stop it from happening, and those who spoke against it were either killed or sent to the Court of Less.

"Don't," Nix whispered as I broke off a small piece of bread. "She doesn't need bread."

To my left, a small fairy hid under a cluster of fallen leaves. Her large, gray eyes darted from Solas, twenty feet away, to the bread I was offering. She looked gray, sickly. I pulled my hand back and cursed. Her teeth sunk into my finger and took out a tiny chunk.

"Her kind need meat and blood," Nix grumbled.

"What are you doing?" Solas stood above me, his hands on his hips.

"Nothing. I cut my finger on a rock," I answered. I moved to stand and put myself in front of the creature.

"Spit it out." Solas, quicker than my eyes could track, picked up the creature by the wings and began to shake her. "Spit it the fuck out."

"Let her go!" I screamed the words, and my magick rolled out of me before I could think of what I was doing. A pulse of wind shot out of me, from every direction. It pushed against Solas with force, and he stopped, shocked. I grabbed the creature from his hand

and knelt down to release her. She darted away before I could urge her to run. She didn't need to be told.

"Does it make you feel good, scaring everything smaller and weaker than you are?" I glared at him. "We all get it. You're big and scary. But there is enough to fear without you causing more of it."

Solas grabbed my shoulder and pulled me to my feet. "It is in your best interest to listen to your little friend here and keep that magick in check. I will not protect you from whatever comes looking for the cause of your magick tricks."

I shoved his hands off me. "Yes, you will. You and I both know that you will. If not, I'd be dead already. And I doubt, very much, that you'll drag a dead body back. You're having a hard enough time shlepping a live one across this hellhole."

"Pack up. We're leaving now." Solas' eyes darkened, and it pleased me. He looked to Nix and snarled. "Control her—or I will. It's only been a couple hours and I'm already wishing I had dumped her off the boat."

"Whatever you say, sir." I spat out the last word in mockery while Nix nodded.

"Crow." He turned on his heel and walked away. The word didn't sting as much as it had just hours ago.

"You don't know what you're doing," Nix scolded as we walked. "He will bloody well eat you and me. Everyone has a breaking point, and you're pushing him to his. He doesn't collect Crows because he's bored, so don't make him show you why he is always the one who is sent."

I rolled my eyes and began to follow Solas. "Unlike you, I'm actually hoping he eats me before we get to the Golden Court."

"Do not use that power here, Perdi. There are things that you don't want to meet, things that will answer your call, and if they don't find what they're looking for, they'll kill us. And although you're marching to a suicidal beat of your own, I'd rather not be eaten."

I shrugged. "If they didn't want a witch mucking up their land, maybe they shouldn't have brought one here, then. But they did, and this witch will muck around if she'd like."

"You do not want to attract something worse than Solas. Do you really want to face something that could take you from him?"

I thought about it for a moment and shook my head. "Is there anything worse than him? In all this godforsaken land, is anything remotely as terrifying as he tries to be?"

"He's not trying, and you don't want to see him try," he replied. "There is always something bigger and badder in Elphame, and I'm not foolish enough to call them by name. Solas truly isn't the worst Fae here." His entire body shuddered. "I'd suggest you keep that part of yourself locked up until you have no choice but to show it."

"How will I know when?"

"You'll be dying, that's how." Nix looked up and grinned. "Use it as a last resort."

I followed behind Solas and Nix. Every so often, I caught a glimpse of the little creature I had fed out of the corner of my eye. I hoped she was curious and not starved for more. When she got close enough, she hopped onto my shoulder. I opened the pocket of my jacket and let her climb in. I hoped she was a pest and would bring hundreds more to the Seelie Courts. *A pest problem brought on the heels of a Crow…* The thought made me laugh out loud.

I let out small tendrils of magick to the displeasure of Solas, who, on more than one occasion, had to chase away the fearless and curious. I wouldn't go blindly into the court of my prison. I had to know what was coming, who was coming and where I was going. I made the trip take twice as long with my magick tricks—or so the king's lapdog informed me. Each time I sent out my Malice, she carried back little snippets of dread and impressions of beasts that lurked up ahead. Maybe I'd attract a big enough monster that I'd be Taken again, before I was dragged before a court that would only kill me in the end. At least this way, Solas might be eaten, too.

"If you keep feeding the monsters, they'll attack the next who comes along and has no food for the taking," Solas pointed out.

"Well then, feeding monsters is now my new hobby," I answered.

"The next one may be an innocent. Careful which hobbies you hone."

I laughed. "Innocent? No one here is innocent."

"You are," he replied. "And those who will come after you are. Do you really want what's lurking in the shadows to develop a taste for Crow?"

I opened my mouth to curse him but had nothing snarky to say in return. It bothered me that he was right.

"Save your magick, little Crow. It's only day one. You still have two and a half thousand days to go," Solas reminded me. "And each day will feel like an eternity."

"Yet, it only takes a minute for the tables to turn," I replied.

"Who said you'd be sitting at a table? But your optimism has improved, although it won't serve you well around here." He called back, and I gave him the middle finger. It was all bravado, nothing more.

Nix scolded me more than Solas did and did so because of Solas. He had hoped I'd survive long enough to escape. He obviously thought we could get away from the Seelie Court and find somewhere to hide, long enough to find a way back to Whitwick. There was nothing in the oaths that said I couldn't escape. Sure, it said I would be the Crow for precisely seven years, but it didn't say I had to serve them all in the court who took me, only that I'd need to remain in Elphame. Nix was right. I had to stay alive. But without a way out, I was going to my death. I was going unarmed, save one gnome and a winged creature stuffed in my pocket. I had a butterknife I stole from the lunch bag and wild magick. I'd be lying if I didn't say I had my doubts on some grand escape plan.

Chapter Five

The day began to fade, and I mourned the passing of each minute. There would only be a few hours of daylight left before the darkness of Elphame wrapped around me. I should fear the dark here, but it settled the uncertainty in my stomach. There were worse things to worry about than the dark, and I was walking toward it and with it. At least the darkness didn't lie about what hid deep inside. It was honest with its horridness. It never asked you to trust it while it leached out your final breaths.

Time in Elphame felt like it moved the same as the mortal realm. The sun rose and set on the same schedule, yet here, it felt foreign, wrong, like it was too much of one thing and not enough of another. But time would move differently once I was in the court, where my promised suffering would begin. Time always slowed to a crawl when you were stuck in moments you didn't want—just as waiting for something good to arrive took forever. I think those moments in between the now and then were precisely the same place—caught between choices and fates not yet decided.

Everything here looked as I'd imagined, yet edged with less of something I couldn't quite put my finger on. Like a painting so close to being done but walked away from or a child born who hadn't yet taken a breath. Where there was an absolute beauty, it lacked true life. Where there were shadows, there lacked a completeness. It was all and nothing. I saw the deepest parts of Elphame the Fae had tried to tuck behind the allure and roses. But no amount of magick could hide the truth from me. I could see the soul of the land. I could feel it slither over my flesh. And if I looked hard enough, most of the glamour fell away, and I could see the aura others had left behind. It stained the pretty flowers and called out from the darkest of places. As I was marched through it, I let the stains from the past dance across my skin as I dragged my fingertips through the grass and along the leaves. One touch was all it took for me to know where I was going, and it was worse than the mortal version of hell. At least in hell, you had earned your ticket down. But here, I didn't deserve this. No Crow ever had, and I knew I'd leave behind my own taint for the next unfortunate soul to feel.

I shuddered out a breath and gagged. The air forced fragrance down my throat like it had been covering up the stench of this awful place. It dried my nose and forced me to swallow my lunch with each wind. "The smell is going to kill me long before the Fae have the chance."

"I suggest you get used to it. Where we're going, it's so much worse," Nix answered.

"I don't think the smell will be the biggest issue I'll have with the place."

"If you live, you'll never forget this smell. It'll haunt you. Why do you think I had refused to grow certain flowers and fruits?"

"Worry not, little Crow." Solas paused to wait for me. "You won't live long enough to learn to hate the smell."

"Lucky for me, I suppose." I glared at him. "You're more morose than I am, and I'm the Crow."

"There are worse things to be in Elphame," he answered. "Though, Crows are fortunate enough to die quicker than the rest of us."

The sun was dropping by the time we left the forests and began climbing a path—or so that's what Solas had called it. A simple trail was not at all what we climbed. It was broken, with sharp rocks that stood in jagged directions. Each step was a choice between destroying my hands or my legs and ankles. The fields and forest had turned into razor rubble, and steep hills, brambles and prickles replaced the once-lush greenery. My body protested each movement. My thighs burned, and my calves cramped with each step up. What didn't burn stung under the sharpness I clung to.

My hands were scabbed with dry blood from gripping rocks and thorns so much that by the time we got to the top, I cradled my hands together. The trek tired me and drained my small well of magick. I knew we were going this route to sap me of my magick, my fight and my will to escape...and it had worked. Resting in my bones was the kind of tired I felt beyond my body and deep into my soul. Even if Solas left me unattended, I wouldn't have made it very far. I simply was too burnt out, and the climb down would have broken more bones than the miles I would have put between us.

Solas walked ahead of me, taking each leap without care. He climbed using his muscled body without hesitation. Everything about him said he had been built for this, for strolling through hell with a whistle on his lips. When I crawled, he slowed and picked his nails. When I stumbled, he leaned against a tree or stone, inconvenienced. I was a dog he was walking, nothing more. I cursed his name with each new injury.

"At this rate, we should make it there by the time your seven years are up. Well played, little Crow."

"You could have found an easier route," I answered when he complained at my pace.

"Perhaps you should have thought of that before you tried to bash my head in with a stump," he countered. "But here we are."

"Wouldn't you have done the same?" I asked and smirked.

He nodded and leaned forward as I got closer. "Yes, I would have. The difference, little Crow, is that I would have killed you."

"The day is still young, Solas. There's still time."

"Not at your pace, there isn't," he replied and moved on for me to follow. "I'll die of old age first."

"But you'll be dead just the same," I called to his back. "I'd rather be the one to do it, but at this point, I'm not that picky."

"This is going to be the longest day of my entire life," he grumbled.

I smiled. "It will be my life's goal to ensure you spend the rest of your days with me thinking that this one was the shortest."

"With a temper like yours, I'm sure those days will be few."

"I'll do as much damage as I can in those few days, then," I taunted.

"Of that, I have no doubt." He stopped talking and put space between us. It gave me joy to see his shoulders slump and hear his exasperated groans.

"He's tiring you out, Perdi. He's trying to wear out your temper before you get to court. If you go in there fuming, you'll die before the banquet tonight." Nix pulled my attention away from Solas. "I'd advise you to stop poking the bear."

"I shouldn't be the only one to remember this day."

I climbed and crawled and poked when I had the chance. The route was rough and treacherous, as was my attitude. Once I had savored the beauty in nature, the only good part of living in Whitwick Gates. I'd spent hours in the hills and forests in utter awe of mother nature. In a place where horror bloomed, beauty could be found if you stopped long enough to look. I spent countless hours hunting, collecting furs for the clothes and trade, picking berries and wild roots. It was only there, in the wilds, where I felt truly free of the oath, of my curse. Coming to Elphame sullied those memories, its beauty casting shadows over the best memories I had.

From a wasteland of rocks and rubble, we stood at the top of the hill. I glanced over the edge and, for a moment, thought about jumping.

"You'd survive the fall if you pushed out far enough from the ledge." Solas was instantly at my side on a light breeze of inky shadows. He, like me, thought I'd jump. "I have my doubts on the landing, though. You would not be the first to try and fail. There's nothing but dagger-sharp stones and bones at the bottom."

"Landings always hurt more than the fall." I leaned over the edge a little more and finally turned away.

When I sat, rubbing my cramping muscles, Solas pulled me back to my feet. There would be no more resting. On tired and stumbling legs, I followed him across a field. Solas walked casually, unafraid. I wished I had the confidence of a monster. My gaze darted around the perimeter of the grounds, waiting for something, anything, to come for us. I preferred the cover of the trees. It felt somehow safer. Being out in the open made me nervous, even though the only creatures to come were the ones I called with the use of my magick. When I stopped, they stopped coming. It gave me satisfaction to watch Solas have to fight off the creatures who came. It was disappointing that none were big enough to bite him in half. I think I would have preferred Solas in two bite-sized pieces, even if I followed him down. Solas led us back into the trees. Once out of the open, my shoulders relaxed.

"We're close, Perdi," Nix whispered from my pocket. "I can feel it."

"I don't feel anything different," I whispered back. "Everything feels…off, just as it has since we arrived in this hellhole."

"Be thankful."

Each step forward brought me closer to my fate. Whatever torture and torment they had planned for me waited on the other side of those trees. The dread was back and pressed on my chest. It gripped my throat and dried my mouth. I tried to slow my pace as much as I could without stopping, but it was of no use. Every step toward the edge of the trees, the line between a false sense of safety and the surety of menace, made me shake to my core. I told myself that I'd likely die soon. I was, after all, half-mortal. I hoped I was enough commoner, enough human, enough lesser than, to die quickly.

I had never experienced absolute nothingness, a void of life so noticeable. It felt as if everything had died off years ago. The trees held dread like cobwebs. Years of hunting the forests of Whitwick, the explosion of life great and small, hadn't prepared me for this…this emptiness. Whatever roamed these lands, which fed on life as the moon ate the day, I knew would be much worse than my mind could possibly imagine.

"Alfheim, the Golden Court." Solas introduced the land with outstretched arms. "We've just crossed their territory."

"It's not yours?" I asked. I thought for sure he was taking me to his court.

"It is, for *now,*" he answered but didn't turn to face me. He walked away before I could ask anything more—though, I doubted he'd have answered me, anyway.

There weren't many firsthand accounts of these lands, only what had been passed down in brief descriptions from surviving Crows before they turned to drink and death. Faolan had told me bits of his history, enough for me to understand them, but it wasn't enough. If I had thought I'd ever end up here, I'd have been more thorough. Though, if it weren't for being sold out, I probably wouldn't be a walking Crow, climbing to my death. He knew I'd end up here and armed me with tales that would help me not. If I saw him again, it would take all of hell to keep me from slapping the snot out of him.

The maps we had showed Elphame divided into two landmasses, Seelie to the North and Unseelie to the South. Alfheim, the Golden Court, was in the uppermost reaches of Seelie territory, bordering the Spring and Summer courts. To the South, the Unseelie Court, the Court of Less, where the Gate was located, bordered the Autumn Court, the Dark Courts and Winter Court. In the Golden Court, King Aelfdene, although Royal to only his court, ruled the others with threats and violence. And his court was now my prison until I died or, by some miracle, lived out my seven years. After seven years, I'd be on the run until I finally died, which I hoped was shortly after, if not today.

The farther North we walked, the heavier my legs became. I could feel what Nix could feel, absolute and utter dread. It felt like standing in the spoils of war after the bodies had dropped and the birds had filled their gullets on the dead. The imprint of all that had happened had stained the earth so brutally that it would never leave. I felt it climb up my legs with each step, weighing them down, making my feet drag.

We broke through the trees and stepped onto perfectly manicured lawns, and my mouth watered from the threat of puking my lunch. Flowers of every color dotted the massive gardens on either side of the grounds. The smell was like a slap across the face. It was harsh and overtook every sense, heating my cheeks as I tried not to breathe it in. I tried to clear my throat, resulting in the stench coating my mouth and lungs. I could taste roses and lilies and lilacs. It was all too much. The Golden Court, perpetually perfect, stank of seasons missing. I felt the trickle of magick dance across my skin. It would never see snowfall or hard rain. It was forever trapped in this dry and stagnant heat—and I was trapped with it.

The estate sprawled across acres of pristine lands. Never in all my years had I seen something so beautiful and terrifying at once. In a perfect square around the grounds, trees of every shape and size and color bordered the estate, trails of ivy and flowers blanketed the limbs. In the shadows of the forest, edging the property, were guards dressed in gold and white, continuously moving. Creatures on leashes, Fae on horseback, beasts crawling and twisting across the lawn tore the beauty away and replaced it with promised viciousness and revulsion. On an otherwise unspoiled property, horrors lurked at the edges, and my gut twisted. I'd never leave. I'd never escape. I'd live out the rest of my mortal life here, however long or short that would be, and in whatever condition they allowed. The reality was harder to swallow than the stench of rotting flowers.

The stone manor, framed by gardens and trees, was as humble as any of the most exquisite gems and diamonds. It stood at the farthest reaches of the property. The front of the manor held three levels of floor-to-ceiling windows. Ivy had been trimmed and cut back to show the massive eyes of the home. Balconies, which looked like they had been carved out of the very stone of the manor, clung under windows. It was as if the estate had grown from the very earth it stood on, like it had been carved into existence by the devil himself. A path of gravel led from the Gate we stepped through to my new prison. Had I not been walking to a fate worse than death, I'd have been in awe.

Under the disguise of gold and riches, I was haunted by it. The beauty of it held secrets and horrors, and I could feel it in my stomach. The manor lived under a relentless shadow. It was as if the sun couldn't reach past the walls or windows. The air was cold, yet it was still bright out. It was the kind of cold that had nothing to do with weather and everything to do with the happenings inside the walls of that manor. As stunning as it was, as breathtaking as it was, no amount of beauty could chase away my fear. Nix crawled up my leg and tucked himself into my pocket, grumbling at the hidden creature still tucked away, but said nothing out loud. I felt them both shake against my hip. They, like me, weren't blinded by the roses.

"Everything is so white. It must be hard to wash the blood off," I muttered.

"The trick is to wash it off right away before the stain has time to set," Solas answered, not missing a beat. "Once it sets, all you can do is toss it."

"I bet you're a real treat at parties." I rolled my eyes.

"Soon enough, you'll find out." He turned his back to me and kept walking.

I would have given almost anything to have a rock in my hand to brain him with. Dreaming of the day I would have that rock, I followed Solas up the path to a fate only nightmares were made of. The stories told to little bad girls and boys didn't come close to the reality of it. There would never be a tale close enough to the truth. This was a shaving of what halflings were told during training for the inevitable. The mortal world tried to prepare future Crows for their Taking. But this, what stood before me, was never covered. I suppose they left out the utter terror of it all to keep future Crows from killing themselves.

I stared down at the gravel under my shoes and shuddered. It wasn't stone or earth. "Are these bones?"

Solas glanced at the bones under my feet and grinned. "How confident would you be, invading, if you were forced to walk on the bones of the previous army to try?"

"Oh my God." The shiver ran over my skin, raising goosebumps.

"Your God doesn't live here, little Crow."

"Neither does yours," I answered. I could feel the terror of the place crawl across my arms and legs. The more I tried to wipe it off, the stronger it got.

"Just keep walking. It'll go away," Nix whispered. "You can't fight it. It's magick."

I nodded. "It feels awful."

"Everything about this place is awful," he replied.

I felt the weight of dozens of eyes. The new Crow had arrived. No one looked directly at Solas. Their eyes were fixed solely on me. When Solas would glance in their direction, they quickly looked away. I wondered what Solas did for the king, for them to fear him in this way. The Darkmore journals spoke of Solas, specifically, as the one who came for the Crows with his flying beasts, the Sluagh. I had watched them out of my window during the Taking. I'd have feared Solas as much as any other on these grounds had I not hated him more than I did. Hate trumped fear, at least when it came to Solas.

"Doesn't look like you have many friends here, Solas," I taunted him. "I thought for sure a man of your stature would have people lining up to greet him."

"Stop needling him," Nix scolded me, and I shrugged. "You're going to make him angry—but not enough to kill you."

"Who needs friends when you have enemies?" Solas countered.

"Me," I whispered and patted my pocket.

"As you wish." He slowed and walked at my side. "But remember, friends and loved ones are the very thing that will cause you to endure, to suffer. They won't save you here. They will tie you to these lands, and you'll pay for every one of them."

"Enemies won't help me, either." I glared at him and pulled away, but he still smiled in return.

"You'll know if I consider you my enemy. It'll be the last thought to cross that little mind of yours."

"I look forward to that day," I answered. "Death at your hands or someone else's… It's all the same to me. This will be over, and I will be free."

"Free?" He barked a laugh. "That's cute, Perdi."

"Do not call me Perdi," I snapped.

"Perdita." He drew out my name and I cringed. "You do not have what it takes to gain your freedom—not now, and certainly not after spending seven years in hell."

"Seven years?" It was now my turn to laugh. "Who the hell said I'd wait seven years to taste my freedom? And when that day comes, if you're standing in my way, I'll be the last thought to cross that little mind of yours, as you see my face standing over your body."

He spread his arms, his body showing no signs of my previous attack. "Bravado so soon? Get it out now, out here. Because in there, they will hurt you for it. They won't hesitate, and they'll do it simply because they are bored of you. There is nothing you can do to me that hasn't already been done a dozen times over. Do it now, because you can't afford it later."

Without a second thought, I pulled the butterknife from my pocket. It had been chewed sharp by my little creature in exchange for another drop of my blood. I slid the blade into Solas' chest, inches from his heart. I jerked it out and plunged it into his stomach. He grabbed my hand and twisted the knife until the warmth of his blood poured over my hand.

"It'll be your heart when I come for you again," I whispered into his ear. "Remember this day, Soulless, for this was the day a Crow chose not to take your life. I won't be as gracious next time."

"Welcome home, little Crow. You'll need more than a butterknife to take my life. You'll need the entire fucking continent for me to even notice." Solas kissed my cheek and stepped back. The wounds closed in front of me, but the blood remained. Although he smiled, I watched the last of his surprise leak from his eyes. That was twice I'd attacked him. Twice I'd surprised him. And twice I'd surprised myself with my boldness. I wondered if I would get a third time before he finally tired of me.

"I'll use iron the next time." I smiled and dropped the knife to the ground. It would be of no use to me here. Iron, cold and raw, would have killed him had I hit his heart. There weren't many tools we had to kill the Fae, but iron was a surefire end to any creature of Elphame. Knowledge of their very few weaknesses was the only reason Whitwick still stood.

"I'm sure you will," he answered and started back toward the manor.

Those around us stared in seeming awe. I almost skipped behind him, happy at my stand against the man who marched me to what I could only assume was my death. I didn't kill him, didn't do much more than amuse him, but it still felt damn good. I hummed and picked the tiny flowers from the lawn and tucked it into my pocket for my creature to nibble on. Deep inside my stomach, held back by sheer force of will, my terror sat. It ate at my soul as the creature in my pocket ate the flowers.

Solas, irritated by my slow pace, grabbed my arm and pulled me to the manor. One colossal staircase jutted out from the earth and climbed to the front door. Its golden banister housed a beast on each side, welcoming none. At the top stood an enclosed deck. Ahead, two massive gold doors opened with a hush before we even reached them. Solas yanked me, and my feet skidded on the marble deck. I didn't want to go in. Every nerve came alive in warning. On the other side of that threshold there was only pain, and in the back of my mind, so much darkness. But Solas pulled anyway. The closer we got, the more I yanked. My brain told me to do whatever I could to get away.

"No, no, no, no…I can't do this," I whispered. The wind in my sails from stabbing Solas was gone.

"Whether you can or can't, you'll come under your own steam, or you will come under mine," he answered and jerked me.

I pulled until the muscles in my shoulder felt like they'd snap. "I'm not going in there."

He leaned into my ear and jerked me into his body. "You will. Do not waste your energy on things you have no control over. Do not fight what you can't control. You're going in there, one way or another. Do not force me to do what I must. You will enjoy it less than I will."

"Bastard." I growled the word.

"I'm many things, but that is not one of them."

My body tensed as we stepped in. My muscles twitched, doing their best to convince me to run. I was bombarded with colors, movement, smells and sounds. White marble decorated the floors and walls. Bouquets of flowers stood on top of tables, tucked into the walls, hung from the ceiling as if the gardens weren't enough. Through the front, doors leading in every direction, stairs sat against the farthest wall, one up and one down. I didn't want to know what was down the stairs. The very moment I saw the stairs, I knew I'd never want to go down there willingly. Something far beyond horror rested in the bowels of this manor, so terrible that there were no windows to gaze upon it.

"Move," Solas barked.

There were dozens of people milling about, waiting on the Crow, chattering. Their voices were too high a pitch for me not to flinch. The noise danced across my brain and gave me an instant headache. They were excited, thrilled at my arrival. They smiled, stared, giggled and glared. I wished each and every one of them a painful death. I didn't know them but hated them all.

I slid across the floor, being pulled forward. "Please, don't. I can't. Please, Solas, *please*."

He leaned in, pulling my body until my ear met his mouth. "Do not make me force you. You don't want to be delivered as a scared little Crow. You don't want to be seen as weak here."

I shook my head. "I can't."

He groaned and stepped forward. He kept his hand firmly under my arm, pressing his grip into my armpit and forced me to step forward, half stumbling and half walking. Each time I froze, Solas effortlessly pulled as though I weighed nothing. I was led through a series of halls and rooms, each more decadent than the last, until we stepped into a room where it felt like all of Elphame stood. I wasn't just intimidated. I was terrified to have every eye on me. Tables lined the walls, and food spilled from plates and bowls. So much waste was all I could think of. People outside of Elphame starved, but here, the food was so excessive that it fell to the floor.

We came to a stop in front of a golden throne. I could feel the deaths it took for that throne to stand. It had been carved of wickedness and bathed in the blood of countless souls who died for the king to sit upon it. Solas had no need to shove me to my knee. My knees gave out once we stood in front of King Aelfdene, and he let go of my arm. The cold floor was unyielding against my tired bones but offered relief against the burning of my muscles. I stared at the white marble floor, veined in gold, too scared to lift my eyes. The room stank of flowers and magick, and now my fear. Fae whispered around me, and none used my name. I was simply 'Crow' within these walls.

"Sorry for the delay. This one was a slow walker," Solas spoke, and the room fell to silence.

"Why ever would you walk her here?" King Aelfdene asked.

"I needed the fresh air," he responded.

"Clearly, the walk was treacherous. You're covered in blood, Solas." There was an edge of amusement in the king's voice.

"She has a spicy temper," he replied.

"Undoubtedly." The king stepped down from his throne, his golden shoes inches from my cowering face. "The gnome must go. He is courtless."

I jolted at the thought of being without Nix and jumped to my feet. I shook my head. I tried to beg, only to fail. No words would come out. My eyes watered, and I backed away. The king didn't so much as nod, and the two men grabbed each arm. I thrashed against them, against being trapped, and finally screamed. I fought, twisted, turned, but made no progress.

"I promised her she could keep her friend," Solas lied. He had said no such thing to me – or had he? Was this how a person ended up owing the Fae, by not understanding the meaning behind their words, by being locked into a deal because of a casual conversation? I had said I needed a friend, and he had granted that wish.

"Why would you make promises you cannot keep?" King Aelfdene asked. He motioned to his men. "Take the gnome."

"No, please, he won't be of any trouble," I begged as guards gripped my arms.

Solas stepped forward, and with one look, the two men dropped me to the ground. "No. I have given my word. You never know when a Crow favor will come in handy."

King Aelfdene froze, and I waited for him to unleash on Solas, but it never came. Whatever monster Solas was for the king, it was enough to earn him a margin of freedom. I didn't want to find out who exactly he was to the king. Leeway was not something anyone received without difficulty, in any realm. He clapped Solas on his back and laughed. His voice echoed through the room. "Do as you please, Solas. You have until tonight. Do not break her. She is our guest of honor."

"Nix?" I asked, my mouth finally able to form words.

"He can stay as long as Solas allows it. He is, after all, responsible for the little creature now," King Aelfdene replied. He turned from me and waved his hand in dismissal. "Show them to their quarters."

I followed behind Solas, back through the gawkers and onlookers. My stomach rolled with anxiety, but Solas wasn't fazed in the least. While he moved with purpose, I shuffled along, jerking at every sound. My mind conjured the most hideous of cells and hovels I'd be placed in. But no image could be as revolting as owing Solas a favor for allowing me to keep Nix or of having the king's dog call in that debt.

Chapter Six

Solas led me through halls of gold and white, marbled and lavish, the stares from those who came to see the Crow followed us from every corner. If it weren't for his arm on mine, I'd have slammed into his back, my eyes everywhere else. From the outside, the manor was massive, but from inside, it was immense, impossibly larger than I had guessed it to be.

We ended on the third story. Behind a carved oak door held a lush bedroom, grander than I needed or wanted. It was a house within a house, my new home. The walls were papered in rich textures and colors, with hints of gold woven throughout. The wall coverings held more real gold than most in Whitwick had seen in their lifetimes. I instantly hated the room for that single reason—excess, extravagance, waste. It made my stomach flop in envy, to want for nothing, and anger for the lavishness while so many others died with empty stomachs. As the daughter of a Guardian, I did not suffer as many had. But both my father and I had skipped plenty of meals and holidays to ensure our community made it through harsh winters.

Thick moldings framed the room, doors and windows. A large four-poster bed sat in the middle of the wall, covered in plush bedding and more pillows than any household, let alone one person, could need. The curtains that hung from the bed and two picture windows were of similar colors and drifted in a breeze that carried with it the scent of flowers and the sound of life carrying on as if the Fae hadn't just dragged a young girl into their realm. More than the anger, I had to hear their laughter. I didn't know which made me gag, the joy or the perpetual flower-shop scents. I wanted to shut the windows just to block out the flowers.

I followed Solas in and stood behind him. I knew he wouldn't protect me from whatever stood in the room with us, but he was still a better option than the unknown. I knew, at that very moment, that if I were willing to stand with him over others, I was in deeper trouble than I could even imagine. I chewed the inside of my cheek and rubbed the middle of my chest. It was all I could do to keep myself from trembling or, worse, crying again. My eyes felt puffy and gritty from too many tears shed. Crying wouldn't fix anything here. It wouldn't bring me home to the comfort of my own room. Crying wouldn't wake me from this terrible dream.

"This is Elswyth." Solas' voice cut through the room like a blade and startled me. It bounced off the art-covered walls and felt like the slap I needed to come back to attention.

I stepped around him and entered. At his front stood a thin woman, no bigger than I was. Her white-blonde hair was tied at the top of her head in tiny knots and twists. She didn't look a day older than I was, yet her ice-blue eyes held centuries of time I had not lived. She was wafer-thin and uncomfortably beautiful. But then again, on the outside, everything looked pretty here in Elphame. Even salt looked like sugar until you tasted it. Elswyth bowed and stayed there, in a position that would have made my legs quake, and eventually, I'd have fallen over. But she held her curtsey as if she were born that way.

"Please, don't bow to me," I finally spoke, my voice quivering. I cleared my throat and tried to swallow down the hard rocks of fear that had caught each word as I spoke. I'd have time to be terrified later and at worse delights than this. "Solas, why is she here?"

"Every Crow is allowed a lady. I've selected Elswyth for your stay in the Golden Courts," he answered and tapped Elswyth. "Go, run her bath. I will return in two hours for the banquet."

I waited for Elswyth to scurry from the room into what I could only assume was my bathroom. She moved as a frightened dog would, skittish from one too many beatings. Her shoulders slumped, and she kept her eyes on the floor. Fear was the motivator of Elphame, even for those who were born of these lands. I disliked her less for that reason alone. We shared a common bond. We were both terrified of this place. I wondered how long it would take for my shoulders to slump as hers did.

I rubbed the tears from my burning eyes. "The smell, what is with the bloody flowers?"

"It covers the scent of death pretty good, does it not?" he answered. Solas lifted his finger to his lips and shook his head. Before I could say anything more, he closed the door, locking us into my room alone. "Keep your head down and your mouth closed, and you may make it through your first night. What you say here comes at a cost. Only ever open your mouth when you're willing to pay for it. And know that payment is always more than what you can afford and never what you want to pay."

"I have nothing to pay with," I answered. "I'm already fated to die. What's one more day closer to my grave?"

"You're a woman. Think of what that means here, of what they'll take from you each time you want to speak," he answered, and I shivered at the dark thoughts that crossed my mind. "You're catching on, little Crow. We only ever pay with that which we'd rather keep. Now, go wash up. You stink more than the flowers."

I glanced at Elswyth in my bathroom, preparing my bath. "I don't need a lady. I don't want one."

"Yes, you do. Being alone here is worse than you think," he answered. "Trust that I know how to survive in this court better than you do."

"I thought I couldn't trust anyone? I'm already surrounded by people I can't trust. Why would I want another one around me at all times?"

"And here I thought you needed a friend?"

I rolled my eyes. "Yes, Solas, because that's exactly what I need right now—a friend who will run me a bath when I need one. However did you know?"

"You'd be surprised. Go wash the stink off yourself and get ready for tonight."

"What will happen tonight?" I spit out the words before I was too afraid to ask.

He shrugged casually like my life wasn't hanging in the balance. "It is different every time. But rest assured, you will remember every last second of it. Even when your mind goes soggy from madness, you'll always remember your first night in Elphame."

I stared at him, surprised at his nonchalant yet jarring answer. "That's not an answer. That's a threat."

"No. It's a promise. I don't know what *will* happen. I only know what *could* happen, hence my comment. Rest assured. You'll remember this night more than any other."

"I don't even know you, and I hate you so deeply."

"You have a lot of pain to feel yet, if this is your idea of hate. Enough time and I'm sure that word will mean much, much more than it does right now. Elphame will ensure that much."

I fidgeted with the torn sleeves of my jacket and fumbled for a better question, one he wouldn't talk riddles around. I swallowed hard and looked him in the eyes. "Will they kill me?"

"Don't get your hopes up, little Crow. They'll try not to kill you for these seven years. But you mortals, even halflings, are far more breakable than most Fae realize or even care to learn. You die at the most inconvenient times and for the oddest reasons. You sneeze or your nose runs, and you're dead by the next day. How does your kind even survive infancy when you drop from sickness within hours?"

"I'm pretty sure, Solas, it won't be a sickness that kills me here," I countered.

"Foolish little Crow, you have no idea how sick this place can be," he replied.

"Stop calling me that."

He smiled and it wasn't friendly. "You have two hours, then I'll be back, and you'll be welcomed into the land of Elphame."

"I could do without a banquet," I mumbled.

"Couldn't we all." His answer was clipped and tired. From the look on his face, I knew he saw how terrified I was. "No one will come in here but me. Fear nothing."

"Trust no one," I echoed back to him.

"Touché." He walked out of the room and left me with a stranger.

For a split second, I wondered if I was strong enough to drown the woman who leaned over my bath. Even with her weak stature, I doubted it, but the thought still made me smile.

"Nice digs," Nix said as he popped out of my pocket, followed by the creature.

"Shut up," I said sourly. "Check the place for wards and ways for others to listen in."

I closed my eyes and allowed my Malice to flow from my core. I could see it in my mind's eye, dark little tendrils curling and slithering about like the arms of a sea creature. While Nix inspected my new room, now my home, I spelled the room as my magick touched each crack and crevasse. If this were going to be my prison, I'd make sure I'd know who was coming and going and who was trying to listen in. My magick brushed up against the magick from the last occupant. They, like me, had done the same. I reinforced decades of old magick and snapped a bubble around my bedroom. The knots of magick I had woven around my room wouldn't keep me safe, but it would keep my cries from those who relished in my tears once I finally had a meltdown.

"It's clear," Nix called from my bed and whistled. "There's a lot of suffering in these walls, Perdi. I can feel it like oil on my skin."

"Yeah, I got that impression when we were walking up the pathway. It feels off. It feels darker than it is, like peeling an orange, only to find it rotten inside." I shuddered.

"It could be worse. Be thankful we are in the Golden Court. There are places I'd rather not go back to—territories and kings that would make this place your relief."

"I don't think it matters much where I am. I think it's going to hurt, regardless."

"Nix?" Elswyth called from the bathroom and poked her head out, and stared at me, waiting for me to invite her from the bathroom.

"Els?" Nix's laughter melted some of my bitterness. "When… How did you get out?"

"My lady, your bath is ready." Elswyth stood to the side of the bathroom door.

"You're not a prisoner in this room, Elswyth," I finally said and motioned for her to come out. "You're not my slave. You're not a slave, period, not when you're here with us. I think there's enough suffering to go around to not inflict it on each other."

"Thank you, my lady." Elswyth bowed her head slightly, catching herself before dropping into a full curtsey.

"And please call me Perdi. I'll draw my own baths from now on, unless I'm a hobbled mess, then I'd appreciate the help," I said as I walked past her. "Thank you, though."

The bathroom was like everything else I had seen since coming to Elphame…luxurious. Everything was gold and white marble. The only color was held in the flowers, plants, art, oils and soaps. The bathroom had everything one would need to wash the stain of sin from the soul. A stand-up shower, large enough for the biggest of creatures, took up the entire right wall, enclosed in glass. The tub sat in the middle and a vanity to the left, with more windows that overlooked the freedom of others. White and gold rugs covered the cold marbled floor.

I peeled off my dirty clothes and slowly crawled into a marble tub with water that smelled of lavender and mint. The change in scent was calming and reminded me of the herb garden in my backyard. I flinched when the hot water touched my cuts and bruises, a sudden reminder of my journey to the Golden Court. My usual pasty-white skin was spoiled in marks. Head to toe, I was covered in the evidence of my Taking. As I looked at each wound and felt the sting of each cut, I knew it would only get worse. Nothing about my trip so far had said each passing moment would be better than the last.

I leaned against the back of the tub and closed my eyes. I listened to Nix and Elswyth talk about times long before I had taken my first breath. I hadn't thought about Nix seeing his friends and family here or how that would make him feel. I was caught up in my own fear. I didn't consider his. He had left Elphame, and I'd dragged him back. A life he no longer wanted, a life he feared, my Taking had forced back on to him. I had been so occupied with my initial fears that I'd forgotten that he had lived this life for decades. How could I have been so selfish not to have sent him back? To have not forced him back.

"Solas bought me," Elswyth said of why she was with Solas, why she was in the Golden Court.

"You were sold?" I called out from the bath. The thought was revolting but not surprising. I was a mortal sitting in a tub in Elphame, covered in wounds from my Taking, and I was surprised someone else would suffer here. That the Fae would treat their own kind in the same manner shouldn't have shocked me in the least. 'Eat or be eaten, kill or be killed', I've learned, were the mottos of the Fae realm.

Elswyth, who hadn't strayed too far from me, leaned around the corner, averting her eyes. "Solas takes people as payments. It sounds awful, but it truly isn't a fate worse than I was already facing."

"That's disgusting," I mumbled.

"No, it was a kindness compared to where I had been."

I didn't know how to reply to that, given where I was. My fate was considered the worst in the mortal realm. I wondered if the Golden Court with Solas was a fate better than if Faolan had Taken me? Was Solas a kindness compared to Faolan? At least here, with Solas, I knew I was hated. There was no lie about it or clever ploy. With Solas, I was simply snatched from my home and told it would hurt. He hadn't spent my entire life trying to convince me I could trust him as Faolan had.

"You will not like tonight." Elswyth broke the silence.

"Naturally. I didn't assume I'd enjoy any part of Elphame," I answered, bitterness on my tongue. "What's on the agenda for this evening? Torture? Pain?"

She nodded. "In a manner of speaking. Whatever you see or hear, it will be done to break you.

Everything, from this point forward, will be at your expense."

"Of that, I have no doubt," I answered.

"Perdi, if they break you here, they will keep you here," Nix spoke at the door. "This is not where you want to remain for the rest of your life."

"Where the hell else would I go? Even if I survive this place, the Gate is one way. I'm here for good." I trembled at my reality. "I'll never go home. This hellhole is my home—these cursed and stanching lands. I've been here for less than a day, and I'm already a mess. I can only imagine what the next two thousand days will bring."

"He did it to tire you out," Elswyth spoke up. "Your journey here."

"So I've heard, but it hurts just the same."

"He did it to keep you in one piece. He does this to those who fight the whole way. It's so that you're too tired later to fight a room of Fae." Her face fell a little. "Some of your kind, mortals, have not even made it to the welcoming banquet. If he thinks you'll be too much trouble too soon, he works it out of you along the way."

"How very thoughtful of him, to ensure I'd last long enough to be welcomed into the land that stole me from my own."

I did my best to tune them out while I washed. It hurt to hear their stories, to know their history, good and bad. It bothered me that I enjoyed the soaps even more. Nix and Elswyth were both from the Court of Less and, from what I could hear, hadn't seen each other since the night he'd come to Whitwick Gates. Elswyth spoke of the king and his court and of the many cruelties performed daily. A never-ending cycle of pain and anguish and I wasn't the least bit shocked.

Why would I end up in a court of kindness? Did they even have that in Elphame? I very much doubted anyone could protect a court of gentle giants. There was no place for a kind soul in Elphame, not if you wanted to live. I wondered if I was willing to let go of my own for survival.

In the corner of the bathroom, under the furthest reaches of the vanity, the only sliver of darkness sat. When I had first curled in the tub, only the brightness of the Golden Court could be seen. But here, now, with me, pitch blackness rested and watched me. It should have made me uncomfortable, scared even. But it calmed me to see that not everything could be forced and broken by the Golden Court. Not everything could be chased away or twisted into their image. I moved to the other end of the tub and stretched my fingertips toward it. At first, it pulled back as soon as I had reached for it. I understood the flinch. My muscles ached from it.

"I won't hurt you," I whispered, "if you don't try to hurt me."

Slowly, it inched along where the wall met the floor, in the cracks. It reminded me of coaxing a wounded animal. The shadows inched up the wall until they grazed my hand and jerked back. I stayed perfectly still, like waiting for a butterfly to land. It reached out again, this time not recoiling. It twisted around my fingers, and I smiled. It didn't feel like danger. It felt like stepping into the shadows under the trees in my backyard. It felt familiar.

"My name is Perdi," I whispered. It said nothing in return. But I didn't really expect shadows to talk. "You should hide before someone sees you."

It twisted tighter, and I sighed. For the briefest of moments, I could smell home. Gone were the bouquets of gagging perfection. I could smell the meadow, earth, moss and tree bark.

"Are you trapped here, too?" I whispered. A wave of salty ocean touched my nose before it finally released.

"Wait. Don't go." I squeaked out strangled words. "Home."

I felt the weight of being alone once again. I didn't want it to go. I wanted to tuck it in my pocket, to stay with Nix and the creature. Another friend, even a shadow, would have been better than not. I watched until it faded, sucked back into the cracks and back to wherever it came from. As it left, I mourned that it hadn't taken me with it. It didn't matter where it had gone, it would have been better than here.

Elswyth helped me from the tub for no other reason than I was weak and tired. I shuffled along the floor, exhausted. Wrapped in a bath sheet, I sat in front of a white dressing desk and mirror and shivered. I wasn't cold. I was afraid. In the mirror, my face was paler than usual, save for the colored blotches and bruises that splattered my cheeks and one eye. Elswyth combed out my tangled red hair and pulled it into a tight braid. She made me eat before I passed out. With my hair away from my face, I looked older. I had aged in hours what it usually took years to do. Everything about me was not me. I left me, who I am, at the Gate. I looked like I had stepped out of that mist with the baggage of several lifetimes in hell resting on my flesh.

The banquet tonight would be the start of this nightmare, so Elswyth said. Everything so far was the build-up. I'd be presented to Elphame, put on display, taunted and ridiculed for the Crow I am. They'd begin breaking me as soon as they could. Thankfully, Crows didn't live long enough to draw it out to its fullest potential. I was happy for that. I would be led in by Solas, who, from what I understand, would be the guard who would keep me in line. As I had thought, he was nothing more than a lapdog for the king.

"Sorry, what?" I finally noticed Elswyth had been talking, and I hadn't heard a word she had said. I chewed on my food, not because I was hungry, but because it was in my hand.

"Nix mentioned you have a temper. I was offering you a kind warning to keep your words to yourself," Elswyth said softly. "I mean no disrespect, but they will punish you for such things here. A long-living Crow is one who learns their place quickly. Nod, smile, keep your head and eyes down and say nothing. If you're asked a question, do your absolute best to be kind with your words. Agree to nothing unless it is from the king himself…or Solas. Do not meddle, do not poke, do not joke. And whatever you do, trust no one. They all want to see you fail. And failure here is not the same as in your mortal world. Failure here is death—drawn out over many years where you won't see the light of day."

"Death doesn't seem like that bad of an idea, Elswyth," I countered.

"Death over seven years, only to die once you've tasted freedom," Nix added.

I groaned. "I'll do my best, but I'm tired and hurting, and crawling into a dirt hole isn't looking that bad."

"You must stop telling yourself that they'll simply just kill you. They won't. They never have and never will. It will be utterly slow and painful." Elswyth closed her eyes and shuddered. "They'll do awful things to you until you finally fall in line. But it will be too late, the damage that will be done…"

"I'm sorry, Elswyth. I'll do my best." I stopped her from going too deeply into memories that hadn't yet scabbed over, still raw as the day someone put them there. I knew, if by some strange and cruel twist of fate, that if I lived, I'd live in the same wounds until I died. Nothing was going to scab over my introduction and survival of Elphame. Nothing, no one, could prepare a Crow.

After disagreeing on several outfits, we finally settled on flat black slippers and a black silk dress that wouldn't get caught up if I had to run. She politely reminded me that I wouldn't be running anywhere. I'd be caught before I got not ten feet away. Still, the thought of wearing heels and a long gown made me cringe. She tried to push me into wearing something bright and colorful, fit for the court we were in. But there was no way I would present myself as already broken, already currying favors, already a member of the Golden Court. I'd go naked before I wore the colors of this cursed place.

"My bruises are colorful enough," I countered. "Now, what are my duties as a Crow? No one has ever told me, not even Faolan. And it isn't like the Crows who had survived and returned had given us a lot of information. I don't think anyone asked. Truthfully, I don't think anyone wanted to ask."

"You will attend all banquets. If we were in a court with Royal children, you would suffer their punishments. But King Aelfdene doesn't have any small children, so you're safe from that." Elswyth smiled as if that were good news. "In some courts, the Crow is the bed partner of the king."

"Sleep with him? I don't think so." I shook my head. My temper flared.

"Eat your temper, Perdi," Elswyth scolded me. "You must be prepared for everything. Whether it happens or not, they will hint at it to gauge your reaction. Whatever you show to be of most bother is what they will do to you, until it no longer troubles you. They will then find something else to torment you with. I can think of a dozen things worse than bedding a king willingly."

"Willingly." I half-laughed. But she was right. It could be unwillingly. I tried to calm myself, but it wasn't easy. "I can't do this."

"Yes, you can." Her voice was firm and much braver than mine. "You have no choice. If you give up, it will get worse. Once they break you, they won't just push you to the side and ignore you. They're far too creative for that. They'll find other ways to entertain themselves. They'll hurt Nix, just to hurt you. We will live and die based on how well you do. I don't mean to put this pressure on you, but we will die and you will watch, and you will be responsible for it."

I froze. Again, I was not thinking of him or that I had pulled him into my nightmare. If they hurt him, I would never forgive myself. "Nix, I'm so sorry. You shouldn't be here. You should go."

"It's too late for that," he answered. "I am already here."

"He came here of his own free will, but he is now tied to you and your seven years," Elswyth explained. "If you die, he will die with you. If you gain your freedom, he is free to leave with you. Whatever your fate is, it is tethered to him—and now to me."

I cursed under my breath. "I hate this place."

"As do most of us, Perdi." Nix plunked himself on my dressing table. "But we do not have the luxury of hate, not here. For us, the only luxuries we have is at the will of the king."

"I see why you left," I muttered. Hate may not be an extravagance I could afford out there, but in this room, it was free.

He nodded in agreement. "Tonight, I can't go with you. Courtless are not welcome here. They're not welcome anywhere."

"What? Why is Elswyth permitted, but you are not?" I asked, my heart racing at the thought of leaving him behind.

"Because, by all rights, I am owned. I am no more important than the dogs the ladies will be bringing tonight," she answered.

"Don't ever repeat those words, Elswyth. You are not a dog, and you are important." I grabbed her arm and turned her to face me. "You *are* important."

"Perhaps to you." She nodded but kept her shoulders slumped. I didn't think she believed me. Had I been in her place, I wouldn't believe me either. I didn't feel any more important than she did. I, like her, was owned. "Do not feel badly for me. Being of no importance keeps me safe, keeps me out of mind. Being on the tip of someone's tongue is a dangerous place to be."

"He's here." Nix stood and looked at the door.

My heart sank to my feet, and I cursed his name.

Chapter Seven

"I trust Elswyth has filled you in on the protocols for this evening?" Solas asked, leading me from my room, my arm tucked in his elbow.

His body was blazing hot under my touch. Each time I tried to pull my hand away, he *tsk*ed me and pulled me back. "Do you really think you can do this alone? You don't want to be here unattended. Trust that, little Crow. There are worse monsters than I wandering these halls."

"I seriously doubt that last part." I grumbled but clasped his arm.

He was dressed casually and looked plain next to me in silks and ribbons. His black dress pants matched my black dress, and it irritated me. His white dress shirt, untucked, flapped behind us in a wind I couldn't feel. In any other circumstance, I'd have said he was attractive with his deep blue eyes, olive skin and wild hair to his shoulders. Everything about him said he cared for the night as much as I did. But unlike him, I wasn't relaxed. Where his shoulders moved with ease, mine were knots of tension. His jaw was clearly relaxed while mine chewed against my inner cheek. Where his lips were smooth, mine were chapped and split. And although I had beaned him in the head twice, not a mark marred his flesh. It must be nice to heal so quickly and look so perfect.

"Some marks can't be seen." Solas leaned into my ear as if my thoughts had been heard. I jerked for a moment and focused on my mind, building up a wall around my thoughts. How utterly intrusive, but could I really expect more from the likes of him?

Elswyth followed behind us and said nothing. She dressed in the bright colors the rest of the court would be wearing—rich purples and pinks, feathers and bows. She had played this game enough times to have learned a place I had just stepped into. She had seen these banquets more times than she'd have liked and kept her eyes down. I almost envied her position of following the Crow, over being the Crow.

I finally nodded to Solas. I didn't trust my words. Elswyth hadn't told me of protocols, aside from reminding me of a temper I got from my mother. Perhaps that was the only protocol worth knowing—look pretty and shut my mouth. Easier said than done, with bruises aplenty and the mood of a cornered animal.

My eyes were wide, and my heart pounded against my ribcage. I struggled for each breath. Solas kept his hot hand over mine, ready to grab me at the earliest sign of me bolting. He was practiced. I wondered how many Crows he had walked to their deaths. How many had run and how many he hunted down, only to drag back. More importantly, did he enjoy the chase, even after all these years?

"Keep your head down, and you'll make it back to your room in one piece." He leaned into my ear again.

"No, she won't."

Solas stopped walking. "Why do you say that?"

I stared at him, puzzled. I had heard the words, but they hadn't come from me. "I didn't say anything."

He looked back to Elswyth, who shook her head. He stared at me again for a moment longer. "Just keep your mouth shut, and it'll be over soon enough."

Ogling faces, sneering gawkers, their eyes focus on me as they had when I first arrived. They littered the halls, High Fae, all wanting to see the Crow marched by. Not a one looked at Solas, yet not a one seemed all that surprised that it was him who had me in his clutches. Solas was far from bland. Everything about him was worthy of another monster's eye, yet their eyes weren't for him.

With glittering glances, far too many teeth and dressed in their finest, they snickered as I moved past each and every one of them. While I cowered under their gaze, Solas was unaffected. Elswyth, if bothered, was well versed in hiding every emotion that didn't please a Royal, a High Fae. I wondered how long it would take for me to break as she had. Would I survive it as she had? Would I find myself drawing a bath for a future Crow? And what advice would I have for them? Smile and shut up, then maybe one day you could be cleaning a tub? Bed the king, and perhaps you'll live long enough to wish for death?

The part of my brain that wanted to survive pulled my attention to the paintings we passed—anything to give my mind the break it so desperately needed. As a child of Whitwick, I could ignore just about anything until it was nipping at my ankles. I focused on things that meant nothing, but everything at that moment, if I wanted to keep my sanity. It was too early in the game to go mad, however lovely it sounded. The paintings that adorned the walls showed history in color. Fae on horseback, gardens with children, weddings, and wars, splashed the walls in perfect detail. It was as if the painter had cast their memories onto canvas, but only the parts of triumph and victories. I suppose one wouldn't want to hang their losses for all to see. I wouldn't want my Taking framed and hanging over my bed.

Solas cleared his throat and brought my attention away from the walls to the room we were entering. The entrance to the ballroom, framed in gold, stood ahead of us. The smell of food and flowers escaped the room and mingled into a perfume of rotting meat in a garden of roses. Two guards stood on either side of the door, dressed in white and gold, each risking a glance our way. It took everything I had not to yell 'boo'.

Solas raised his eyebrows as if asking a question if I was ready. I didn't nod. I would never be fully prepared for this to happen. I didn't want to go in, but his smile said he didn't care. I was going in regardless. With a slight jerk of his elbow, we stepped through open double doors into a room filled to the ceiling with only the very best for a king. While the mortal world struggled and starved, Elphame stuffed themselves to their fullest. I swallowed the hate and my wish that they all dropped dead in a display of twisted pain. The brief thought of their deaths had settled the storm brewing in my stomach.

The banquet room was a grand hall, to say the least. It made my first impression of the manor seem less than this. The hall dripped in opulence. The cream-colored walls were splattered with paintings, gold, marble statues and bouquets of lavish and pristine flowers. It was all too much and not enough at the same time. It was over-the-top gaudy. Massive marble tables lined the walls, eating up the vastness of the space, offering a hint of romance and slapping you in the face with a fist of gold coins. Gold tablecloths covered in food and drink, dared the guests to gorge themselves. Tall, gold candelabras commanded attention from the center of the tables, holding gold candles with wax that never dripped. Clusters of chandeliers hung high above the crowd and cast shadows that made me step back. It was as though the fog had never left me. It hung above the room and waited.

I froze, and Solas tugged.

"Walk, or they will put a leash on you and lead you through the room." Solas leaned into my cheek. "Don't force me to drag you. This is not the place to show weakness or fear. They'll eat it up and come back for more. Is that what you want? Or are you going to go in on your own steam and own it before they can own you?"

"Tonight, I'll pray for your death," I responded.

"Not your own death? That's progress, I'd say." He yanked me forward. I either walked, or I fell. Was he baiting me or giving me a target for my anger?

I stepped into the room with Solas and Elswyth at my back. The laughter and merriment rose around us and did nothing to steady my nerves. My cheeks burned as every eye turned toward me. I suddenly felt underdressed. Everyone else was dressed in gowns and feathers and furs, everyone but Solas. His black hair hung loosely around his collar, where others had spent hours perfecting theirs. His face was blank, a perfect mask I wish I could master. He pulled me through the gaping crowd, each tug making me wince in pain.

The laughter had all but disappeared, but the music hadn't skipped a beat. The classical music was fitting for my march through the hall. I kept my eyes on the floor and followed Solas as he led me to the front. I didn't need to wait for him to push me to my knees. I dropped before he had the chance. My knees, already bruised, didn't need another crash landing. I blinked as rapidly as I could to keep the tears from my eyes. I fidgeted with my dress and tried not to vomit on the floor. Butterflies slammed around my stomach, threatening to tear their way out. This moment, this must have been what every animal I hunted had felt right before I'd dragged a knife across their throat—the hopelessness, the deprivation, the fear. I'd never hunt again. I swallowed my hate for Elphame taking away another fond memory of home and replacing it with something grotesque.

"Allow me to present our newest Crow, Perdita Darkmore," Solas announced to the room.

King Aelfdene stood from this gold-and-marble throne and hushed the whispers around the room. "Yes, the last Darkmore, welcome."

"Breathe, or you're going to pass out. This is not the place you want to be unconscious." Solas nudged me with his boot. The crowd burst into laughter, and the party started back up again. No one cared for a scared little Crow. "Get up."

Elswyth helped me stand on weak legs. I stared at Solas, begging with my eyes. I didn't know what to do next. It was an awful thing to have him as my only lifeline. He motioned to the side of the room.

"Go stand over there, against the wall. I will be with you in a moment. Do nothing. Say nothing. Be nothing. If you want to survive, learn to become a fixture and nothing more," He said and left me with Elswyth. I watched him walk into the crowd. It parted without him needing to ask.

It didn't take long for me to get to the other side of the room. I scurried like a rat in the night. The horde moved as I neared and kept a reasonable distance once I passed. Not even a feather grazed my skin. I didn't acknowledge a single one of them for fear they'd want to talk to me. I tried to keep my head up, to show no fear, but I cowered, nonetheless. My shoulders slumped, and my teeth chattered in fear. There was a twenty-foot void between me and the others, but it didn't make me feel better. There had been a Gate and realms between us previously, yet that hadn't kept me safe, either. A few feet were nothing. A few feet wouldn't help me any more now than it had this morning.

"Drink. It'll help," Elswyth passed me a gold-rimmed glass of wine and leaned into my ear. "Be thankful for Solas. As much as you dislike him, their fear of Solas outweighs their curiosity about you. For a Crow, that is a good thing."

"Why do people fear him?"

"You don't?" she asked.

I shrugged. "No. He's terrifying, but so is a swarm of bees."

"Are you comparing him to your mortal honey makers?" The moment she said it, we both laughed.

We stayed at the edge of this new world, and I counted myself lucky not to be center stage. I drank my wine, wishing it were poison. It was not, and to my disappointment, I would live through the night. Elswyth whispered in my ear and pointed out each person in the room. Every Royal of the Seelie Court was present, along with their lovers and enslaved people. Elswyth told me of each person as if she had been taking notes for centuries. Some she hated more than others, and some she said were no worse than they absolutely had to be. We watched as each new person made their rounds, straight to the king, then circled to see the Crow, finally. I was thankful none of them spoke to me. I kept my eye on Solas, and he kept his close watch on me. Each time I thought I couldn't do this or the panic would begin, Solas would casually motion with his hand for me to calm down, to remember to breathe. His movements were practiced and went unnoticed by everyone but me. He, like Elswyth, knew this song and dance, and it pained me to think of being thankful to have him in the room with me.

As the night dragged on, Elswyth kept my mind busy with court gossip. And after several glasses of wine, I relaxed, and the need to dart from the room was all but silenced. When I couldn't see Solas, my heart hammered. I scanned the hall almost desperately. Elswyth pointed to him, standing with four other men. Solas didn't look happy, but he never did, save the moment I'd run. Solas looked back at me and shook his head slowly. When I stared back in confusion, he motioned to my right. My eyes tracked what he was looking at. Faolan was coming my way.

All the hate and anger I had swallowed through the night threatened to come back. My stomach rolled, and my heart pounded in my chest with such force that I staggered. If I had been in high heels, I'd have toppled over. I blinked through blurred vision and grabbed onto Elswyth for balance.

"Why is he here?" I asked Elswyth. My voice came out a little too high-pitched, as if it had to force its way past a scream that I had locked up tight.

"You didn't know?" she asked.

"Didn't know *what*? Why is he, of all people, *here*? Is this part of my torture? That I must see his face while I suffer? I thought he was Unseelie?"

"King Faolan is a friend of the Golden Court. They have treaties amongst their courts. I fear you will see him more than you would wish to," she answered. She motioned toward Solas in an attempt to get his attention. "Perdi, don't do anything I wouldn't do. For the love of Gods, do nothing at all. It'll end very badly for you. I beg of you. Bow, greet him, but say nothing."

"He sold me out. I wouldn't be here if it wasn't for him." I squeezed out, a sob catching in my throat.

"You wouldn't be the first he's hurt..." Elswyth covered her mouth, surprised at what she'd said. "Forgive me. I spoke out of turn."

"It's okay, Elswyth." I breathed past my panic in shuddering breaths. "Always speak freely with me. I won't survive off lies alone. The truth is all that will keep me alive."

"And your ability to keep your mouth shut." Solas moved to my side and passed me another glass of wine. "Are you ready?"

"For what?" I asked. My chest was so tight. I swore I'd pass out at any moment.

He leaned in, his hair brushed my neck and I fought the urge to push him away. "I never lied, little Crow. As I promised, Elphame would teach you what true hurt and hate really mean. If you are smart, you will endure and say nothing. If you don't, you'll learn the hard way. It's your choice how much you want tonight to hurt, and how much you will suffer."

Faolan stood in front of me. He was dressed as the others were, head to toe in the finest of silks and fabrics. I had never seen him so grand or regal. It made me want to vomit on his spit-shined shoes. His hair was pulled back, exposing a face I had grown to trust and cherish. Now, all I could muster was revulsion.

"Perdi," Faolan finally spoke. I'd never love his voice again. Never, for the rest of my years, would I look forward to my name on his lips.

"Don't, Faolan. Please, just don't." I turned my back to him. I didn't want to look at him. I *couldn't* look at him. My heart broke to see him here, celebrating my Taking, enjoying a party in honor of a Crow he had come for, had sold out.

"Perdita Darkmore, welcome to Elphame." Faolan's words felt like a kick to my stomach.

I breathed out shaking breaths and finally growled low. Solas shook his head and closed his eyes. It was a warning I wouldn't listen to, but I still counted to ten. I counted to twenty. I breathed deeply, as I had been taught. I told myself to calm down. I tried to focus on three things I could smell, but all I could smell were the cursed flowers of this cursed land that this cursed man had handpicked me for. Instead of calming down, I continued to boil deep inside. Solas cleared his throat and gave me another look that told me to control myself.

Faolan leaned into my ear. "If you want to survive Elphame, you will need to learn how to be a Crow. Learn to play the game better than everyone else. Learn to eat it, or Elphame will eat you."

I pursed my lips and fought not to snarl. I could feel myself growing hotter. I wanted to do so many things to Faolan, all of them ending in my hands around his throat.

"Stop, little Crow," Solas warned, and I glared at him. "You cannot afford this show of temper."

"Shut up, Solas!" I snapped at him. I turned and threw my wine in Faolan's face. "I'm only here because of you!" I screamed at him. When he didn't move, I slapped him as hard as I could and damn the consequences. It felt good enough to die for. "Get the hell away from me. Haven't you done enough?"

The music came to an abrupt end, and the room fell uncomfortably silent. It was quiet enough for me to hear Solas' groan.

"Crow." One word from the king.

"Nothing in this world is free, and now you pay." Solas shook his head. "Don't ever say I didn't give you the chance to make it through the night unscathed. I warned you, and Elswyth warned you."

He pulled me to the front of the room. His fingers dug into my arm, sending a burning jolt right down to my fingertips. I cried out in pain, but his grip didn't lessen in the least. If anything, he became rougher. He pushed his way through the crowd when they weren't quick enough to move out of his way. Behind him, I staggered to catch up to his pace. And when Solas finally stopped at the front of the room, I slammed into his back. He pulled me to his side, lifting my arm higher toward the king. I thought my arm would pop out of its socket, and I stopped struggling against the hold.

"It is a crime to attack a Royal." King Aelfdene's face was red with anger and far too many glasses of wine.

"He's not *my* king, but he is my traitor," I answered.

"Stop, damn it." Solas squeezed my arm until I screamed out once again in pain. I struggled once more to pull free from him, free myself of the pain and his warning. "For the love of your flesh, you'll shut your mouth. You won't die. Do you understand? There is only pain here."

"Let go of me." I tugged at Solas' grip.

"Enough!" He jerked me hard against his body and leaned into my ear. I froze under the heat of his temper. "If you listen to anything this night, listen to me now. They won't kill you. You'll wish for a death that will never come. No one here can protect you, not even I can. You do not want to pay the cost of your failure. Do you want your gnome and lady to die in your place? Because they are the only ones who will die on this night."

I stopped fighting and looked to the king. I felt tiny and hot from a shame I shouldn't own.

"Faolan is a Royal while you're in Elphame." The king walked away and snapped his fingers once. "He is a king, whether you care he is or not. Your hate of him does not change his station."

Solas released my arm, and for a brief moment, I was grateful. Solas stepped back and was replaced by two guards, who each pulled my arms out wide and led me to the doors entering the hall. They didn't drag me from the room as I thought they would, as I hoped they would. Instead, they held me for all to see. I was stretched to my limits. My shoulder muscles pulled until they'd tear with any more force. I couldn't move without ripping off my own arms.

Solas stepped to my front, close enough for me to smell the oils on his skin. "Now comes the pain I promised."

"What?"

"This is what real hurt feels like, Perdi," Solas answered. "When the person you love most in the world watches and does nothing to protect you. That's the truest hurt you'll ever feel. From this moment forward, you will measure pain based on tonight being the worst you've ever felt. Pain in your heart will always trump pain of the body."

"Don't leave me," I spit out, frantic. "Please, don't leave me here."

"I won't leave you here. Control your magick. Eat it down or we'll be here all night." He whispered and stepped away.

Even as he walked away, I knew he'd stay in the room. I watched Faolan step in front of me, not but ten feet away. I stared into his eyes as a crack in the air froze me to my core. Faolan let out a hiss of air as the first lash of magick across my back sent me sagging in the grips of two guards. The shock of the pain stunned me. My brain focused on nothing but the excruciating burn with each lash. It felt like being hit with fire and rocks and sliced with glass at once. Each blow felt more brutal than the last. I struggled against it, but it was useless. Faolan stood and watched, as did the rest of the room.

Every drop of hope I had that he would somehow save me was whipped from my body. The promises he had made me so long ago flowed from my open wounds to the floor. He didn't just betray me. He'd be the reason for my death. And up until I had vomited blood, in the deepest parts of my heart, I had hoped he wasn't a traitor and had done this to protect me, that he'd come running to my rescue, that this was nothing more than a ploy. But as he watched me and did nothing to help, I knew he was a traitor. I realized, as my flesh broke open, how silly my thoughts had been, how deadly my hopes were and how utterly stupid I had been to trust a Fae. Every warning I had ignored and paid for with a pound of flesh. I had watched from the safety of my home what the Fae were capable of, and still, I'd trusted. Generations of Crows, and here I was, one of them, because I had put my faith in a being born to destroy us. I hated him, as he hated me.

As I prayed for the death that Solas said would never come, I wanted this world to swallow me whole. I watched through blurred vision as the hall beyond the ballroom entrance danced with shadows. I wanted more than anything to crawl inside those shadows and disappear to a place where no one could hurt me. I reached with my soul and begged them to help me. No one else here would. They inched closer, tentatively, the more my mind screamed for them. As soon as I thought they'd whisk me away, they were gone, pulled back to the place where they had come from.

"Come back," I whispered then sagged. Not even whatever haunted the halls wanted me. I was alone.

"Enough," Solas commanded, and the guards dropped me into a pool of my own bloody making.

Solas dragged me to my feet, gliding on my own blood and vomit. When I couldn't stand or walk on my own, he picked me up and carried me from the room, not up the stairs but down. I didn't even know what sat below the Golden Court, but I didn't want to know.

With each step he took, the walls felt tighter and told me everything I needed to know about where I was going. *Hell.*

"How am I still awake?" I asked, my throat raw and burned from screaming.

"How is this a punishment if you pass out?" he replied. "It isn't fun unless you're screaming."

My head lulled from side to side, catching glimpses of stone walls and candlelight. "Where are you taking me?"

"The rest of your punishment will be held in cells. You will wish for lashings once you've spent time in the dungeons of the Golden Court," he answered, and I began to fade out of the awful world of Elphame. "You will always choose the lash over this place for as long as you live."

"I don't know what hurt more, being lashed with Faolan watching and doing nothing, or having to be carried by you, Soulless," I whispered. "Next time, don't stop them. Let them kill me."

"Next time, keep your mouth shut and you won't be lashed at all," he answered. "Being a Crow can be as easy or as hard as you make it. Choose wisely, Perdi. Spend your anger on that which is worthy of your blood."

I smiled. "It was worth it to slap him."

"No, I don't think it was. It cost him nothing. Next time, make sure you're not the one to pay for your temper."

"When I leave, I will burn this place to the ground on my way out," I whispered.

"*If* you leave," Solas replied.

"You don't have to believe me, Solas. Whether you think I can do it or not means nothing to me."

"Little Crow, I have no doubt you will try. But trying and succeeding are two very different things."

"This is true. But the only way I'll succeed is by trying, and I can light a great many fires before I die."

"This is going to be the longest seven years of my life," he grumbled.

Against my better judgment, I left him with parting words that I knew I'd regret. "I won't leave you here. If you're trapped here, I mean."

"*You* are going to save *me*?" He laughed, and I bounced painfully in his arms. "That's rich, coming from a Crow."

"Or maybe I'll leave you for the birds," I answered, but knew I wouldn't.

"*Sleep,*" Solas whispered with a small push of magick.

As the sleep finally tugged at my edges, I smiled. I fought to stay awake, even through the pain. As Solas had said, this was not the place to be unconscious. I couldn't protect myself if I were asleep. Truth be told, I couldn't defend myself while I was awake, either. Knowing I'd die no matter my alertness, I let myself go into the darkness with the sound of my cell door opening on hinges rotten from years of use. The last thing I felt was the sting of being dropped from too high and landing on my back. The cell door squealed shut, locking me into a room that already smelled of death. My last thoughts were of the warmth that blanketed me. I prayed that's what death felt like when he finally decided to visit. But I knew better because it came to visit Whitwick often enough for me to appreciate that it was nothing like warmth and coziness.

Chapter Eight

I slowly came back from a fog of my own creation, my temper's creation. The first time I woke, I didn't know where I was. I didn't understand why I stared up at a stone ceiling and not in my bed, safe at home in Whitwick. When I moved to touch the walls, pain surged, and the reality of where I was crashed down on me. From a sliver of light from under the door, I saw where my temper had brought me. I had been warned repeatedly but had allowed it to take control, and I paid dearly in strips of flesh and blood. I'd never make it to the end of seven years if I left pieces of myself on the floor each time I came out of my bedroom. I, like so many before me, would finish off my years as a twisted mess. I'd never survive, never be able to run, if I were hobbled in the Golden Court.

Each time I woke, I was both thankful and filled with regret. The pain was unlike anything I had ever felt. It burned and throbbed. But it was nothing compared to the pain I felt in my heart. I couldn't do much more than lie there and cry. The tears brought an inability to taste and smell, and I was more than thankful for not smelling the rotten stench held in the air. Gone were the flowers, replaced with a disgusting odor that soured my empty stomach. Everything smelled of the dead and the prayer for death. I've learned that there are things worse than death, and one of those things was knowing the smells of rot were coming from my own body. I stank of infection and dying meat still hanging on the bone.

My prison cell was nothing more than a blood-stained cot on a wet, stone floor and a crude toilet in the form of a used bucket next to the steel door. There were no windows and one drain in the middle of the floor. It wasn't a cell as much as it was a roomy coffin with better lighting. From under the door and cracks in the frame, a low flicker of light rolled in. When in complete darkness, not much light was needed to see. My eyes adjusted quickly. And once I could, I wanted to have remained blind to it all. Nail marks scarred the stone, claw marks on the floor of someone being dragged out made me wish the room had no light at all.

At the door, two plates of food and a jug of water sat, and I wondered how long I had been out. Did they feed me three meals a day or just enough for me not to die? I slowly sat up and ate my screams behind a clenched jaw. My head pounded from hitting the floor after the lashes, my skull bones taking the brunt of the landing. I swallowed back the bile. If I were to heal, I needed energy. It took three tries before I could crawl to the door. The movement pulled my ruined dress from the dried blood and wounds on my back, opening them once again. When I made it back to my cot, I was bleeding. I hoped the fresh blood would clean my wounds, since I wouldn't dare put the water on my back.

I ate what I could and curled up but didn't sleep, although I was exhausted. I was not the only prisoner, but I was the only one not currently being tortured. I tried to block them out, but the harder I fought against it, the more panic and fear built in my chest and crushed me, crushed my soul. I pushed myself against the far wall and cried. I had tried not to imagine what was happening to them, but each crack of a whip sent me back to the banquet hall. I tried not to allow myself to think of what they were enduring, but each scream reminded me of my own pain.

From under the door, shadows slinked across the floor—the shadowy tendrils I had seen in my bathroom and while being lashed. Painfully, I reached toward it, and it pulled back. My knuckles slammed into the floor with a thud.

"Please, don't leave me," I croaked around my sob. It left as quickly as it had come. "Please, come back."

I was in hell, the kind of hell they taught us about in church every Sunday. There was no other word for it. I would die like this, in a dungeon, locked away, suffering, alone. I was sure every other Crow had met the same fate, punished and tortured until their human bodies could take no more. This is what it meant to be a Crow. We were the sacrifice, and they ensured we gave everything to this godforsaken land, from our hope and tears to our blood and bones. We would leave our souls splattered on the marble floors.

As much as I felt sorry for myself, I more pitied those in the cells. I pitied their Fae blood. They could be hurt harder and much longer than a human. They could take what would break me. Fae blood would allow them to heal time and time again. I covered my ears and wept for what they would suffer. Solas was right. This prison was punishment greater than lashes, and it pained me to think of just how bad it really was. I'd have preferred to be tied up and whipped by everyone in the court overhearing the begging and screaming of those in the cells next to me. Every sound was a reminder of how lowly I was in the pecking order.

A high-pitched shrill brought my swollen eyes open. My creature was pushing herself under the door. Behind her, the darkness I had begged to stay, rolled poppies from the crack under the door to my bed. They hadn't left me. They'd gone for help. I watched her make a small hill of plants as the shadows slinked away and left her with me. I recognized the plants and was grateful Elphame held similar herbs as home. She had carried me painkillers and plants to help with the infection that even I could smell. I could only imagine how badly I reeked to her tiny nose.

"You shouldn't be in here. If they catch you, they'll kill you," I whispered and held out my hand to her. "Thank you."

She hopped off my hand and pulled at my shoulder. I rolled onto my stomach. She ground up the poppy seed and a few other leaves with a stone from the floor and placed them in my mouth, then climbed onto my back and began working. My little creature flinched each time a scream echoed across the stones of my cell. She trembled as she worked. She hopped off my back and sat a few inches from my face. Her wings hung. Even in the darkness, I could see her tear-stained face. I was thankful for the break, but it pained me to see her so sad. It had hurt more to fix what the lashes had done than to have it done. But I'd have endured the lashings all over again if it kept her from crying.

"Do you know them?" I whispered.

She sniffled, and her body trembled, but she made no actual sound. She finally nodded.

"Can you help them?" I asked.

She shook her head and shrugged. She couldn't and didn't know how.

"I'm sorry." I didn't know what else to say. "If I could save them, I would."

I reached my hand to hers. It was tiny but gripped enough for me to feel her squeeze. She stood and got back to work. Her sobs escaped her as she worked, and we cried together. It didn't matter to me who the others were. No one deserved to be tortured endlessly. Either kill them or let them go. This in-between, dragging it out, sickened me. Only monsters did this. Only the Fae did this. I may have hated them all, but my hate didn't include being sadistic. Then again, I'm still new around here. Who knows how deep my well of hatred would be if I lived another day?

My body began to relax as the painkiller kicked in. Eventually, I passed out just as my little creature started to chew at the rotten flesh on my back. The skin and meat were dead, the pain of it was either too minor to keep me awake, or the medications she gave me were more potent than I had thought. I was thankful for either.

I woke to the door hinges squealing in protest as they opened. I jerked and moved through the pain when someone walked in. The brilliance of the hallway lighting blinded me and ruined my night vision. I didn't need to see him to know it was Faolan. I knew him even in the darkest of shadows. Him, Faolan, deserved the torture I had just condemned, long and drawn out. But I dismissed the thought. I didn't think I could ever order him to suffer like that. I'd just simply kill him for his deeds. I wouldn't even make a decent Fae. I wasn't cruel enough. I doubted being a Crow would be any easier because of that.

"Why are you here?" I asked, my voice cracked. I pushed myself to my knees and gritted my teeth through the waves of pain and dizziness that followed.

He stood a foot from my front, forcing me to look up at him like a begging animal would. "To give you a choice."

"Whatever it is that you want from me, the answer is no." I didn't want whatever he was he was offering. "If you came to offer me promises or oaths or deals, I'd rather die down here. You could give me my very freedom and I'd choose this cell over owing you a damn thing."

"Perdi, you can choose to stay down here and die or..." He covered his mouth and gagged. I heard his meal try for an escape. "Or you may come with me now. God, Perdi, you smell of things worse than death."

"*You* sent me to a place worse than death. How did you expect this to play out?" I asked.

"I certainly didn't expect you to throw your wine in my face and slap me. I thought you had more sense than that."

"More sense? How did you think I'd react when I saw you? You betrayed me. Because of you, I'm here. How should I have behaved?"

"Like someone who doesn't want to die."

"Oh, but I do." I clutched my ribs as I laughed.

"Come with me, Perdi." He held out his hand. "You don't have to suffer like this."

"Why would I go with you, now? I mean, look at this place. It has everything a prisoner would need. Why would I want to leave this fine establishment?"

"Because you will die here if you don't."

"Why, Faolan?" I asked. "Excuse me, *King* Faolan. Why did you sell me out?"

"We would both get what we wanted. You would have a safe place to be a Crow, and I could protect my people. You were coming here, no matter what. You were cursed to come, whether I collected you or not."

"This was to protect your people? And only for them?" I asked.

"Of course… I'd never do anything to hurt you. But my people, Perdi, I can't abandon them because I love a halfling girl. I can't sentence them to war and death, not even for you."

I smiled and closed my eyes. I had waited years to be loved—to be loved by him. *And he says it now.* I didn't need to be Fae to know he was lying to me. I knew him well enough to know when he was lying. Even as he stood in front of me, he didn't flinch to the sounds of bones crunching or flesh-tearing open. The begging and pleading of prisoners didn't so much as stir a single emotion in him. He would have known that this cell, this pain, would have been my fate, and he willingly lured me to the place. He wasn't just a liar. He was a coward, and as monstrous as those carrying out the punishments of the dungeon.

"Leave," I said after moments of letting it sink in. "You never loved me in any way that didn't hurt me. And that's not love, not real love. You never bothered to tell me the truth. Not even now, after it's already out. This was to protect yourself, and to hell with me."

"You'd rather die? You could come with me and be safe, or you can stay and grovel like a Crow from the bottom. This will never get easier, only harder."

"Yes, I'd rather die," I said and meant it. "There are a million tortures I'd sooner endure than spend one more minute with you."

"Suit yourself," he answered. "Whether you come or stay, you'll still see my face wherever you go. I won't simply leave."

"Faolan, before I am dead, I will see you lose everything you've ever gained. Mark my words, I'll see you when this is over." I smiled up at him. I meant every word I said.

His laughter was a slap in my face. It was a mix of surprise and frustration. "You have no idea, Perdi, what this court is capable of, what Elphame will do to a Crow. There is only suffering served in Elphame, and Crows eat the most of it."

I pushed myself to my feet. Sheer will and grit got me but inches from his face. "You, Little King, have no idea what *I* am capable of. You have no clue what you've dragged into these lands and the blight I'll release on you all. My desire to see you fall, see your court fail, outweighs everything you could possibly send my way."

"That's what Aoife said before she died. I was offering you freedom, but I'll take you when you're a broken Crow, just the same. If I have to drag you broken back to my territory, I will." The look in Faolan's eyes was the only warning I had, as Faolan grabbed me and pulled me to his front. The force of his body against me pushed me back and back until he held me against the wall. He leaned into my neck and breathed me in.

"Stop." I fought the urge to scream and cry. Faolan released his hot breath against my pulse, and I squirmed, repulsed at his touch.

"No one can help you here, Perdi. You can scream all you want. No one will care. This is what Elphame is. This is what the Golden Court is. It's hell, and I'm offering you a way out before you burn in it. I am giving you freedom. With me, you wouldn't suffer a single day." Faolan pushed against me and sighed. "Why must you be so bloody stubborn?"

"No." I pushed against him and winced at the pain in my back. I wanted to tell him that I would not be the one to burn. This court would feel those flames long before I would. But no great plan came to fruition by spilling them before fulfilling them. "You'll have to kill me first."

"It won't be me that kills you, here," he answered. I froze as the light leached from my cell, leaving us both in complete darkness. "Stop this, Perdi, if you know what's good for you."

"It's not me," I whispered. "I'm not doing this."

The darkness danced throughout the room, opening pockets in the dark where I could see Faolan's face. He lifted his hand and formed a small globe of light. Each time he pushed against me, his light was eaten by the shadows. He stepped back, and his light returned. It was a warning. From where? I didn't know. When Faolan moved toward me again, the shadows gobbled up everything in the room, every sight and sound and breath. But when he'd back off, the darkness eased.

"Is the darkness sweet for you already?" Faolan asked, and I frowned. "Don't end up like every other

Crow to walk these halls, ready to bend over for any favor they can curry. You won't like who will be forced to become."

"I don't know what you're talking about," I answered, and I didn't.

"Soon, Perdi, I'll come for you, and you'll be thankful it is me coming," Faolan whispered.

My cell door opened, and Solas stood at the entrance. "I think you've overstayed your welcome, Little King."

"Is it your turn already?" Faolan spat his words at him and left me standing there, trembling, fresh blood trickling from my back.

"Come back here again, Faolan, and you'll never leave these cells alive." Solas stepped out of the way for Faolan, and for the briefest moments, I feared him stepping in. I feared what Solas would do to me. I prayed he would beat me or pull out my fingernails, anything but what Faolan had just tried to do.

"Thank you," I finally said.

"I warned you, little Crow. It doesn't get better than this, but it can always get worse." Without saying another word, Solas dropped his eyes from me and closed the door, locking me inside. I eased myself back down and sobbed. I pressed my back against to cool stones of my prison and pulled my knees to my chest, tucking my head into my legs. My back protested when I hugged my legs, but the fear overrode my pain. The darkness didn't leave, not entirely. It hung in the corners and along the walls, heavy and moving like a beast I didn't want to poke.

"Whoever or whatever are you, thank you," I whispered into the darkness and got no answer. "Thank you."

I counted three more days in the cells. The food came once a day. I was there for five days total. My little creature came twice a day to heal my back and swelled-shut eye. She, unlike Faolan, didn't fear the dark, and it didn't move against her. She milled about and ignored it as if she noticed it not. Each night, the darkness wrapped around me and brought with it smells of the ocean, earth and visions of mountains, treetops and the songs of the forest. It wasn't Whitwick, but it felt like home. The shadows couldn't give me freedom, but they could help me pretend.

On the fifth day, Solas stepped into my room and found me curled in shadows. It blanketed me, warming me, protecting me. I had once feared the dark, and now, in the bright Court of Summer, I feared the light. It was only when I was covered, head to toe, with the swirling midnight sky did I feel truly safe. My dreams were calm, my body at ease.

Solas pulled me from the shadows and smelled the air. "What did you give it, Perdi?"

Half asleep, I stumbled out of the cell, dragged by my arm. "Give what? To who? What are you talking about?"

"What did you give the darkness to protect you?" he asked. His face was inches from mine. His anger was palpable. I could almost taste the heat and chew on his words. He shook my arm and rattled my body. "What did you offer in exchange for help?"

"Please, you're hurting me." I winced in pain. A small cry escaped my lips. "I didn't offer anything to anyone. It just came, I swear. I don't know what you're talking about. Please, Solas, don't put me back in there."

"It doesn't just come. It wants something from you. Whatever you do, do not bargain with anyone, especially down here. Trust no one, no matter who or what they are, especially what lurks in the shadows."

"Starting with you." I pulled my arm from his grasp and scowled.

"If it weren't for me, you'd have suffered a great deal more than you had," he snapped back.

"Don't do me any favors."

He let out an exasperated groan. "I am the only reason your heart still beats."

With each step forward he took, I backed up. I watched the darkness crawl from my room like mist. Solas watched the shadows dance over my feet and edge to the tips of his shoes. One stomp from him, and it rolled casually across the dirt from and into the cracks in the stone wall opposite my room. It hadn't jerked like I would have. It wasn't scared of him, but also felt no need to test his patience like I had.

"Let's go."

"Where?" I asked. "Please don't put me back in there."

"To your room. You smell of a rotting Crow."

I shrugged. The pull of my almost fully healed wounds made the movement awkward. "You get used to the smell."

He turned. "You never get used to the smell."

Even though the cells were silent, I could still hear their screams, forever stained on my soul. Through the hall, following Solas, I stopped. The silence was as deafening as the torture. I knew when lying in my hovel when each prisoner had stopped screaming because they had no screams left to give and when a soul was finally snuffed out. My Malice felt them all. I don't know which was worse, hearing it or feeling them endure it.

"Why are these people down here?" I asked. "There are children down here."

"Like you, they are those who have displeased the king. They have no one to bargain or pay for their freedom or to protect them."

I pressed my hand into the wall. "I will."

"No, you won't," Solas called from the end of the hall.

I froze to a pull in my gut, like a string I couldn't see. It gripped my stomach with panic and need. I closed my eyes and leaned into the sensation. I knew whatever tugged at me lived on the other side of the rock wall. There were no doors, no way through unless you took the dungeon apart. But I could still feel a pulse, through the stones, on the other side of the wall, steady, in pace with my own. It was familiar. I breathed deeply and heard a sigh on the other side of the wall. My magick flared to life. I felt nothing but shadows and darkness on the other side of the stones. But in that pitch, it felt like home, and I was homesick for a place I'd never see again.

I searched for what felt like miles and felt no one. No one was there. *Perhaps an imprint of someone from years gone by,* I thought, at first. But I knew better. Whatever was on the other side of the rock was like me, trapped. Whatever rested on the stone felt me, in the same way I could feel it. I was familiar. I tilted my head and smiled.

"Move it." Solas grabbed my arm and pulled me.

"You have the manners of a greedy boy child." I pulled my arm back. "All you have to do is ask, and stop reefing me around like a toy."

"It is in your best interest to just smile, do as you're asked and keep your mouth shut."

I stared at the wall and nodded, not in agreement with Solas. In a silent pact that I'd come back and keep coming back until I found a way to open the wall.

"Good, you catch on quickly."

I kept my mouth closed and followed him up from the basement. I paid attention to the twists and turns of the Golden Court, and there were many. Solas didn't speak, and as we passed others, they didn't utter a single word to us. They froze and dipped their heads. I understood why people cowered when Solas neared. He made me do the same. I put on a pretty good front each time I saw him, but my soul hid in the deepest corners, out of his reach.

At my door, I stepped inside and turned to face Solas. "Go to hell."

"Perdi, our hells are one and the same. Welcome to my little slice." He stepped back and spread his arms. "Wherever you go, I go. So, get used to the flames, my little Crow."

"I. Am. Not. Your. Crow." I slammed the door in his face. It would be the only satisfaction I'd have today. The movement burned and stretched my destroyed back, but it was worth the pain.

Chapter Nine

Closing my door felt like locking myself away from the world of Elphame. One small chunk of wood and I was in an entirely different place, away from what stains souls. I wasn't two steps into my room when Elswyth threw herself to my feet, sobbing.

"I'm so sorry. I should have offered to take your lashings."

"Why in the world would you do that?" I was shocked.

"It is what your lady would be charged to do." Nix climbed up my front and hugged my neck. "I was so scared."

"I'm okay," I answered and helped him perch on my shoulder.

"No, you're not. I can smell your back," he replied. My little creature fluttered at eye level and squealed. Nix flinched at her piercing sounds.

"Elswyth, get up. I can't bend down to hug you." I pulled on her until she stood. "If anyone asks, tell them I forbid you from taking my punishments."

"I couldn't do it. I just… I've had to… I can't…" she cried. "I couldn't do it again."

"She was used as a whipping boy for years. She took the punishments that were not hers to take." Nix spoke softly. "You can't tell anyone that she was scared, Perdi. They would take her away. If she can't do her duties, all of them, there is no use for her here."

"Elswyth, I'd never expect you to take my punishments…period. And no one will ever know. If ever you're asked, tell them I ordered you not to."

She helped me into the bath. The moment the water touched my back, I screamed until I cried. I clung to the side of the tub and vomited until I shook as she cleaned my back. My creature tried to calm me with more painkiller paste, but there wasn't enough medicine in the world that would take my pain away. It wasn't just the physical pain. I screamed at the emotional pain, Faolan, the screams of others in the basement. I told Elswyth and Nix about them, but they already knew. This was standard practice throughout Elphame. Once I was covered in salve and bandaged, the pain lessened.

"Elswyth, could you excuse Nix and me?" I asked.

"You can trust her, Perdi," he interrupted. When I disagreed with a shake of my head, Nix turned to Elswyth, "Els, tell her—or I will. She will never trust you unless you're honest with her."

She stepped forward, her eyes already watering. "Solas bought me after I was a prisoner in the Winter Court. After they were done with me and I was thrown out, Solas bought me from who found me. He bought me when I was near death."

"Nothing surprises me about this place, but you've already told me this," I answered.

"No, Perdi, Solas got me from Faolan's land. I suffered greatly in that court, things I'd rather not repeat. Faolan killed my parents when they disagreed with a law that allowed young women to be forced into the marital bed too soon. I was told that he killed them."

My mouth dropped. "You were a prisoner in his court?"

She nodded. "I was owned, all of me, in ways that make the Golden Court look like a mercy."

I closed my eyes. Tears rolled down my cheeks. "I'm so sorry."

"After I was all used up, Faolan dumped me outside of his land, on the border of the Dark Courts, the Court of Shadows. There, I was taken again. The Sluagh found me, and as horrible and frightening as they are, they do not delight in the scraps of torture. They brought me to Solas. He purchased me from my new captors and took me in."

"What a bastard." I didn't bother hiding the hate in my voice.

"That's a nice way of putting it," Nix said.

"I saw Faolan down there," I blurted out.

"What did he want?" he asked, disgusted at the idea.

"For me to go with him," I answered. "But that's not the weird thing. When he attacked me, the room filled with darkness and pushed him back. What the hell is down there?"

"You don't want to know what they keep in those prisons." His entire body shivered with the answer.

I nodded. He was probably right. "Solas came when Faolan was in my cell and threatened to kill him if he came back."

Elswyth stifled a laugh. "Solas is not Faolan's biggest fan."

"I can't see why not. They're both monsters," I replied.

"Solas came up here, too," Nix interrupted.

"Did he hurt you, threaten you?" I felt my anger begin to bubble. If he let me keep Nix only to abuse him the moment I was gone, I'd make every single day feel like an eternity for him.

"No. He kept checking with her." He pointed at my creature. "He was ordering her about, telling her how to better fix your wounds. We're the lowest in Elphame, as if we don't know how to fix what they've done to all of us several times over."

"Why would he care what condition I'm in?" I asked.

"I don't know," Elswyth said. "He didn't mention it, and it's not my place to ask. It could simply be that you are his charge, his responsibility, as much as he is tasked with keeping me alive until I'm of no more service to him."

"Who knows," Nix answered. "No one ever knows why Solas does what he does. No one is brave enough to ask."

"Thank you for coming," I said to my creature, who tipped her head. "When I was down there, I could hear others and what was happening to them. Those in the cells, the women and children, the weak, we need to get them out."

Elswyth's eyes got wide, and she jumped up. "You cannot say things like that out loud."

"I spelled the room when I got here. No one can hear us. It's a small magick. No one would even notice unless they tried to listen. But I'd feel them break my spell before they heard a word," I answered.

Elswyth scanned the room and finally sat. She was still uneasy and took to whispering. "The only way they're leaving here is if they're dead or purchased."

"How much do they cost?" I asked.

"We are not in the human realm. It is not dollars the king will want. It is magick, favors, oaths," she answered. "Even if we could pay the cost, we are not free. We are owned, ourselves. We cannot bargain for their release."

I sighed. So much for trying to steal enough to buy them. "Can we break them out?"

Nix laughed. "Perdi, are you sure your head isn't more injured? Sure, we can break them out if we want to die with them."

Elswyth started to pace and finally nodded her head and came to a stop in front of us. "Hear me out. You can probably ask for a few additional servants of your own. It is customary for you to receive maids during your stay."

"I don't want one. And don't call them that." I frowned at her suggestion. "They're prisoners, trapped like I am."

"But you want to save them, don't you? The only way one will be released is if you own one yourself. If you owned them, we could find a way to get one free from here."

I smiled now. "Okay, how do I do that?"

"Ask for an audience with the king," she replied. "You must do this very carefully, Perdi. One wrong move, and the punishment would be severe. And I mean this in the kindest of ways, but you do not appear to be able to withstand another punishment. You can free no one if you're dead."

"Help me write a letter right way. I need him to agree, and if I do it on my own, I'll screw things up." I pulled Elswyth to my desk.

"You will need to win him over, Perdi. Charm him, or you will never have enough freedom to help anyone, much less yourself," Nix added. "Now would be the time to use a small power, show him you are his. You are a broken Crow."

"And how would I do that?" I asked.

Nix raised his eyebrows. "You're already on death's door now. Test the waters with your Malice. Even if you're caught, they can't kill you twice."

Elswyth stood quickly and stared. "You have the ability to wield Malice?"

"It's dark magick, to mortals, that's all," I answered. "It's not really dark, though, unless I will it to do horrible things."

"No, that is not *all* it is, Perdi. That is a rare talent among anyone, Fae or not," she countered. "We could use this carefully."

"It's a curse. I feel every soul around me. I feel their desires, fears, loves, wants and wishes. But here, I just feel pain," I answered. "It doesn't matter, though. Solas said it doesn't work on him and not to use it on Royal blood or High Fae."

"Aelfdene is not born of Royal blood. He took the throne," Nix said. "But, High Fae, he is. I believe Solas warned you away from being caught. It is a death sentence to use magick against a Royal or High Fae."

"If I'm careful, I could try." I looked to Elswyth. "Do you think it would work?"

"Aelfdene wants a child, a halfling. I believe that is why he chose you as Crow. A Darkmore child would be tempting enough that he may not notice," Elswyth said, and I stared at her, eyes wide and shaking my head. "I'm not telling you to have a child with him. I'm saying that Aelfdene believes that if he were to have a halfling, it would allow him to walk between worlds, to become the most powerful of the Sidhe. That, alone, may blind him."

"I thought the Fae couldn't make any more halflings?" I asked.

"The oaths between your realm and ours says anyone who enters Elphame cannot return. But, if the king were to find a willing Crow, he could create a halfling. A child of this much power, he believes, would be able to cross, and in turn, Aelfdene would rule both realms. I don't think he believes the Gate would be able to hold a Darkmore from crossing."

"You're suggesting I lead him to believe I would be willing to have a child with him?" I asked, and she nodded. "And what happens when he calls my bluff and tries to take what he wants?"

Elswyth's face soured. "I'm sorry, Perdi, but if that is what he wants, there is no bluff to call. He will simply take it. But a willing child, a Darkmore child? That would be worth waiting on. It would be worth being kind to you, earning your favor. He cannot just will a child into the world without your agreement. The child would simply not take in your womb. Birthing in Elphame, I believe, is not the same as in your mortal world. We must agree to the bedding. Children are not born of rape here. Elphame magick does not lend itself to that horror."

"As a Crow, you are cursed not to conceive unless you are willing while you are in Elphame," Nix added.

"I've nothing to lose," I agreed.

"Except your life," he added.

I nodded. "Well, there's that. But it's not really mine anymore, is it?"

I paced behind Elswyth as she penned a letter. We disagreed on what to write, but I heeded her judgment. She had been playing the games of the court long before my great grandparents were even a thought. We read it over and over until I finally worked up the nerve to send it to the king. I passed it to a guard outside my bedroom door. "I'd like an audience with the king. I must apologize for my behavior and beg his forgiveness."

We dined, and I was schooled on the protocols of court and how to grovel, which was not my best skill. It went against everything I was and believed to be right in the world. Elswyth and Nix prepared me for my audience. They coached me on what to say and how to say it, how to behave, what to do and not do, right down to how I should move and how I would glance at him. I would wear my hair a certain way and wear the colors and clothes of the Golden Court. The king had a particular type and responded to only one kind of woman—weak, calculating, devious, wanted by all, had by none, terrifying to most, but above all else, broken and agreeable to only the king. I would become the woman the king wanted to keep, a woman others feared and only he loved. In essence, I would become a Crow of desire and horror, someone who only Aelfdene could love.

"Weakness will paint a target on your back," Elswyth said. "You need to master the fine art of cruelty. Become the Crow you were destined to be. Only then will he feel like he's won. Make him believe he's broken the last Darkmore. Appeal to his greed and ego. Appeal to his brutality."

We paced, we waited, we wrote a new letter each day, and each new letter was crafted expertly by Elswyth. A week had passed, a week where I hadn't been summoned or tortured. As much as I wanted to gain freedom for those in the dungeon, I was happy not to have been called from my room. On the evening of the seventh day, Solas knocked on my door. The king would see me. I dressed as I had been instructed, and Solas led me from my room to the dining hall.

"I see Elswyth dressed you today." He finally spoke on the last landing.

My mind was a whirlwind of thoughts. It took several tries to clear the fear from my throat. "Yes, she was gracious enough to assist me in my selections."

I wasn't used to wearing gowns or heels or rare gems. I didn't hate it, but I also didn't like it as much as the others appeared to. It felt stuffy and tight and itchy. I made noise whenever I moved and struggled for each breath I took, from a corset tied too tight. But I didn't stand out for appearance. It was because I was a Crow.

"Whatever you're about to do, don't." Solas grabbed my arm before we entered. "Why could you not have just been happy that the king has left you alone? Why must you stir the pot?"

"I was bored," I answered and got a glare back in return.

"You should know, Faolan is in there. So whatever stupid thing you're about to do, don't do it."

I smiled, but it didn't reach my eyes. It was a mask, nothing more. "Faolan is no longer an issue. Now, lead the way."

"Learn to lie better or keep your mouth shut, little Crow," Solas replied.

I pulled my arm back. "Learn your place, little dog, just as I have."

"Do you really want to play games with those who have had countless mortal lifetimes to master them?"

"I don't know what games you're referring to." I motioned toward the door.

The dining room was simple compared to the banquet room I had seen previously—simple, in Fae terms. It was grander than any dining room I had been in or had ever seen. The human realm, although also known for extravagance, did not compare. In the center of the room, in front of a massive marble fireplace, King Aelfdene sat with six others, one being Faolan. I eyed the knives beside the plates and wished it was iron. I'd have taken my chances and stabbed Faolan. Instead, I swallowed my need for revenge. That would come later. At the start of this all, I'd promised myself I would make them all pay before I left. It was a promise I planned to keep, and I couldn't do that from beyond the grave or the cells below. That alone held me steady on my feet as I entered the room and began a game I was only just learning.

I dipped my head and moved quickly to King Aelfdene and dropped to his side. I lowered myself into a bow I'd practiced with Elswyth. I knelt and waited to be acknowledged. I didn't make a sound, although I wanted his attention. I was patient, like a spider to a fly. He finally pushed his chair out and cleared his throat.

"What is it, Crow?" King Aelfdene finally spoke. He sounded irritated by my very presence. "You've pestered me for days. Spit it out and take your leave."

"Thank you, My King." I wanted to puke, just saying the words. They still came out smooth as butter. "I fear my behavior at your very gracious welcoming party for me was unacceptable. I am truly grateful to have been selected for your court, when it could have been so awful in one of the others. I am thankful for your hospitality and apologize to you and your guests for my outburst. I showed you great disrespect, and it will not happen again."

"It was not I who you slighted," he answered coldly and motioned to Faolan.

I swallowed a rock in the back of my throat. "King Faolan, I apologize for my behavior. Please understand that I was scared and overwhelmed, and to be honest, I did not expect to see you after my Taking. My very mortal emotions got the better of me, and I hope you would see it in your heart to accept my sincerest apology. It will *not* happen again."

"That's fine," he answered. His voice was flat, like I was intruding on his meal. He sounded nothing like how I remembered him. But those days were long gone. He was not the man I had built up in my mind. Then again, I didn't hate him then, as I did now.

"I appreciate you accepting my apology." I kept myself calm and focused. Now was not the time to stand and scream at him. I'd only end up punished again and that much further from my goals, however lofty they may be. "Allow me to waste no more of your precious time and, if it pleases you, discuss why I've come to you, My King."

"Oh, and why is that?" King Aelfdene was amused.

"If it so pleases you, I wish to have ladies to teach me of your customs?" I asked. "No one of any importance, of course, as I am not deserving of favor from my king. Perhaps someone of low value, which you will not miss."

He lifted my chin and stared into my eyes. "Another lady?"

I nodded and fought to squirm against his touch. But his touch was exactly what I needed. I opened the smallest of doors to my power, and with a death grip on it, I allowed the smallest tendril to snake out and glide over his skin. He didn't pull back.

"Yes, My King. If I am to be in Elphame, in your court, I must learn to survive, I must learn how to behave. Your grace, I must learn to please you." I sent a wave of lust through my touch. "I am, after all, a mortal woman and do not understand the ways of Royal or of Fae. I cannot be of any service to you, ignorant as I am in your ways."

I touched his leg with my last words and closed the loop on my magick. "Please, My King, give me the chance to make it up to you." I touched his leg again and risked a shy glance. "I am young and inexperienced. I cannot…please you, as I am right now."

"I agree to this. You may take two ladies." The king grinned and accepted my flirt and touch. "Solas will assist you in the dungeon. There's no one important down there. They won't be missed."

I bowed all the way to the floor. "Thank you. I will endeavor to show you how grateful I truly am."

Solas lifted me by my armpit to my feet and led me from the room. I didn't raise my eyes or even look back. I let Solas pull me until we were out of the room, where

I pushed his hand from my arm and held my head high. He led me back toward the stairs leading to my room.

"No. I would like to select from the cells." I stopped him.

He turned and shook his head. "I know what you are doing, little Crow."

"I don't know what you mean."

"You cannot save them, do not even try. Having them as your slave doesn't protect them. All you'll do is extend their suffering."

I showed no cards to Solas. "As the king has spoken, shall we?"

"As the king has spoken? No, little Crow, as *you* have spoken. I am not a fool. I could smell what you were doing. And if I could smell it, who else in that room did as well?"

"I have no idea what you're talking about. Now, my slaves?" I smiled. But he was right. I couldn't risk magick in front of anyone but the king. I'd take Solas' questioning as a warning.

He sighed, deep from his chest, but said no more. He led me to the stairs and down the winding steps, back to the basement, back to the smells and death. I had thought it would look different now that I was not a prisoner but it didn't. It was the same hell. It grated on my soul today, as it did while I was an occupant.

"Solas, if you had to select two people from these cells who are so close to death that it would be a waste of my time, who would you select?"

He cocked his head, a confused look on his face. "Why would you want two dying servants?"

I shrugged, then smiled. I allowed all my fear, hate and anger to cloud my face. "Maybe because I want to watch your people hurt. If I have to suffer, so do they.

If I can never leave this hellhole, neither can they. Every time I am punished, I will punish them in turn, twice as bad. This Crow wants a whipping boy of her own. Every time you try to break me, I will break another of your people. I will find the weakest and will take their last hope away from them. I am, after all, a Crow of Elphame. And the worst part is, you can only thank yourself for this, Soulless. For it was you who brought poison to feed their lands."

Solas froze in his steps. He couldn't hide his surprise. I watched it play over his face, from first thinking I was trying to help, to him hearing what I had planned to do to them. In a sentence, I had shattered every good thought he had of me. He turned and rushed to my front. I surprised myself when I didn't flinch. I smiled instead, pleased at my bravery.

"Do you think this is a fucking game? Do you think any of these people deserve to be here?"

"No. But you all seem to think that playing with *my* life is a fucking game." I pushed myself into his chest and let go of any lingering fear I had of him. "Do you think I deserve to be here? Do you think I should suffer and me alone? If the Fae can play with me, I will be damned sure to play in return, before this cursed place takes my life."

"Your very brief life, if you keep this up."

"It takes two to play this game. You all just climbed onto the board with me, willingly, and I'm just getting started, Soulless. Find two, or I will go back to the king and inform him you will not aid me because you care so much more for them than you do of doing what your king commands of you. I'm sure he'll find someone else more than willing to play my little games. If it is not the king himself standing center stage with me."

"You are playing with fire."

I laughed in his face. "And you all will burn with me."

He pulled back, repulsed. I thought he'd vomit if I kept pushing. I was tempted, but I wasn't there for him. I came for an entirely different reason. He stopped at the last door on the right and opened it. The smell made my eyes and nose water. I wretched and covered my nose and mouth with my sleeve. Inside, curled in the far corner, a young woman holding a younger boy in her arms. Both were bloodied, covered in filth, and near death in the corner. They didn't bother moving or cowering. They welcomed death. They hoped for it. I knew that is what they prayed for because I had done the same thing and hadn't even endured an ounce of what they had.

"Clean them before you bring them to my room," I cleared my throat and finally said, thankful my voice didn't betray me. "They stink of death and of filth. I'd never get that smell out of my linens."

Solas leaned against the door. "I see why Faolan has always loved you so dearly. You're just like him."

The words stung, but I still smiled. "Come now. You're hurting my feelings. You know that's not true. I am much worse than he ever could be. My hate for all of Elphame runs deeper than his hate for me ever could."

I left him standing in the basement. I forced myself not to run but to walk casually. I held in my tears and vomit and forced a smile for the outside world to see. I didn't cry until I got to my room, alone in the shower, scrubbing off the disgust I had in myself.

"It's just a game, just a game." I rocked myself in the corner of the shower. "You can do this. You *have* to do this."

My little creature dragged a towel across the floor and tapped on the glass door. She pointed to my bedroom. My newest slaves had arrived. My work had just begun. Now, we had to fix them, tell them of our plan and pray they wouldn't tell a soul or we'd all be dead, and I wasn't ready to die just yet.

Chapter Ten

I became a lie, and it made me sick to my soul—a lie so good that Solas had questioned Elswyth's well-being and asked her if she wanted to be removed as my lady. During one of the endless parties, we performed the entertainment for all to see the monster I had become. Elswyth did not bow when Faolan approached us. I slapped her across her cheek hard enough to send her to her knees. My hand stung as I lifted it again. I would hit her while she was down, nothing more than a show at who was stronger and more fearsome. In Elphame, it was not the physically strong who survived the longest. No, Elswyth would simply die because she was lesser than everyone else in the room—less evil, less monstrous. When she cowered and lifted her arms to protect herself, I told her to apologize to Faolan, to grovel like the dog she was. I demanded she remove her face from my sight and sent her to my bedroom, where she was to wait for me to return, and we'd finish the conversation in private.

It was carefully choreographed, down to how many tears she would shed, how she would stagger from the room as if I had beaten her many times before. Elswyth had chosen Faolan because of what he'd done to me, and it would shock the others all the more for that reason alone. It had surprised Faolan, as it did everyone else. The moment Elswyth left the ballroom in tears was the first time everyone in the room had taken a collective step back from me. A hint of fear mixed in with their curiosity, but it was nothing more than a lie I wore as armor. I was in the middle of a battle for my life, for the weak and defenseless, and I'd be damned if I would lose, even if I had to beat my friend for all to see. Behind closed doors, I cried. Hurting Elswyth in front of everyone broke something inside of me, something I'd never repair.

I had spent my eighteenth birthday watching a young man, a lesser Fae, have his wings brutally cut from his body. I became an adult on the eve of a man losing his life. I celebrated my birthday as the others celebrated horror. But I still smiled, laughed, complimented the king on his creativity and thanked him for the entertainment on my birthday. That night, I puked until my face swelled, and I couldn't see through the tears.

For weeks, I crafted a new Crow, a character I played for the outside world. It was an intricate design built from many nights of tears and an endless pit of fear. Every outfit was calculated down to the smallest detail. My hair was always up, showcasing my expertly placed makeup and jewels. I flirted shyly. I touched the king casually and blushed when he touched me in return. I had rolled my Malice over his body each time we had been alone until he began to seek me out in a crowd.

Soon, the king openly found reasons to touch me, give me gifts and compliments, all in front of his people. And when they questioned him, I played insulted until he punished them in a brutal fashion. I forced myself not to shrink away from their pain but to revel in its delights. I smiled, I clapped and I stroked the ego of a heinous monster. I coaxed him every chance I got. I led him to believe that one night, I would come to his bed. One night, we would enjoy the cruel pleasures of his court together. Together, we would show his court what real entertainment was. I had promised that he would see delights that only I, a Crow, could produce. And I would do it all for him, my king.

And when my rage bubbled up and I couldn't stand it any longer, I'd use it to my advantage. Many suffered for me to become who I needed to be, for the king to grow to want me. After my promise to bed the king, my room was no longer guarded. For weeks I allowed him to believe he was turning me into the perfect submissive and broken Crow he so desperately needed. And for weeks, I cried myself to sleep, ashamed of every act, even if it were just an act. I watched myself fall into hell, and it burned every moment I stayed there. This was worse than anything they could do to me, willing myself to become just like them.

With my newfound favor, I told myself it would be easy to leave. I could walk the halls, and no one would stop or question me. I was, after all, the wicked Crow, the newest tormentor. I became a threat the king dished out to those who displeased him, a night at my mercy. But I couldn't leave, not yet. I would not just save myself, however easy that would be. I could not leave behind those who had no one to fight for them. I daydreamed of the day I stained this white court with the blood of its people. I convinced myself that the revenge would taste better aged, like a fine wine. And that wine would come from the basement of monsters. That thought alone got me through many nights and festivities.

Every day, I sank deeper and deeper into my persona. And every night, I clawed my way back up and held on for dear life. I'd stand in the mirror and tell myself I was not lost to this court. I was not as awful as I felt. The moment I couldn't look myself in the eyes would be the moment I had to leave. I wouldn't be of any help if the parts of me I was protecting died on the floors in the Golden Court.

Tonight would be just another party. I had grown used to the fact that the Fae celebrated everything and nothing. They held feasts and ceremonies several times a week for no other reason but to be the monsters they were. I attended banquet after banquet and watched as the lesser Fae were used as entertainment. I had thought I hated all of Elphame until I was forced to watch them tortured. The lesser Fae hadn't deserved their fates on the floors of the Golden Court any more than I did or those in the dungeons. Every show was more repulsive than the last. But through my disgust, I performed my act for the court with Elswyth at my side, prompting me to laugh, to look at the king, to clap and cheer. She had seen hundreds of these shows that I hadn't, and I barely had the stomach to get out of bed, let alone watch someone be tortured over and over. The show never changed, only the star, but they all screamed the same, they cried the same—and so did I.

The woven web of lies was a balancing act, one Elswyth and I perfected, and it gnawed on my soul like a starved animal. Solas was the only one not to buy my charade fully. He was always my guard, uncertain of what I was getting up to. He followed me everywhere. He was an unwanted hangnail that never healed. He was shrewder than I gave him credit for, but I was more conniving than he gave me credit for. A cornered animal has very few choices, but becoming the hunter was mine.

I stood with Elswyth at my side, where she always was. I went nowhere without her. The king began to refer to Elswyth as my shadow. She was. Tonight was different, though. Something about it was off. The air was charged. It prickled with static. My skin crawled with magick and excitement I didn't want near me.

"Faolan just walked in," Elswyth whispered.

I laughed and touched her arm as if she had said something witty and amusing. I was far from amused. Faolan dressed as he always had, light blues and whites and sparkled with fresh snow. I watched him move through the clusters of High-Born Fae in their pearls, stones, furs and skins. Both Solas and the king saw Faolan as well and made their way to me. Solas, likely because he did not like how I treated Elswyth when Faolan was around. The king only came because he enjoyed the entertainment. It's the only reason his heart beat, so he always came to see what game I'd play with Faolan. Punishment for my behavior toward Faolan stopped coming the moment the king thought I'd bed him.

I bowed when Faolan reached us. Elswyth followed suit. "King Faolan, what a pleasure it is to see you. You look charming, as usual."

King Aelfdene lifted me to stand and pulled my arm into his. I fought not to cringe from his touch. It didn't matter how much I practiced. Touching the devil would never grow pleasant. "Faolan, you come to see my little Crow again? What has she done to win this honor of yours?"

Faolan's eyes moved from Aelfdene to me, and a smile slid across his face. He was better at these games than I was. "I pay my respects to all of your pets, King Aelfdene. I was just in your barn, as well."

"You're too kind," I said sweetly. I had been in that barn, and what was housed in there was grotesque. "Those are, after all, prized animals and highly sought after. I hear two were gifts from you. I suppose I have something else in common with them, for I was a gift from you as well."

King Aelfdene kissed the palm of my hand but kept his eyes on Faolan. "Welcome to my home, Faolan. Enjoy the party. We have a wonderful show this evening."

Faolan leaned in and kissed my cheek. "It seems everyone has grown sweet on you, Perdi. What enchantments have you shown him to be granted such freedom from his madness? I smell your magick on your skin as thickly as on his."

I pulled back. He'd caught me off guard. Aelfdene stepped forward, and I touched his arm. With a knowing look, he nodded, giving me permission to handle Faolan on my own. "King Faolan, jealousy ages you considerably. I am merely a Crow, ready to bend over like a dog for any favor I can curry. Why would I not pick the most powerful bed in all of Elphame to bend over on?" I smiled on the outside and crumbled on the inside. Everyone already thought I was the king's harlot. Why was it a surprise that Faolan thought the same thing?

"But I wonder, why ever would it matter to you what my king does and doesn't do with his Crow? Are you questioning his judgment? Or how he rules his land and people? Or do you just have a problem with who he chooses to bed? Do you think you can do better? We both know you're not that good, but if you'd like to try again, I could make myself available for a few minutes."

Faolan's face paled. "Of course not."

"That's too bad. I would have loved the night to end in blood, even if that blood isn't worth me stepping over." I pushed out my bottom lip and grinned toward Aelfdene. "There is only so much dancing that can entertain a girl before she grows bored."

King Aelfdene's laughter boomed through the room. He patted my hand and nodded his head with a proud smile. "Cruel woman. Always a delight."

Faolan followed behind Aelfdene, explaining he was not at all questioning him. Aelfdene ignored him and waved him away. I smiled one of the most authentic smiles I had had since coming to Elphame. It felt good to screw with Faolan, toy with the mechanicians of this awful place. And the more I twisted and turned the palace, the more Solas watched over my shoulder. He didn't trust me, and I didn't blame him. I was, after all, not trustworthy in the least.

I stayed against the wall, at the edge of the party, as I had so many times before. I watched. I waited. I drank from golden goblets. I ate frosted gold cakes. I numbed myself from the horrors the night always unfolded, screams of torture and laughter to follow. Like a rerun, a memory, nightmares I could never wake up from. It was never-ending and always played the same song, night after night—fear and screaming, begging and pleading, joy and laughter, repeat.

Elswyth grabbed my wrist and nudged my attention toward the front of the room. A young woman, human, who couldn't be a day older than I was, was led into the hall. Every now and again, one witless mortal made it through the gate and lived through the deadly mist. It wasn't a broken oath if the fools came looking on their own. She tried to get away, but she was surrounded. It wouldn't have mattered, anyway. They had let others go before, only to chase them down in a hunt. She was better off dying now. How I envied her death, albeit it would be slow and painful, as it always was. But it was better than the alternative, being left for living.

Even from a distance, I could see her regret plastered on her wide eyes and quivering lips. Her body shuddered at her reality. She had been willing, they always were, until they got here. They came freely at first, always the curious, which turned invariably fatal. Before the night was over, she'd be dead and eventually replaced with another who believed they'd be welcomed into the land of the Fae. No one was welcome here, not even the Fae.

I felt the heat of his stare and turned to see Solas. I smiled and lifted my wine glass to him, toasting to the night's festivities. As the young woman was tortured, he watched me. His eyes burned into me, and I fought not to squirm under their weight. I pulled back a little from the room. I picked at the food I had no intention of eating and breathed through my nose until the waves of nausea settled. I stood at the edge of the room, leaning against the wall as though I were bored. It hadn't mattered who I had tried to become. The real me was always under the surface, begging to be let go. For all to see, I smiled, and I would wait until I closed my bedroom door to cry.

"Don't leave," Elswyth whispered as she slid into her place beside me. "You can't show them weakness. You must put on this front or all is lost. It will have been for nothing."

"I can't watch this." I drank down my glass of wine and grabbed another. My head swam, both from wine and from grief.

"You have no choice," she reminded me. "Remember why you are doing this. This is but a small payment for the reward."

Elswyth kept me planted, one arm linked through mine. She nudged me when I was to clap and when I was to smile. I drank until the room was blurry, until my body was hot and I couldn't help but laugh. Drunk, that's where my nights ended, always. It was the only way I could stomach the parties, the earsplitting screams, the gut-wrenching beseeches for life.

The woman crawled through the crowd. She clawed at the ankles of those who would walk on her before helping her stand. They laughed, they kicked her, but they did not help her. She would find no help anywhere in Elphame. And when she grabbed my foot, I was too numb to recoil. Everything hit me at once. She cried for help, and the room swirled as it caught up to me. I puked on her as she begged me.

"Get off of me." I finally found the words.

The room roared with laughter and clapping. I had become part of the entertainment. As cheers went up, chanting for her end, the woman was dragged away, her eyes on only me. I wanted to vomit again. I couldn't help her. She was dead long before she'd crossed the

Gate. Her fate had been sealed the moment she decided she could trust Fae, just as mine had been.

"Get her to bed." King Aelfdene put my hand in the hand of the man who brought me to this hellhole…Solas. "She's had a little too much fun, and the drink has her."

I giggled. It was that or cry, and I could only afford the laughter. He kissed my hand and made a show of saying good night, proving to the others I was broken and that he'd done the breaking. I did nothing to persuade them that he was wrong. I was a monster, *his* monster. Deep down, I felt like I didn't deserve to be called anything but that. The woman would haunt me for the rest of my life. Her eyes, how she begged… I'd never forget her face.

Solas led me from the room, the others asking me to stay and pulling on my arms. I tried to stay, to make a show of my desire to be with them. Solas pushed through them like a storm, with me trailing behind, staggering. Elswyth followed behind me, her face blank. She didn't like the parties any more than I did but was better at hiding it than I was.

"You find somewhere else to be right now," Solas barked at Elswyth once we got to my bedroom. She didn't argue and scurried away. Inside my room, he tried the same thing with Nix and my creature. The creature laughed hard enough that she dropped from the air and landed on her side, like a bumblebee in sudden darkness. Nix and she walked to the other side of the room, laughing. Pests, he called them.

Solas let go of my arm, and I fell hard on my hands and knees. He quickly tried to pick me up, and I pushed him away. I used the bed to help myself stand and caught my reflection in the mirror. My eyes were sunken, and makeup was smeared over my ashen and sweaty skin. My hair was a mess—stringy, faded, as lifeless as I felt. I tried to swallow my rage, but it came out in tears. Solas grabbed me again as I stumbled toward the bathroom. His arm had been the only thing that kept me from smashing my head into the marble doorframe.

"What a joy this is for you. You must love this show, me breaking, again and again, night after fucking night." I pulled away from him. "It must give you such delight to see me a shattered mess—the evil and monstrous Crow."

"I don't enjoy this any more than you do," he answered.

"You have a funny way of showing it."

"As do you."

I shambled my way into the bathroom and stripped from my dress, leaving my full slip on. I climbed into the shower and sat on the floor in the pouring hot water. I tried to clean the vomit from my hair, but my shaking hands were useless. I screamed and cursed and puked again.

"Let me help you," Solas offered.

"I don't need your help," I mumbled back.

"You need someone's help, Perdi. Your mask is slipping with each night that you try to be the monster you're not."

"I'm not a monster," I whispered, more for myself than him.

"I know, and that's why it hurts."

He sat quietly while I retched. Nix and my creature came into the shower after my screams had turned to sobs. They helped me clean myself up, as they had after every single party. Solas didn't poke at me or yell at me as he usually did. He sat with his back to the frosted glass of my shower and let me suffer in peace. It was probably the only decent thing I had seen him do for me.

"I can't do this." I cried until I heaved. I slumped to my side, feeling empty of things that I could rid myself of but filled to the brim with that which never would leave.

Nix rubbed my back until the dry heaves finally stopped. "You *can* do this."

"That poor girl," I cried. "I couldn't help her."

"You can't help everyone. You can't risk it," he said. "You can only ever save yourself."

"What would happen if you ran?" I asked. "If you, Els and my creature ran away from here?"

"I don't know, and I'll never know. I won't leave you."

"You must. You all could get away. Get to the Gate and leave. You could go to my father's cabin. You liked it there. You'd be safe. You'd be free. Please, Nix, go."

"No. Would you leave me?" he asked, and I shook my head. "You're not even willing to leave this godforsaken place unless you take every feeble body with you. You're going to kill yourself for them."

"Death in place of someone who cannot protect themselves doesn't sound like a bad way to die," I answered. "I'm the only chance they have. If not even the Crow cares about them, there's no one left who will."

"I know, and you'll suffer all the more for it." Nix kissed my nose. "We all will suffer willingly with you, Perdi. You're not alone."

The creature dragged a glass of cold water across the tiled floor and produced a small bundle of greenery. I chewed on the leaves and swallowed the icy water. My stomach settled the moment it went down. My body relaxed, and the world seemed to lighten from off my shoulders. The game I was playing, still burdensome and weighty, dulled just enough for me to stop shaking. But it wasn't a game, not really. People were going to die. People were already dying. And some deaths I'd cause and others only because I couldn't save them. Some I'd watch, and others I'd only hear of their last words.

"Leave me, please," I told the others. "Let me wash the night down the drain, so I can do it again tomorrow."

I curled on my side. The water dropped like rain and hid the tears. The shadows in the corner of the shower closed in slowly. When I didn't flinch, when I stared into them and reached for them, they surrounded me, covered me, and since the last time I had seen them, I finally felt safe. The rumble of the shower was gone, replaced with the rushing of blood in my ears. With the world blocked out, I could finally breathe. The ice I felt in my veins slowly warmed. I felt like anything could have come through the doors but couldn't touch me inside the void I had wrapped around myself. Nothing could see me or hear me or hurt me over and again.

"I can't do this," I whispered.

"But you must." The darkness whispered back, for the first time, in a drawn-out hiss, as if dozens of voices had formed into one, and called to me from miles away.

"I'm going to die here."

"We all die," they replied. The truth of it was a bitter pill to swallow. "It is a rarity for us to be given the choice of how we die. Very few of us are given a glimpse into our destiny."

"I don't want to be a monster. It hurts."

"Everything here hurts," they answered. "We're all monsters, in one way or another. It's what you do with that power that counts."

Silence was a luxury—one I didn't often receive. The shadows gave me all that I wanted, and I didn't want it to end. Out there, in the light, is where the pain lived. I stared into the nothingness and let my guard down, finally relaxed. I didn't fear the dark. If it wanted me dead, I'd be gone, and I'd be thankful. Even in the complete blackness, I could see memories from long before, memories that weren't mine. The world of Elphame, before kings and queens made it into the nightmare it is. The darkness was always there, ever watching and waiting, devouring the souls of those deserving. It punished and killed without flinching, without a second warning. Deep inside the pitch, voices of men and women. They brought law and order. They also brought peace and war—and so much death. I saw the faces of those I'd never met and felt sadness and rage. I tasted blood and tears. Just as my chest was about to burst in grief, I heard the cry of a new baby, the laughter of children, face upon face of reasons why wars would come and why warriors would always fight.

I rolled over in the shadows and felt weightless. "Why do you come to me?"

"You call us as a flower calls to a butterfly. You taste of home and familiar things."

"You smell of home." I breathed them in.

"Unless you would like to be locked away as well, we would not tell anyone else you attract the dungeon shadows—and certainly not that we taste of home."

I didn't understand why, but I understood very little about the why of many things in Elphame. "Why are you here?"

"We are trapped here. Wards keep us from leaving."

"So am I. I'm sorry you're here. If I could, I'd let you out."

"We know." The shadows jerked around my body. "But you can't save all. You will die trying."

"So I've been told."

"We're sure Solas has said a great many things to you." They didn't ask. They knew it would have been him.

"How do you know him?" I asked.

"Everyone knows Solas."

"Do you trust him?"

"We trust no one."

"But you trust me."

"You are not no one. You are home," they answered. The shadows vibrated, just enough for me to feel a slight hum. "The little creature is yelling. Your little friend, Nix, is not happy with Solas for taking you from your home."

Through the shadows, I could hear Nix's hushed voice. "She is going to die here, and you watch her wither each day. You push her to hate you more than you will her to live."

"I can't change her fate. Not you, or I, or anyone else. I did not pen her destiny any more than I did my own. She was fated to come here, just as I was to Take her." Solas' voice was soft yet heavy. "Her hate for me will keep her alive. Don't you see that? Do you know what happens to those who align themselves with me? The king slaughters them as a show of power. If she were to show care, even once, she would die faster than the slow crawl to the finish line she is currently on."

"Please, Solas, help her." Elswyth's voice was pained enough for me to taste her tears fall like rain in the shadows.

"I'm doing the best I can."

"Then do the job of someone better than you," Nix snapped. "You're failing her."

"She doesn't exactly make it easy for me. Every time I try to warn her, she ignores me. I have to stalk her like prey, every hour of every day. I'm like her bloody shadow. You both should be schooling her better. It can't just be me."

"You could try to be kinder," Elswyth said. I could hear her voice catch in her throat as if the very idea of telling Solas what to do scared her.

"She can't afford my kindness. Her hate will keep her alive, and that's all that matters."

"This is eating her up inside. Little by little, I can smell her soul die," Nix replied, and I curled away. The shadows closed down the echo and wrapped back around me in the shower.

"He's right," I finally said to the darkness.

"He's not. Your soul is exactly where it was when we first met, albeit scarred and bloody. But there is no soul we've ever met that doesn't hold scars or gaping wounds. Rest assured, yours is still in one piece," the shadow replied.

"It doesn't feel like it."

"For you to leave, as you wish, with those you can save, it's going to hurt a lot more than this. You will be forced to become who you were meant to be. Once you truly face your fate, you will be free, but you will pay dearly for it."

"And what is my fate?"

The shadows rolled around me, thinking. "To suffer. To skin your soul alive. To pay for the sins of your foremothers. To do what is needed."

"I don't think I can do it."

"Then don't. Run. Tonight. Run hard and fast and don't look back."

"I'll never make it. Solas would find me."

"Would you make it? Perhaps...perhaps not. But surely yes, without a doubt, Solas will find you. He could find the darkest shadow in the deepest pits of hell, under one thousand years of ash." The shadows stilled around me. "Solas is here."

"Do not call on the shadows, Perdi. Never let anyone see you with them," Solas' voice called out to me, strangled in anger. "And whatever you do, do not answer it when it calls back. It is not a place for little Crows to be."

I felt the shadows flinch as soon as Solas walked into the bathroom. I knew he was in the shower with me long before his words cleaved the darkness, and they drew back from me. Once he had chased away every shadow, I felt naked. I felt the moment they were gone completely, and they'd taken a piece of me along. I could have stayed there until my final breath, and now I was alone again.

"I didn't call them," I answered. But perhaps I had, like a flower to a butterfly. Not with intention, just by being there—on my first night here, when I needed to fade into nothingness, when I needed help. And when I had been lashed, I didn't want to be alone. When I was in trouble in the cell, the shadows had come to help. Now, in the shower, when I felt the weight of all my actions and thought I could go no further, they came to settle me.

"Do not meddle with what you don't understand. You risk your soul when you reach into the shadows. You would risk your life if you were ever caught with them." He picked me up from the floor and carried me out of the bathroom. He was rough enough for me to fall from his arms and land on the floor.

I didn't cry out when I hit the floor. I somehow felt deserving of it.

"I'm sorry." He scrambled to pull me into his arms. He cradled me and dried me. His apology felt unusual. It was the first he had given, and I wondered if it was real or something someone said because of habit. He peeled my wet slip off, and I flinched.

"Is this how it happens? How you will show me *your* version of hurt? Is this how you plan to school me, for me to fall in line? At least I'm drunk and won't remember it." I half-laughed, only to finish in a sob. "I pray I don't remember it. But I have the feeling I'll remember every hour of every day, like a book I've read hundreds of times."

"No. I have no taste for such things as that." His answer didn't surprise me. Aside from his roughness with me, I hadn't seen him touch another, though I didn't know what he did after he locked me in my room each night.

"Yet here you are in a court that only delights in force."

"Not by choice," he replied. "I'd never come to this goddamn place willingly."

"Finally, we have something in common."

"We do what we must when our options are few."

"How do you live this life?" I asked when he pulled a dry gown over my head. I stared at him through teared lashes.

"This isn't living for either of us. This is surviving, and we do what we can to save those who we can."

"I can't save anyone, can I? There's nothing but horror and dread here. It's a game that I can't win."

"This isn't about winning. Just save yourself, Perdi," he answered. "There is no one here that needs saving more than you. The more you try, the more you will suffer."

"I can't leave them all behind. I'm not that person, as much as I wish I could be."

"I know. But if you don't, you will never make it. And if you don't make it, all this suffering will have been for nothing."

"I want to go home," I cried. "The feeling won't go away, my desperation to go home. I try to let it go, but it won't. It eats at me."

"We all want to go home, and that feeling never goes away. But you, little Crow, cannot."

I buried my head into his chest. "The day you took me and I ran, I prayed your monsters would kill me. I begged you to kill me."

"I know," he answered. "Crows always run, always beg for death…except for Aoife. She never ran, never begged once. But you are the first to land a strike."

"But it wasn't enough to be the end to my life as a Crow." I smiled weakly.

"You don't really want to die or you'd have done it already. No one, not even me, can force a person to survive."

"I can't, not yet," I answered.

"And that is why you'll suffer."

"How do you sleep at night, knowing you've Taken us to this place, to this hell?"

"I don't, little Crow," he answered. "I haven't slept a true night in longer than I can remember."

I clung to him and sobbed until I was nothing more than tired hiccups.

"I will save them," I said quietly.

"You will try," Solas answered and tucked me into bed.

"I will win, and we will all be free," I mumbled.

"No one is ever free."

"I will be," I answered. When I felt him move, my stomach twisted. "Don't leave me alone."

Solas pushed my hair from my face. "You're never alone. I'm always near."

"I won't leave you behind," I told him. "When I burn this place to ash, run."

"Put your mask back on and take it off for no one, absolutely no one," he finally said. "*Sleep.*"

He sent me to sleep with a slight push of magick, where I dreamed of the girl begging at my feet and me laughing as the Fae slaughtered her alive, opening her like a butterfly. We dined on mortals, bellies full and drunk on grotesque blood wine. And I finished the night dancing with Faolan, my hands tied behind my back. Even in my dreams, I couldn't escape being a Crow.

Chapter Eleven

Elphame had now been my home for just over five months. They were the longest months of my life. And not a day went by that I didn't feel it as a loss, a waste. Each morning I cursed the perpetual sun, the stench of flowers, the laughter of high tea and the bootlicking and bribing favors from anyone and everyone with power. On the outside, the Golden Court was all one would expect it to be. But on the inside, behind the glamour and gold, it was in a constant state of rot and ruin. Souls came here to die, and we all toasted our glasses to their deaths. I felt each one. My Malice could, as well, and although she was in a constant state of hunger, not even she liked the feeling.

Months passed since my breakdown in the shower. Solas and I didn't talk about it, what little I remembered. The reminder of how close I came to revealing my plan was enough for me to stay clear of him. I couldn't risk Solas finding out what we were doing, what the newest monster of Golden Court was about to do. Not even Elswyth spoke to Solas, for fear he'd command her to tell him what game the little Crow was playing. But he was never far away, always watching and waiting for me to slip up. Solas lurked like a constant shadow and was around every corner I turned. He attended every banquet and only to watch me watch the show. He looked for a crack in my carefully crafted exterior. He looked for Perdita, the girl he'd dragged to Elphame. He'd never find what he was looking for, but whatever he did see made him come back again and again. I didn't entertain him. He feared my next move. But now, he was not the only one watching. I was watching him. I was not the only one in these Golden Lands to be wearing a mask.

King Aelfdene was a disease that rotted Elphame from the inside out, and his followers spread it wherever they went. Each day the king graced me with his presence. He looked a little less High Fae than he had before. Little by little, the glamour of who he wanted me to believe he was fell away, leaving behind fragments of who he really was—a monster. His skin was paler, not yet white, but sickly. His ears were more pointed, his hair stringy and oily. Each time I saw him, the rage in my stomach—the living, breathing hate I had for Elphame—blistered as it rolled through me. But I swallowed it, just as I choked down my night terrors and constant prayer for freedom.

Days that bled into weeks and months, nursing the prisoners back to health, built up to this very moment, on the edge of the property, standing at the riverbank. My little creature landed on the bank at my feet and nodded. As we had practiced for weeks, I started an argument with both my servants, slapping them, beating them down for being worthless and disobedient. I had spent weeks treating them as insignificant creatures in front of the court. They trailed behind me, shuffling on wounds that just wouldn't heal without being broken again. I spoke of them to others as though they weren't worth much more than the ratty shoes on their feet. Many laughs were had at their expense, and each night, when we returned to my room, I hugged them and apologized. It may have been a show, but the humiliation was painful, regardless of whether you knew it was coming or not.

With a nod of her head, the young woman yelled obscenities, and I slapped her with enough force to send her into waters no one dared to venture into. She was pulled under before all her body was even thoroughly wet. The other, the young boy she had clung to in the dungeon, confronted me and yelled at me. I pushed him in next. I laughed as he screamed. He fought but was pulled under with ease, as I knew he would be.

Nix and my creature had bargained for the help of the nymphs. The water nymphs would take them across into the waiting hands of the forest nymphs. From there, they'd be brought to the border of the Court of Less. Nix would have his people bring them to safety, take them home. It was a risky deal and required me to steal an awful lot of gold and jewels to pay the nymphs, but no one had questioned me or my need to be covered in gems and gold and never asked where the last hoard had gone when I asked for more.

We made a show of it, and my laughter was genuine. I was happy, even though I reveled in their demise on the outside. I had rescued two. If nothing else, I knew two would be free—and it felt absolutely glorious. If this was all I got, if two lives were all I could ever save, it was worth whatever I would now pay for them.

Nix and Elswyth didn't laugh with me. They played the part of fear, fear of me, for all to see—and all did. Nix hid behind Elswyth, shaking in his boots. When Elswyth fanned a cry, I scolded her and threatened her. I tugged at her, pulling her toward the water. She cowered as we practiced. When she was good and truly scared, I pushed her up the bank and marched after her. The others ran from the field the closer I got to them. I took my seat at a picnic we had packed earlier in the day and proceeded to eat my lunch. I smiled and laughed as if nothing had happened. With each bite I took, I realized I was actually hungry. For the first time, I enjoyed a meal in Elphame. I, the Crow, had saved two lives, and it felt damn good.

"The king would like to see you." Solas stood at the edge of my blanket, casting a shadow over me.

I looked up with a smile and shielded my eyes from the sun. "Right now?"

"Yes, now," he answered and lifted me to my feet by my wrist.

"Oh, someone isn't having a good day," I taunted him as he pulled me toward the manor. "Can I interest you in a swim? Perhaps you can swim better than the last two who tried."

"I saw what you did," Solas answered. "If I saw, others did."

I tried to shrug, but his grip on my arm tightened. "They were defiant. I absolutely cannot have disobedience in my servants. As King Aelfdene has shown us, that leads to rebellion and all kinds of trouble I cannot afford."

"Disobedience doesn't deserve what you did." He jerked me hard and fast, but I was ready for his anger. It was the only emotion he ever showed me. He whispered his last words for only my ears. "Lie better, little Crow. You're walking a dangerous path. Choose your words carefully. Choose only ones with enough truth that I can lie with you, or you will die when you go in there."

"It wouldn't be Elphame without the risk of death around every corner."

I tilted my head back and laughed a full-bellied laugh as Solas marched me into the manor. I stumbled behind him and snickered. The laughter was nothing more than a confused cover. I wondered what he'd seen, what he'd really seen. More than that, had he just offered to lie for me? Why would he care if I died today or tomorrow?

"Have I missed a joke?" King Aelfdene sat behind his desk.

"Just his surprise. He's a constant source of amusement for me," I answered.

"You asked to speak to her." Solas pushed me to my knees in front of the king.

"My Crow, I've been told you killed your servants this morning?"

"My King," I whispered and touched his leg. I looked up at him with sweetness in my eyes and Malice on my fingertips. "They were defiant, unruly. They wouldn't listen. I tried to punish them, but today, when they overheard me speaking to Elswyth about preparing to come to your room, they spoke cruelly about me. They called me awful names. It was heard by all who were outside. They said I shouldn't go to you, that I should go with Faolan as he offered. They told me to leave before it was too late, before you sullied me."

"Go with Faolan? He offered to take you from here?" Aelfdene looked confused and angry at once. That another would turn against him truly baffled him. He was a foolish and egotistical man, just as Elswyth said he was.

"Yes, he came to my prison long ago, when I was in the cells, and offered me freedom from you if I left with him. He said he would allow me freedom in his court if I left you. But I told him I would not leave, that I wanted to stay, and he has come to every party and has hounded my lady and me. You've seen him. I've had to discipline my lady because of him. I speak no lies." I weaved a web with bits of truth and hoped I'd be alive to watch Faolan burn for it.

Aelfdene offered his hand for me to stand. "If you are telling untruths…"

I smiled. "My King, you would know if I were lying, no?"

He looked at Solas. When I turned to face him, Solas nodded his head.

"So far, she is telling the truth. I found Faolan in her cell," he answered. I had skirted the truth so meticulously that he couldn't say I was outwardly lying. It was the truth—my version of it, anyway.

"My King, I am not lying," I pleaded with him. I grabbed at his hand and squeezed. My eyes begged him to trust me, believe me. "Today, I just snapped. Then something dragged them under before I could do anything about it. They were just gone. I thought, at most, they'd get wet and have to sit in soggy clothes. But they didn't come back up. The water isn't even deep enough for them to not have stood back up."

"Water nymphs," Solas answered. "The waters around here are filled with them."

"Perfect. Go ask them, then. They will tell you what happened," I added for good measure. "They would have seen the argument. It will prove I speak only the truth. Come, please. I will take you to them. They will tell you. I swear to it."

If, and that was a big *if*, the nymphs answered the call of Aelfdene, they would lie as I'd paid them to. They would give a similar story and add that the two Fae I had pushed into the water were theirs to eat for entering their territory without permission.

"I believe you." Aelfdene smiled and ran his thumb down my cheek. "Little Crow, you can't just kill your servants because they won't listen to you or they hurt your feelings. If it happens again, let me know, and I'll have new ones sent to you."

I nodded and pouted for show. "Up until the moment they didn't bob back up, I was having fun, and now my fun is over."

"You still have that other one, Elswyth, or did you drown her, too?" he asked with a hint of laughter in his voice.

"I still have her, but one isn't enough to entertain me." I grinned. "I need more, and I'll pick them this time. The last ones were almost as bad as having Solas as my shadow."

The king laughed and patted my head like a dog. "He can be bothersome."

"Please let me pick new ones. I'll try not to break them this time." I fluttered my eyelashes and wanted to puke at my display. "But truthfully, I also cannot tolerate them speaking poorly of you or of me. I simply will not abide that behavior. I may be a Crow, but I am *your* Crow."

"Of course, but keep these ones alive. They are an annoyance to replace."

"I shall try, but I cannot promise." I winked. My stomach rolled. "I bore easily."

The king leaned in and whispered, "Let us dine tomorrow evening?"

"Perhaps," I said playfully and kissed him on the cheek, the corners of our mouths touching. It was the closest he had gotten, to date, to a real kiss. "Now, get back to work."

I skipped from the room, my hair bouncing behind me. Solas stormed at my back. His anger pulsed in the air and pushed me forward. I didn't turn. I left him at my back, showing I wasn't as scared of him as the others were…because I wasn't. Not because I had the king's favor… No, the king would kill me as quickly as he'd bed me. I gave Solas my back because it tormented him to know I wasn't afraid of what he'd do. At worst, he'd torture me in ways that broke me. And if I were broken, I wouldn't care what he did. At best, he'd kill me—and the dead had no worries.

"I saw what happened at the river," Solas said when I got to the stairs of the basement. "I saw more than you think.

"You saw nothing," I answered. A part of me wanted to trust him, to have one more ally, but I couldn't risk it. I would take off this mask for no one, not even him—the only warning of his that I'd bother to listen to. "I am owed two more. Go fetch. I have a picnic waiting for me."

I followed him to the basement, counting the stairs and the turns and plotting, as I always did. I stood at the head of the hall into a dungeon that buzzed with flies for the dead. It was the only place that didn't smell like the rest of the Golden Court, save for Solas. He never smelled of flowers. Whenever he was near, I could smell mint, lavender and fresh earth, like he had spent his days in an herb garden. Although I'd never admit it out loud, his scent was a respite from the constant pounding smells of the Golden Court.

"You look like a starved animal hunting a beast," Solas breathed out his words, sending them over my skin.

"Let's not pretend you haven't spent every day here doing the same thing," I answered.

"I'm not starved, and I am the beast."

I smirked. "Isn't that the truth."

Solas leaned into my neck, and when I didn't pull back in fear, he sighed. His hot breath made me flinch, but I still stood my ground. "I'm warning you one last time, Perdi—enough of this."

"Or what, Solas?" I asked and turned to him. "What will you do? What can you prove? Whatever would you say to the king of his little Crow? You have no idea what I am willing to do and have done to me in order to win. Blood will splash these walls, and I really don't care if it is my blood or yours."

"You will force my hand."

I smiled. There was no joy on my face. "And you will force mine."

"Do you want freedom so badly that you'll risk innocent people?"

"You have no idea what I'm willing to do."

He nodded. "And I will do a great deal to stop you from harming my people."

"I'm glad we each know where the other stands. But tell me, if you are the beast, why are you down here fetching? Why are you even in this court if you are as monstrous as you claim?" I put my hands on my hips. "You are the Great Solas, the nightmare of Elphame, the terror of Fae. Yet, here you are, down in the dungeons, taking orders from the Crow you dragged here. Why?"

"To see how far you're willing to go. To see how much you're willing to risk," he answered then left me standing alone at the head of the hall.

"Whatever it takes," I replied.

"I'm counting on it," he said in less than a whisper.

I waited for him to search the cells for two sickly Fae. I made him open every cage of despair and show me who was inside. I made a mental note of how many we would need to rescue and how many would be dead before we could get to them. Each time he pointed one out for me to take, I'd shake my head and make an excuse as to why I didn't want them. The truth was, I had to see every square inch of the basement prisons. He cursed at me, yelled at me and belittled me, but I still stood firm.

"This is utterly disgusting, Solas. He is not coming to my room. He has nine eyes. How do I go about my day with him slinking around and staring at me?" I ran out of sickly reasons not to take a Fae—illnesses, oozing wounds and I even resorted to esthetic reasons. I wanted those about to die, those whose life depended on freedom. Most of what I saw could be healed if left alone for a day or two. I wanted the absolutely broken and shattered. I knew how it felt to give up and how badly I ached for compassion and a savior. "How do you expect me to eat a meal served to me by someone who has tentacles for arms and four of them to boot? Next."

"You're sick," Solas growled in my face.

I stepped around him, light on my feet, and waltzed the halls again. "No, actually, I feel fine, fit as a fiddle. I'm not sick in the least. But I do appreciate your concern for my health. It's such a delightful change from your usual cursing of me."

"You once asked how I could sleep at night. I now ask you the same thing."

"I sleep just fine."

"No, you don't. I hear your screams, even through the Malice wrapped around your room."

I shrugged. "Just because I scream doesn't mean I haven't learned to enjoy it. Let's move this along. I didn't come down here to discuss how damned my soul is. It was damned the moment I was born. You've just hastened things for me."

I made Solas start over. This time, I waited in the hall and didn't look in each cell. I really didn't want to see the show again or smell the mess the Golden Court had left down here. For a moment, I wondered if those in the cells even deserved help after years of Taking Crows. Should a Crow, who they had a hand in Taking, help them? Wouldn't leaving them in the cells to rot be some sort of justice? I scolded myself for the thought. I pushed the hate aside. I knew better than that. Who would be brave enough to stand up against kings? Who in their right mind would risk their families for a Crow? I couldn't blame them, not really. Back home, we would have sold our neighbor's unborn child for one more year of freedom. I sympathized with and understood the things others were forced to do when desperate to survive. Those in the cells were as deserving of freedom as I was.

I leaned against the wall and calmed myself. I couldn't blow it. I couldn't break down or all would be lost. He already knew more than I was comfortable with, more than I trusted him with. The truth was, I hated being in the basement. It smelled of memories I'd sooner forget. My heart hammered in my chest. There hadn't been many times since becoming a Crow when I wasn't terrified, when I wasn't afraid of being caught or tortured. And now I was playing with fire, not the kind that simply burned my hand, but the kind that would rage against me and those I loved. If I were found out, we'd all be dead, and I'd be responsible for the burned bodies.

The brick warmed against my flesh, and a low rumble filled my chest. It calmed my racing pulse. It reminded me of a cat's purr back home. That small memory of barn cats and home, and I felt my pain leach out of me and into the wall. I pulled back slowly, placed my hand on the stone and closed my eyes. On the other side of the wall felt like home, freedom and utter sadness and despair. I wanted nothing more than to take back my pain. It already had so much.

"I'm sorry," I whispered to it.

"Not every prison has a door." Solas startled me, and I flinched. I hated that he snuck up on me and that my response was fear.

"Who is bricked behind the wall?" I asked.

"Monsters," he answered.

"We're all monsters in one way or another," I replied and thought back to the night the darkness came and wrapped around me in the shower.

"Then I would be afraid of what the other monsters were so scared of that they bricked it up."

I pulled back and stared at the wall. Whatever was back there had wanted out in ways that trumped my own. It felt familiar in how stars were, no matter where you called home. Behind that wall felt like looking at a different sky but still knowing you were home. The nails that clawed on the other side felt like the same claws that raked down my soul each time I had gone to a banquet and had clapped when a head came off. It felt like me, behind the wall—the me I locked away when I decided I'd escape this place.

"Are you afraid of it?" I asked Solas.

"No."

"Neither am I," I answered.

"Why not? Everyone else with half a brain is."

I smiled. "That doesn't say much about the brain in your head."

He shrugged. "It takes a lot to scare me, little Crow."

"I hate that you call me that."

"I know."

I closed my eyes and breathed in the scent of wet moss and starry nights. "It smells like home, like pushing my face into my pillow and breathing it in—like the rain at night, tucked safely in bed. It feels like all the good parts of my soul, before I came here."

"Most have said it smells of death."

I grinned. "Not my death, but the death of those who will come against me. And there's no better smell than that."

"Careful what you say out loud, little Crow, for you may find yourself bricked in there with it."

"I doubt whatever is holding it back could keep us both," I answered. I breathed it into the very bottom of my lungs and held it as if I could take it with me when I left.

"We'd eat the fucking world together."

Solas pulled me from the stone. "What did you say?"

I tilted my head and knowingly smiled. He heard the voices as I had. "I didn't say anything."

"Don't, Perdi. Don't ever come back down here. You risk too much with your curiosity. What has been bricked has not spoken in centuries. That you've awoken its interest will be your death if any other were to know."

I risked another glance at the wall. "It's awake now and wants out."

"Good luck with that." Solas leaned into my cheek. His hot breath edged on painful. "This is not the path you want to walk. This path, what is bricked up, will swallow the world. It starves for food you cannot possibly feed it. If anyone were to know it speaks to you, you'd die, and all your careful planning will have been for nothing. All these months of horror you've endured will be for naught, and you'll never escape."

I pulled back with a genuine smile, one of the first I had in months. My smile turned to laughter, and it was full-bellied. "He's going to burn this hellhole to the ground."

"With you in it," Solas countered.

I shrugged. "I don't think he would, but I also don't think I care."

"You should."

"I should do a great many things, Solas, and I don't care about those, either."

* * * *

Solas had brought me two more from the basement. Both were in worse shape than the last ones and smelled as if death was already upon them. One died within hours, painfully, starved of food and love. We held her, cried for her, loved her for her last moments. We gave her peace in her final time, and it ripped my heart in two. I knew Solas had done it on purpose, to punish my cruel heart. The other would likely die before the morning came, and there was nothing I was able to do to stop it. She wouldn't leave this place, but she'd soon be free. We gave her painkiller paste, cleaned her broken body and dressed her for her final hours. Someone would remain with her until her last breath. If nothing else, we would not let her die alone. She deserved better. Her crime was saying no to the offer from a Royal. He took her against her will anyway, and she was punished for her audacity to fight back. I hated the king for this. I hated Faolan for this. I wanted to hate all of Elphame, but I couldn't. I loved a very few of them, and they loved me back.

"I need to get into the basement," I told Elswyth. "There's something down there I need to check out. It could be our way out of here. I've felt it stirring since the day I got here."

"Don't do it, Perdi. Whatever you found down there is down there for a reason."

I motioned to the broken woman on my bed. "I found her down there. Are you going to tell me she was down there for a good reason? They put me down there. Would I have deserved this treatment?"

"No, I never meant…" Elswyth shook her head. "No, you're right. Regardless of why any are down there, none deserve what has been laid upon their bodies. I'm sorry. That wasn't right of me to say."

Sneaking through the Golden Court was dangerous—not because I was scared that I'd be caught, but because I was afraid of who would catch me and what they'd do to me before anyone else realized I was gone. All Fae were cruel and hateful, but some are demented and twisted. I didn't know which one was worse. I crossed my fingers that whichever flavor of monster snagged me would be a complete lunatic and would just eat me on the spot. I uncrossed my fingers. For the first time since coming through the Gate, I prayed I wouldn't die. There were too many people counting on me for me to just give in to death.

It was an odd feeling to realize you no longer wanted death, no longer felt it would be a mercy. Everything I had done, recreating a version of myself to be dark and cruel, had been to survive, to not only survive but ensure others were saved with me. To know that I didn't want to die raised the stakes incredibly. Now I no longer had to just protect the others. I had to protect myself as well. And during my journey from my bedroom to the bowels of the manor had felt like walking along a tight rope during a hailstorm. It was beyond any measure of risk I had taken to date.

I stood in complete darkness with my hand pressed against the stones. The basement was pitch black, save the flickering of candles high on the wall. From their position, they lent no usable light to someone of my height. But the darkness was not something I feared, not when there were worse things in this land to scare me. The stones were cold at first touch, like a stone from a riverbed, icy at first but warmed quickly in my hand. The warmth, though, had nothing to do with me and everything to do with what stood on the other side of the wall.

Behind the wall was a prison. Within the prison were shadows of a monster I couldn't see. I pressed magick into the stones, but they did not budge. Wards tickled the back of my mind and held the rocks firmly in place. Knots upon knots pulled an ancient spell together. The force it would take to break the spell would bring the wall down, crumbling in rubble. It was a risk I couldn't make, not yet, not this soon.

I leaned my forehead on the wall and sighed at what sighed back. "What are you?"

"Nightmares and darkness and terror and death," he finally whispered.

"That sums up the entirety of Elphame."

"I assure you, little Crow, the others are but a faint shadow to my darkness."

"Why are you here?"

"The same reason you light a candle at night. Fear. You fear what you do not know. You lock away that which scares you most," he answered, but on the edge of his voice, rested dozens of other voices, answering together.

"Who put you here?"

"I came willingly."

I frowned. "Who the hell comes here willingly?"

"You did," he answered.

"Fair enough. What did you do?" I asked.

Claws scraped against the wall. I could see them flex along the stone in the back of my mind as clearly as if they were in front of me. "Wouldn't you wish to keep the darkness at bay?"

"No. The darkness is the only place that doesn't lie. Darkness is the only way I can hide. No one looks too deeply into the pitch for fear it will glance back." I smiled at the memory of the shadows wrapping around me. "Is it you who is coming to me?"

"In part."

"Why?"

"Curiosity. Much like why you have come to me."

"I can feel you, your pain." I whispered and rubbed the center of my chest. The pain and sorrow squeezed my lungs. "I felt you the moment I stepped foot on these grounds. I can feel you always. When I wake from a nightmare, I can smell you."

"As did I feel you when you arrived. You are the first to come to see what the Golden Courts fear so great that they've locked it away. You are either foolish or brave. Which one are you?"

"I'm neither foolish nor brave. I am desperate. I only wish to save as many as I can before I'm killed here." I pulled my hand back. "When the light can't save me, who else do I turn to but the dark?"

"Foolish, that is what you are," the darkness replied. "You can save no one but yourself."

"I've heard the story before, yet here I am," I countered.

"Why would you not save yourself?"

"My freedom would just be a different prison, always on the run, always hunted. I won't leave Elphame alive, so if I could save more than myself, why wouldn't I?" I asked. "Why would I leave, knowing I could have taken others with me?"

"Saving others means you suffer more. Why would you want to suffer more for those you care nothing about? You owe no oaths to them. You owe no favors. They are not your kings or queens. You own them no allegiance."

"Saving others isn't about what they owe me. It is what I owe myself. I owe it to myself to try. And I will suffer regardless. Adding another reason to why won't keep me from feeling the pain in the end," I answered. "If I only cared about the suffering of others when it benefited me, I'd deserve to die here. If only my life mattered, I wouldn't deserve to live it."

A collective sigh rolled through the darkness.

"If I release you, what will happen?" I asked.

"If you survive long enough, little Crow, to release me and all I am...that is the only question that matters."

"I could kill them all," I whispered. "I can see it in the back of my mind. If I let out my Malice and stopped holding onto her so tightly... If I let her breathe, she'd eat them all. I know she would. She's so hungry all the time. I want to let her out, to punish them."

"I would not test your theory. You are not strong enough to eat them all."

I sighed. "Are you?"

"Yes."

"Will you kill me if I let you out?"

"I don't know yet."

"Will you kill the prisoners?"

"No. They've done nothing to bring me to their doors."

"Will you kill the Golden Court?"

"Yes."

"How do I get you out of there?"

"You'd have to unweave spell after spell. We can do the rest... Someone is coming. It's time you run along, little Crow."

"What are you doing here?" A guard stepped into the hall of horrors. His voice echoed down the chamber and shocked me to my core.

My heart hammered, and I searched for a believable lie. I had been in such a rush to get to the basement in one piece that I didn't think about getting back in the same condition. "I…I."

"She's tormenting the prisoners. What does it look like?" Solas walked in behind the guard.

"She's not allowed down here."

"By order of the king, she does as she pleases. And since she kills every servant she takes, she's likely looking for her next victims." Solas stared past the guard to me. I didn't need him to touch me to feel his scorn. The look in his eyes had said all that needed to be said. "She didn't have her last ones for more than a few hours."

"I heard that about you." The guard chuckled. "Did you find one who tickles your fancy?"

It was one thing to be a monster and another to be thought of as a monster and not be one. It oddly hurt my feelings. I shook my head, and by sheer will, I didn't cry or run. "Not yet. But I only just got here. Had you not disturbed me, I would have."

I marched past the guard, who fell over himself to apologize to the king's Crow. I pushed past Solas, who followed me to my room. I felt his eyes on the back of my head with each step. I tried to keep as much distance ahead of him as I could, but he was bigger and faster, and I just wasn't.

"I don't know what game you're playing, Perdi, but you need to stop before it costs you your life—before it costs others their lives," Solas said, holding my bedroom door open for me, like the gentleman he clearly was not.

"You could have stopped me at any time, but you didn't. I suppose it is both of us with blood on our hands, not just me," I answered.

"I'm trying to save your life, and you're doing everything you can to end it. You're making being your guard a full-time job."

"Trying to save my life? Here I thought I couldn't afford your kindness?" I snapped back, and the look on his face told me I had said too much.

"How many need to die before you stop this?" he asked. If he knew I had heard him talk to the others, he didn't mention it.

"As many as possible," I answered and could taste the truth on my tongue. The look on his face said he believed me. He didn't need to know who would die by the time I was done or why. For the first time, I willingly touched him, and he jerked back. We both stared at our hands, as if we both could feel them tingle.

I grabbed his shoulder and pulled him to my whispers. "Solas, you need to leave. I can't save you and everyone else."

"I don't need you to save me. I need you to save yourself," he replied.

"I'd hate to set this place to burn with you inside to save them all. But for them, I would."

"I pray you will."

Chapter Twelve

The second prisoner died an hour before my dinner with the king. I sat at Aelfdene's dining table, laughing, smiling, when I was crushed inside. My food tasted of tears and cardboard. My heart was shattered, and my soul felt like it was on the brink of destruction. I tried desperately not to tremble and blamed the copious amounts of wine during the day for my behavior. We mortals—the weak, feeble creatures we were—suffered greatly when it came to such things as spirits. The king was amused and agreed that mortals were far too weak to keep up with the likes of Fae, and I should stop trying.

Each time I wanted to scream, the shadows across the room moved just enough for me to notice. They were both a warning and a reminder that I wasn't alone, even if I felt I was. They kept me from dropping the mask I had painfully created. I was grateful. I couldn't afford anger. Not yet. But it was almost worth it.

Dining with the king was never a highlight of my evenings, especially when I'd sooner be in my room, mourning another needless death. What made things worse was not that Solas sat beside me and stared at me the entire time. It was the guest for dinner that made my temper flare. To my surprise, but not Solas', the Captain of the Guardians was at the dinner table. He looked nothing like how I remembered him. Gone was the intimidating and powerful man that once sat at the head of the table. Now he just looked frail and desperate against the backdrop of the Fae. His garb, once a symbol of resistance against the tyranny of Elphame, was nothing more than a shabby cloche over his traitorous frame. From his scruffy blond hair to his dirty nails, he was his truest self now—disloyal, a defector, a murderer. He fit in nicely at this table. Now, more than ever, he and I had something in common. Neither of us could be trusted, each for different reasons. But death would follow us both.

He'd come to renegotiate the oath, on his own, in his favor. He wanted the Gate open in exchange for riches and a Fae wife. He asked for eternal life and to live those days out in Elphame, free of the mortal world. What he didn't understand was that he could be given all that while locked in a cell in the basement of the Golden Court. He was a selfish and foolish man who would die for his own greed, whether at the hands of the Guardians or at the hands of Fae.

I nibbled on my food as I learned it was the Captain of the Guardians who'd convinced the king to take me. He'd told them the Guardians would finally wage war for Taking a Guardian's child, and the oath would be broken. For promises of gold and fortune and a Fae wife, he'd sold us all out. He felt no shame in what he had done and even pointed out how well I had done for myself here in Elphame. How lucky I was. I didn't correct him. I silently put his name on a piece of paper in my soul. I'd make sure he got what was coming to him if Elphame didn't do it for me.

"You seem so calm, Perdi, given the news you've just heard." Solas turned and faced me. "The Guardian has said he helped to ensure you would be Taken as a Crow. He didn't protect you as he should have, and you have no comment? Where is this dark Crow everyone so fears?"

I shrugged him off. "I'm sure he has his reasons, just like the rest of us. He, too, had a child he was protecting."

"You're not angry?" He needled me, baited me, as he had every time I had to sit with the king for dinner. "This man is responsible for what you're feeling this very minute, and you've not a thing to say to him?"

"We all do what we must to survive." I looked into his eyes and meant those words. I, too, would do what I had to. "If selling out his people, damning himself to a fate he deserves, is what he feels he must do, who am I to tell him differently? I'm just a Crow, Solas. What would I know?"

"They're *your* people, little Crow," Solas corrected me.

I smiled. "Have you failed to notice? I am here, in Elphame, and not in the mortal world? Who should my people be, Solas? Those who let me go, those who sold me to improve their lives or those who now keep me safe? Since you have all the answers, who the hell do I give my allegiance to?"

"He looks mighty healthy for a mortal to be in Elphame lands," Solas pointed out. "I wonder just how many times he's come here to not feel Fae sickness? How long has he been selling out your people?"

"Stop poking at her, Solas," Aelfdene intervened, as he often had to. Solas was unrelenting most nights. And when those moments came, I usually excused myself and ruined any chance the king had to coax me to his chambers. I didn't know if Solas did it on purpose, to save me from the king, or if he really liked needling me as much as I enjoyed needling him back.

I kept my smile on, kept my conversation light, but soon excused myself. The look I gave Solas blamed him for my leaving. He'd hear about it from Aelfdene, as he always did. But it was a show, nothing more. I left them to discuss the particulars of their deals, the pending doom on my people and the growing homesickness I had in my chest.

I returned to my room, dragging my feet. This time, Solas didn't follow, and I was grateful. I could hear Solas cut into the Guardian, slicing his loyalty to the bone. He said the words I couldn't afford to say. For a brief moment, I was glad Solas had been there. He could pay the cost for whatever came from his mouth, and tonight, he held back nothing. I, unfortunately, could say nothing at all. Once inside my room, I leaned against my door and slid to the floor.

"There's a Guardian down there," I told Nix. "Captain Ridley Hilliard."

"What?" He jumped from the bed. "Was he Taken?"

I shook my head. "Nope. He came to renegotiate the oath in exchange for wealth, a Fae wife and eternal life within Elphame. What's funny is, he doesn't look like this is his first time through the Gate. I was sick for half a day, and he's fine."

"He's likely of half-blood and probably has come many times." Elswyth's voice carried through the room.

Nix laughed. "Stupid man. He will die here."

I nodded. "So will my people."

"Desperate times reduce men to greed and despair." Elswyth sat on the edge of the bed. "They feel free to act as they choose, as long as they can prove they were desperate and had no other choices."

"He does have choices," I answered.

"But not ones that bring him wealth and long life," she countered. "To him, there are no other choices with the same results. So, he tells himself there are no others."

"How do I get word back to Whitwick and the other Guardians?" I asked Nix.

"We can't. If they're planning on doing this, Perdi, we'd never get there in time. We have to leave this place first, make it out alive and get to safety—then get to the Gate," he answered. "If we go sooner, we'd be bringing the fight to their doorstep, with all of Elphame hunting us."

"I can't just do nothing," I protested. "If I do nothing, I share in the blame."

"We all do, Perdi," Elswyth agreed.

****

The king celebrated his victory over the mortal realm with a banquet. I didn't hate it more or less than any other one. They were the same, no matter the why behind the dancing. Tonight, Captain Ridley was showered with affection and sat beside the king. He took it as a great honor. But there wasn't another in the room who wanted to take his place or that intense interest from the king. Ridley's laugh echoed through the room like nails on a chalkboard, dragging over my soul. Elswyth did her best to keep my mind away from the chatter and bets on how long the mortal land would stand once invaded.

There wasn't enough wine in all of Elphame to keep my rage in, which was already drunk and wanted nothing more than to stand up and yell curses. But my temper wasn't the one that would suffer. It would be my flesh that split. I pulled from Elswyth and walked out. I had given them the hours I'd always regret I gave. I moved from room to room, looking for a balcony, anything that was away from the party. I would hide until this day bled into the next, where I would do the same routine over again. I could still hear the crowd laughing at the pending deaths of my people. I bit my lip and swallowed each scream until my stomach was too full to keep them down. I covered my mouth and fought it tooth and nail until I found myself running.

"You can't be out here!" A guard grabbed my arm as I bolted onto the back veranda.

Another guard stood from the banister. "And where do you think you're going?"

I jerked my arm back and took a step back. "Don't ever touch me again."

"Just doing my job. You, Crow, are not allowed outside without a guard."

"Gentlemen, what seems to be the problem?" Solas' breath was hot against my neck as he appeared from nowhere. I knew he saw me leave and knew he'd never be too far away.

"She is not to be out alone," the guard from the banister called out.

"This is the king's Crow, and he lets her do as she damn well wants. You're obviously new to the court, but the rest of us know well enough to leave her the hell alone." Solas stepped around me. Wisps of hot air flowed from his body. "And she is not alone. She asked me to escort her for fresh air. The stench of the traitor has bothered her delicate senses."

"I apologize. We didn't know." The guard stepped away from me and tipped his head. "My apologies."

"It is not me who you put your hands on. I would pray she doesn't choose you the next time she's bored. She grows tired of those used up souls in the basement. I'm sure you'd last longer than they could." Solas' laughs stung deep inside. He looked each man up and down and laughed a little longer. "Perhaps not. Run along. You've wasted minutes of my life that I'll never get back. Any more and I'll come to collect them as you sleep."

They scattered like mice.

"Must be nice to be feared that much." I pointed toward the guards scurrying away.

"It has its perks," he answered. "But you should know that by now. There's never been a Crow the Fae have feared—until now, until you."

Solas passed me a glass of wine and took a seat as far away from me as he could. I didn't blame him. I wouldn't want to be near someone like me, either. I sipped my wine and wondered if the guards ran from him or from me once they were reminded of who I had become. My money was on Solas.

"You look lovely as usual." He broke the silence with small talk.

"What? This old thing?" I smiled. "I hate it. It's too much, and bloody hell does this stuff ever itch. I have no idea how the others wear this without clawing off their own skin or fainting from the heat. You should see some of the stuff she tries to make me wear. Bloody hell."

"I much prefer you in your pants and a sweater."

"You saw me once in pants and a sweater, and I puked all over myself," I answered.

"I saw you a lot more than once, little Crow. I've seen you during every single Taking, from the day you were born to the day I made you come here."

"I forgot about that part…you leading the Taking." I sighed. "Did you like doing it?"

He shook his head, and for the first time, I had no desire to poke him further on the subject. "It never got easier, either."

"Thank you," I changed the subject, "for helping tonight."

Solas looked over once and nodded.

"You could have just watched me meet my fate," I called over the distance between us. "It's not like you don't think I haven't earned it."

He huffed a laugh. "Some of us don't like to watch this…" he waved his hand in the air, gesturing back to the celebrations.

I nodded. It wasn't often that anything came out of his mouth that I agreed with. "I'd wager more do than do not."

"Would you have left if given a chance?" he asked. "Would you have run if the guards hadn't stopped you? If I were to go back inside, would you go?"

The thought was appealing, but I'd never leave without my friends. I couldn't leave without saving who I could. "I want to say yes, but, no, I wouldn't have."

"Foolish little Crow," Solas muttered. "Are you enjoying yourself that much that you've given up on the thought of freedom?"

"I'm not enjoying myself," I answered. I felt my face redden. My embarrassment was mine to own. I had built up the Crow the court saw day in and day out.

As always, it took so very few words from Solas for me to feel the shame I deserved. It wormed through my body with every beat of my heart, and I couldn't stop it. I couldn't keep anything from happening. I couldn't keep anyone safe. And now, I couldn't keep my people safe. The Guardian had seen to that. My heart hammered in my chest with the realization that I might never stop any of this. I could dig myself into an endless pit, where all of Elphame was terrified of me, but it would not be enough. If I could never leave this place, I couldn't save anyone. I couldn't end the suffering. This would be for nothing. All the pain and horror would be for nothing. I would fail, and so many would die for it. My Malice swirled. If I just let her out, this would be over. I could almost taste her freedom, and it tasted like souls and death and the promise of freedom. She twisted and turned and threatened to come out, whether I willed it or not. She made promises I knew she'd keep. Before I died for her, she'd make as many as she could, pay dearly…and I believed her.

"I can't…breathe." My words were strangled. Fearing my own failure and the promise my Malice made me, she snaked her way through my stomach and dumped gas on the fire within. My power grew with each lick of the flame. "It burns."

"Breathe, Perdi. Slowly. In through your nose, out through your mouth," Solas whispered as soon as he had closed the distance between us in a blink. He pulled me from my chair and wrapped us in the midnight sky and a cold breeze. "Don't do this. Eat your power."

"Can't... Hurts..." My stomach burned, and I choked on the flames.

"It'll hurt more in the long run if you lose control here," he replied. "You don't have room to show your cards yet. You are too close to give up now. Just a little longer. Hold on just a little more."

I tried to say I didn't know what he was referring to but only managed to squeak out garbles and groans. I struggled against his grip, wanting nothing more than to let the flames pour from my lips. Anything, just to get it out of me.

"Of course not," he answered, understanding my jumbled words. He gripped me tighter. "This is going to hurt, little Crow. I trust, by now, you know how to swallow a scream."

Solas pulled me into his chest. The wind I had felt before now dragged the fire from my pit. I wanted to fight him, to keep it for myself. I greedily wanted to burn the court to ash. But there was nothing I could do to stop it from going to a willing host. It blistered on its way out as it extinguished in my belly. It felt like claws ripping at my fire through my belly button. I chewed my lips to keep my screams from escaping. As the flames lessened into nothing more than coals to save for a different day, Solas leaned my tired body against the banister. The midnight sky still wrapped around us.

"Dear God, that hurt." I groaned and rubbed my stomach. "Why didn't you just let me burn? I would have burned this place to the ground. It would have solved a lot of your problems with my death. No more full-time guard duty."

"What would be the fun in that?" He grinned. "Not all of us want to see the Crow burn."

"I doubt that very much. I suspect I'm the only Crow you've actually hated. The only one you've never pitied. You did once, feel sorry for me, when I first got here. But not anymore."

"You don't really care if I hate you, and you don't need my pity," he answered but skipped around what I had asked about letting me die. "All truth in here, Perdi. No one else can hear us."

I laughed. "The truth kills everyone in Elphame, and it would take my life just as quickly, whether anyone but you could hear it or not."

"You've been praying for death since the moment I met you, so what's the difference?"

"That is the question, isn't it?" I asked. "I don't want to live, but I have to survive."

"Touché," he answered. "A Crow who dresses like the devil but has the heart of an angel. What an interesting mask you've chosen to wear."

I shrugged. "It's the only thing I have, Solas."

"We all wear masks to protect our people, but you can't wear yours forever. Eventually, they have to come off. It's as true for you as it is for me. Are you ready for the day that happens? For all of what you've done, to finally come to a head? Are you ready for the game you've been playing to only have final moves left?"

I stared at him for a long minute. "I don't know what you're talking about."

He shook his head and let the entire weight of his eyes press down on me. I fought not to squirm. "You've gotten better with your lies. I'll give you that. But you need to learn how to lie better. Feel the lie become truth as it rolls from your tongue. To tell the truth with a lie woven so tightly around it that it could only ever be known as the truth."

"If I've gotten better, why do you never believe me, then?" I asked. "Everyone else does, except you."

"Everyone else is not me. When you've lived an entire life with lies over lies built around you, you can smell another from a mile away," he answered. "Or perhaps I'm just unwilling to see you as the monster you've so carefully crafted. I can still see you in there, struggling to keep your head above water."

"And I can see you behind yours," I replied. "Eventually, oh wise one, even *your* lies will surface. You can't live forever on half-truths and bullshit."

"You have no idea how long a lie can feed those who care nothing for the truth." I watched a sneaky grin form on his mouth. He raised his arms to gesture behind us. "Sometimes the truth is much more terrifying than the lie, and very few ask questions of those they fear. Look around. The only honesty people here are looking for is the one that bring them more power."

"Or protection and freedom," I countered.

"You, little Crow, want protection and freedom. For the others, who've lived hundreds of years, death doesn't mean anything to them anymore. It's hard to fear something that doesn't come knocking all that often."

"And you? What do you fear?" I asked.

He shook his head. "Tonight is not the night for spilling my secrets."

"You ask for truth, words that will kill me before dawn, yet you never offer anything of yourself. If you won't tell me a truth, tell me a lie you've told me," I asked and prayed it was worse than what I had done to still be alive.

He laughed. It was soft, almost friendly. For the briefest of moments, I wondered who he would have been had he not been here. "Very well, I will give you one secret, then you will give one in return. I'll tell you the why of me being here, locked into this hellhole *with* you, not against you. I had a friend once, if you can believe that. In a place like Elphame, having a true friend, one you'd give your life for, is the rarest of treasures. He was taken, and I can't save him. I'm here because I can't save him. I took you to save his life."

"That's not really a secret, Solas. I knew this court had something over you to force you to do its bidding. We're all here because we're powerless, because someone has taken something from us, because we have no other choice," I sighed out the pressure beginning in my chest. "No one chooses this. It's pushed into our laps, and we make do. You, on the other hand, seem to have fared just fine. The entire court, and likely all of Elphame, fears you. Nothing I do will cause enough fear for me to be free. I'd have to live a hundred lifetimes for that to happen, and I do not see myself surviving the one I've got, let alone one hundred."

"You don't want the fear I've created. But that's a secret for a different day." He leaned in closer. "Do you really think I'd stand here and wag my tail for that…king, if I didn't want to be here? If I didn't *need* to be here?"

"Why don't you leave?" I asked. "I would."

"Yet, here you are, not leaving," he countered, and I shrugged. "The real secret, little Crow, is that my friend came here, knowing you'd save him. I took you, willingly, because he believed you'd save him and yourself. That is why I'm here. I am tied to you both, and my curse is watching you both fail."

"Me?" I asked. "I don't understand."

"Yes, you. When Aelfdene came for us, my friend went willingly to save my people. He said a Crow would come for him, and this was how it was meant to be. My friend could have slaughtered them all, with one hand behind his back, but chose not to. He said you'd need him here. You'd need his help as much as he would need yours. You would end up here, sold out by a Fae and mortals, one way or another. It would have to be this exact way, this Taking, for you both to survive. If one thing were to change—a day late, a nudge in the wrong direction, a choice not of your own—no one would survive."

"Have I met your friend?" I asked.

"You've never been introduced to him formally, no."

"Then how could I save him if I don't even know him?" I asked. "Hell, how will I save anyone? Your friend is wrong. I'm not the Crow he's waiting for. Even *you* have told me I won't save anyone. Hell, you *just* said your curse is to watch me fail."

"That's the question, isn't it? Before he was taken, I told him the very same thing. A Crow would not come to his rescue. The very idea, putting his faith in someone so easily broken, is ridiculous," he answered. "I doubt very much that you'll have what it takes to do it. Sadly, I do not share the same confidence my friend has in you. Your guilt and shame stop you every time you come to a fork in the road. When you have a choice that you know will stain your soul, you choose the least painful route."

"Most people do that. They take the route that doesn't scrub off chunks of soul," I answered.

"And most people die here because of that."

"Death is a mercy. Who the hell wants to actually live here? How can I live here, doing that which makes me wish I was dead?" I asked. "I can't think of anything worse than being a Crow, except surviving the seven years and going home, only to be named a Crow again and having to come back."

"As I said, when you have choices that'll hurt you, you take the easy way, every time. The easy way is not always the best way to go. More times than not, you have to walk a hard path to find freedom. Sometimes you have to be feared by all Fae to find what you're looking for," Solas replied.

"You make it sound so easy, but it isn't. You instill fear in anyone who even breathes the air you wanted for yourself. I do not have that luxury or that ability."

"And you don't want to do what I've needed to do, to instill that fear," he answered. "Your fear rests in realities that haven't happened. You're so stuck in this indignation of becoming a Crow that you've forgotten what it means to be one. You're a halfling…a witch, as you call it. You're not without power. You're not without options." His answer held a hint of frustration in his voice. "You're here. Get over it. You can't change it. Why waste your time and energy trying to change that which has already happened? And because of that, you carry around all these little wounds, and they're dragging you down. Soon, you'll be so bloody cut up that you won't get out of bed. And when that day comes, I'll tell my friend he gave up his life for nothing, for no one. It will kill me to be wrong, but I know he wasn't right to put his faith in you. And, little Crow, you'll know what hate truly feels like. Because I will hate you for costing us all. I will hate you for what you've done to my friend, to my people and most of all, to yourself."

I smiled, but it wasn't friendly. I believed him when he said I'd probably fail. But somehow, hearing him, of all people, tell me in the rawest form that he thought I'd fail made me want to succeed all the more. I wanted it to spite him, to prove him wrong. Sometimes motivation can be found in the oddest of places.

"Like fear and pain, hate is no worse and no better, but at least I understand hate. All of this, this court and the hate I feel sticks to my skin. I've grown used to it. You hating me doesn't change who I am, what I am and what I will become. You may think I will fail. Hell, I think I'll fail, but my hate has yet to paint these walls. I will rain down on this court, not for myself, but for my friends, for those trapped here, like me." I pushed away from him. "Truthfully, I'm counting on your hate if I fail. Because then this will finally be over. I may never go home, but at least I won't have to stay here."

"You're counting on me to kill you." He didn't pose it as a question.

My smile faltered. "I believe I've had enough truth for the night."

"I didn't think I'd ever hear you say something real, something so utterly Perdi that it made my stomach roll. Here I thought I had scared the guards away for no reason." He grinned. "You don't need to say your truth out loud. I already know. I believe, little Crow, your truth doesn't rest in what you've done here but in what you'll do to leave here, and you're more scared of that than of doing nothing at all. I think you're more scared of leaving than you are of remaining. Because if you go, you're going into the unknown. If you stay, you already know what hell looks and feels like. Your truth, Perdi, is the fear you have in yourself. Know this… It is not only your life you gamble with."

"You seem to think this is a simple matter of which piece of soul I start burning off first."

"You can't change anything that is meant to be. If you're meant to shred your soul off on the gravel of Elphame, it's going to happen, whether you will it or not. You might as well get what you came for before that takes place. Because I promise you, if you're meant to suffer, you will."

"And I promise you, Solas, if I suffer, the rest of you suffer with me," I replied, and it was my turn to whisper secrets into his ear. "I'll burn this court down on my way out. But I'll kill him, the Golden King, before I strike my match."

"Put your mask back on, little Crow. You need it more than I do."

I took a step forward and stopped. "Why did you help me? Why do you keep helping me?"

He shrugged. "To protect my people."

"I'm not the monster…" My words caught in my throat. I wanted to tell him I hadn't killed anyone. I wasn't the monster he thought I was, but I chewed back my words instead. He was right. I needed that mask and wasn't going to drop it because he had told one truth in a lifetime of lies.

"I know you're not," he answered. "I wish more than anything that you were. This would be so much easier if you were. Run along, little Crow. The party is coming to an end, and you don't want to be the only lady awake in this court. Sooner or later, he will take you to his bed, and no amount of my poking at you will stop it from happening."

"Mark my words, Solas. If he tries to take me against my will, I will eat his fucking soul like an apple before my dress hits the floor. There is no one this side of hell who could stop me."

"Good night, little Crow." Solas' gaze felt like he was picking through my mind and soul and didn't like what he saw. He tilted his head and closed his eyes. From behind me, we both could hear the night coming to an end. My heart sank in my stomach. I hated the end as much as the start. "Stay with the shadows tonight."

"I thought I was meddling?" I asked. I imitated him the best I could. *"Stay away from things you don't understand."*

"You are, but it's a little late for that now, isn't it?" he asked. "Final moves are all you have left. Make each and every one of them count."

Chapter Thirteen

I didn't sleep. Each time I closed my eyes, I pictured the horrors of Elphame bleeding onto the streets of Whitwick, with Solas standing at the side, watching—a never-ending banquet at the expense of my people. I jerked awake each time I faded, the shadows creeping around at the foot of my bed, ready to pull me from my nightmares if I couldn't do it on my own. I didn't want the dreams. They left me only half-rested and anxious the following day, but I couldn't stop them from coming.

With the shadows remaining much longer than before, it didn't bring me comfort. They only stayed when I needed them—and now I waited for the other shoe to drop, the why of their remaining. I sat at my window and stared out into the night. I could never see beyond the forests of Alfheim, but the stars reminded me of home when I wasn't so afraid to notice. Bits of this place held just enough beauty that I could imagine I was there and this reality was a nightmare I had woken from. I could almost smell my father's bread cooking over the fire, the lavender from my garden or the dewy grass of a morning hike. It was barely enough for a whole memory, but it helped on nights when it was all just a little too much. Even after months of this, it still became more than I could bear.

Final moves were all I had left. I rolled the words over in my mind. Solas had told me to stay with the shadows. Did he know, as I felt, that something was coming? What did he know that I didn't? What did he see that I couldn't? I replayed every conversation I had had with him until I unraveled each word and held them in my mind. How many warnings had he given me that I'd pushed away as cruelty?

The shadows pulled up from the floor as my ears twitched at an echo. A terrible, gut-wrenching scream pulled me from my daydream. I jerked as the sound bounced off my walls and jumped from the window. I ran to the door as the screaming continued, a woman's scream. I could feel her terror, feel it pierce my heart. She was foolish enough to beg for help, help that would never come, not here, not ever. These halls would remain empty for her. Who would dare? These screams came after every party or dinner. It was how the king celebrated the very sun setting. The shadows swirled around the doorframe, pushing back against me each time I reached for the doorknob.

"Go see what's happening." I motioned to my little creature. I could imagine, but I had to know. My heart needed to know. Someone needed to feel pain for the giver of the scream. Someone had to remember their names.

Although my creature was in and out in seconds, it felt like hours had passed. She flew to my hair and yanked it, frantically trying to tug me out of my room. I pulled back and shook my head. Whatever was happening, I didn't want to see it. I didn't need another image stained into my mind, only to haunt me later when I laughed or enjoyed a moment of peace. My creature tugged again, ripping hair from my head. Her eyes begged me into action, action I couldn't afford. She hovered, and tears fell to the floor. She lifted her hands and brought her knees up as if she were kneeling, and in a very mortal movement, she begged me.

"I can't," I whispered. "I'm not going in there."

Her hands clasped tighter as if to say 'please'.

"I can't do it. I'm not taking her place." My heart pounded with impossible decisions.

My creature had never begged me before. She had never asked me to put myself in the middle or in any danger. Solas had been right. Until tonight, I had always made the easiest choice. Albeit they were still painful and I still suffered, they were still the lesser of two evils. I released a hot and shaking breath then stepped into the hall. I was surprised not to see a single guard. When I heard the woman scream again, I knew they had left their post. If the guards couldn't stomach it, I knew it would shred me, but I still let my creature pull me toward the calls for help. The shadows parted and let me pass. They were gone now, sucked into the cracks of the baseboards outside the king's bedroom.

I stood in front of his chamber door at the other end of the hall. Could I really take the woman's place? My mind flipped and flopped with bravery and cowardice. Could I give myself willingly to a man who wouldn't care if I were willing or not? I had no plan. I had no careful lie to tell. It took another scream for me to put my hand on the doorknob.

"Don't do it." Solas stepped from the shadows at the edge of the hall. "If you open that door, you'll not like what you see."

"I know." I swallowed the pulse in my throat. "Leave. Save who you can and run."

"It is you who will need to be saved, once you step into that room."

"No, I don't think it will be me who suffers tonight." I shook my head. "When I'm done, you don't want to still be here."

"And why is that?"

"Because it's time to go," I answered then paused. "I hope you're not foolish enough to try to stop me. I'd hate to kill two men tonight."

His eyes flickered, like tiny stars trying to blister the clouds from their view. "Little Crow, we've all been waiting for you to light the match. Burn it all."

"Before I leave, I'm going to unlock the monster who is feared by all, brick by brick, if I must."

"He's trapped, Perdi. Just save yourself. Please, Perdi, don't do this. Run. Please."

"If I only wanted to save myself, I'd have left the day I was released from that basement." The woman's scream brought my attention back to the horrors of Elphame. "Go, Solas. But you'd better save who you can on your way out or your door will be the next one I open."

"If you do this, you can't take it back. You'll be hunted."

"I'll be hunted no matter what, so I might as well go to my grave knowing I took a king with me."

"Find the Court of Less. The courtless lands are the only place where you won't be hunted," he replied. He stepped away and paused. He turned back to me. "Burn it all to the ground, all of it."

"I hope the flames find you last," I replied, and he left me with my hand on the door to my fate.

I slowly pushed the door open and slipped inside. It wasn't the first time I had been in his room, but it was the first time he had been awake. I had stood over him on many occasions, willing myself to kill him in his sleep. I had come close several times but always stopped myself for the sake of the others.

On the floor in front of a fireplace, the king held a young lady on the ground, ripping at her clothes. Her minty green hair caught my eye. She was so young, younger than she should have been. I froze. I could feel the rage boil in my belly and did everything I could to breathe past it. I knew of cruelty. I had been on the receiving end of it. But this? This was worse. This was horror and terror and every sick feeling I had ever felt all smashed into one event. During so many Takings, young women came across. And I knew, at that very moment, what their fates had been. I felt powerless and hateful. In an instant, I wished him dead. I wanted it to be drawn out, with him begging as she was. I wanted him to suffer—for his very soul to feel the same fear that he created.

The woman fought a pointless fight. She'd never win, not here. There was never any winning here. We all suffered for the king. But this, on the floor, was beyond suffering. It was everything being a woman in this court had meant. We were good for very few things. This was one of them, whether we liked it or not. I couldn't help but think of my face on that girl. One night, I'd take her place, and that would be me, fighting an unwinnable fight, my screams and pleads to echo in every hall and chamber. I, too, would be ignored.

My creature tapped my leg. She had dragged an iron knife to my feet. Her hands sizzled at the touch of cold iron. It was the same knife I had seen the king use to torture others, to scar them horribly with iron. She pushed the knife handle into my foot and pointed to the king. The rage on her little face ignited mine. I nodded. I agreed. He had to die for this. He had to die to protect everyone else from him, because some things are worse than death. King Aelfdene was a fate worse than death. He was the creator of nightmares and the reason so many women took their lives when he paid them notice. When he had told them to come to his chambers, they'd sooner die than risk his advances. And by taking his life, I would sentence myself to a fate I wasn't ready for. But it would be worth it, even if he killed me before I left his room.

I picked up the knife and moved to stand beside the king. I was calm. For once, I was more at peace than I had ever been. I knew I could never turn back. I couldn't take this back once it was done. I'd seal my fate and the fate of every other Crow who came after me. The world came into hyper-focus, and I was the steady hand of my own destiny. He turned his head to look at me and smiled. His smile told me he thought I'd join. He thought I'd enjoy the torture. His leer told me I was a monster to him. I dragged the knife across his throat before he knew what had happened. His hot blood coated my hand. I had never killed a man before, but I had killed elk and deer. I felt worse for the meat than I did this man. The woman stared at me but didn't scream. Her gaze connected with mine, and for the briefest of moments, we understood each other.

"Raewyn," I called her name, bringing her focus back from the dying king, to mine. She was one of the ladies who brought my meals to me. "Go to my room. Do not make a sound."

"Thank you," she whispered. She grabbed her scraps of clothes and left quickly but quietly.

I rolled Aelfdene onto his back and climbed onto his stomach. He opened and closed his mouth as the life dripped from his neck. I knew he wouldn't be able to scream. I had cut deep enough to slice open his windpipe, much like the animals I had hunted back home. Blood sputtered out of his mouth onto my face. I smiled. I knew I shouldn't have but found one forming before I could think that only a monster would truly smile at death. The shadows leached from every corner and pulled tightly around us. Not a soul would hear what I was about to do. From the look on the dying man's face, he knew what had befallen him.

"You made what now sits upon your chest. You did this, and you deserve worse than this," I whispered. "You should not have Taken a Darkmore. Pray you die and not bear witness to what I will do next. Because, Little King, I'm going to burn your fucking kingdom to the ground."

I don't know how many times I slammed the knife into him. I stabbed until my little creature flew into my line of sight. She placed her hand on mine, and I pushed the knife into his heart and twisted it. I climbed off the king and spelled him to sleep. He would not heal quickly from cold iron, if at all. It would be hard to mend a broken heart, especially from iron blade carving out the middle of it. I prayed he bled out long before anyone else woke up, long before he could be found and saved. I would have cut him to pieces had I more time. I reach the door, only to freeze. The shadows pulled at my hand. I was not done yet.

I turned and reached with my Malice, pulling the energy from his body, the little he had left. I wouldn't leave him with enough to heal. I would leave him without a soul. I'd need that energy soon enough. My little creature left the room, and I followed her back to my chambers. I closed the door quietly. The darkness slithered along the floor and was gone. I would follow soon enough. The once-warm blood that covered my hands and arms to my elbows had grown cold and sticky, and it would be my blood to spill if we didn't hurry.

"Where were you?" Nix started then stopped. One look at my blood-soaked nightgown told him more than enough. "What the hell is…?"

"We leave now." The words spilled from my mouth in a rush.

"What did you do?" he asked and sniffed the air. "Whose blood is that? Is the king…"

"I killed the king," I said quickly. "We need to go, *now*."

"You did *what*?" he asked, shocked, but moved into action quickly.

"I stabbed Aelfdene," I answered. "I left him for dead on his bedroom floor. Now, we can stand around and play questions and answers, or you can save it for later."

"They'll kill us all for this." Elswyth clutched her throat.

"They were going to kill us anyway. It was only a matter of time." Nix snapped his fingers at Elswyth, pulling her attention from her dread. "Get your stuff.

Perdi is right. We must leave right now. We have less than an hour before they come to collect the girl."

I pulled out the sack of supplies from the back of my closet, packed for this very moment. I put on the clothes I had set aside for escape and strung the small sack over my back and pulled it tight. I would leave my dresses and slippers behind, the gowns I wore for balls and festivals, the shoes the young woman had gripped when I'd puked on her. Elswyth was ready with her gear, and we left my room with the servant girl, who followed us without question. Elswyth and Nix knew the plan by heart, without us needing to review it again. We had practiced it for months, with dozens of dry runs. We climbed down the stairs into the basement and, one by one, opened the cells and freed every soul held down there, including many we shouldn't have dared release. They left in the hush they promised for their freedom.

I sent Elswyth through the escape route. She would lead the others to safety. We didn't want to say goodbye, but we each had a job to do, and hers was ensuring as many prisoners made it to the Court of Less. She would lead the way. I trusted her with every soul that followed her into the tunnels under the court.

Splitting up was our only option if we all wanted the chance at freedom. All of us would certainly die together, especially since they'd be looking for me. I was the one who'd killed their king. I'd be the one they'd punish most. But in the end, we'd all die just the same.

The shadows danced along the wall. I stopped and pressed my hand into it.

"Leave it alone," Nix called. "We don't have time."

"I can't," I replied. "Who is in there?"

"Those who eat the night and those who eat…souls."

"Darkness?" I whispered. I took two steps away from the wall. I contemplated leaving them, wanting to punish Solas for all he had done to me, but stopped. "I can't leave him, Nix."

"*Them,* Perdi. There's a hell of a lot more sitting on the other side of that wall, and none of them should we wish to meet," he replied. When I didn't budge, he groaned. "And how are you going to release them? Do you plan to dig them out?"

I touched the brick and whispered through the wall. "What happens if you're freed?"

And through the stone, it whispered back, "Death."

"Mine?" I asked.

"Perhaps," it answered truthfully.

Nix grabbed my pant leg. "Perdi, even I heard that."

"And what would we owe you, should you release us?" it asked.

"Nothing," I answered. "Have your freedom and save whoever you can, *if* you can."

"For that, I'll give you a head start, Perdita Darkmore."

I leaned into the wall with both hands and pushed magick. Every drop of my Malice poured from my skin, igniting a fire within my soul. I used the energy I'd sucked from the king and forced it into the stone. When it wasn't enough, I watched as more shadows leaked from the cracks in the rock to wrap around my arms and hands, lending me whatever energy they had.

Seconds felt like hours. The walls were a jumble of wards that prickled my skin as if my limbs had fallen asleep. Old magick. Dark magick. It crawled across my hands and up my arms, seeking energy and power. It would find nothing at my door. My magick was Darkmore, from the richest of wells. It was linked to me and powered by my very soul. Through my mind's eye, I twisted the spells tied tightly around each brick and found the knot that held the entire thing together. I pushed every drop of power I had, given to me from the shadows into those bricks. From the other side, I felt them use their own magick. Together, we would wake all Elphame. When my spell came back threefold, I didn't know what price I'd pay, but it would be massive.

I fractured the spell cast that encases that which ate souls. I was thrown back, into the opposite wall, dazed. My ears rang with power. I couldn't bring the wall down, but I could give them a fighting chance. Behind the wall, a rumble came. They needed no more help.

"Run!" Nix yelled.

I stood on shaking legs and ran behind Nix as the basement erupted in rubble and chaos. Darkness ate every drop of light. I muffled a scream as the memories of my Taking came back like a tidal wave. It felt like the fog was eating me again. I ran. I ran as fast as I could, through the basement maze, through the escape route I had practiced for months. The tunnels curled and twisted their way into what felt like infinite darkness. I had known darkness before, the fog, the shadows, my own soul. This was the kind of dark that robbed you of your senses and replaced it with stunning fear. My shoulders hit the walls, sticky wet, and stunk of death, a path built for one and not for running, but I didn't fall. The dwindling light at the other end of the tunnel played with my mind. Shadows moved from side to side, ready to pounce and drag me back. Although I was born to be the prey, tonight, I was no longer the rabbit in a snare. I readied myself for an assault, but the shadows never came for us and were gone before we reached the opening of the passageway.

At the end of the tunnel, we crawled up a small, wet bank. Creatures who had been caged in the hellhole of the Golden Court all struggled to climb out to the freedom I had offered. A tiny, winged being, no bigger than my hand, thrashed in the mud. His wings were tattered from years of abuse. Without help, he'd die in the slop after having been so close to freedom. I felt his fear, as it was the same that strangled my soul.

"I've got you." I stopped, and I dug him out of the mud.

I plucked him up and tucked him into my pocket. I ran my hands over the rest of the earth, making sure no one was trampled and no one was left behind. I took one more glance down the hall to make sure everyone had gotten out.

Before the basement erupted in shadows and wings, monsters from hell, I saw Solas at the end of the hall. He had to know what I was releasing into the Elphame. I watched him move to the mouth, his sword drawn, the darkness swallowing him whole. But he was not as scared of the darkness as everyone else. If Solas called them monsters, those less scary than Solas probably didn't have words to describe them. I wondered how long it would take before the monsters killed everyone in the Golden Court? If they were smart, they'd leave their vengeance behind and run away from that hellhole as fast as they could. I couldn't help but hope the monsters I released on the court ate Faolan before they left.

"Run!" Solas' voice echoed off the stone hall and rolled up the bank. "Take your freedom!"

"I said I'd save you, too." I climbed down, back through the mud, and reached into the darkness for him. "I won't leave you behind."

"It was *me* who would not leave *you*. I stayed here for you." His hand found mine and brought it to his lips, kissing my palm. After one squeeze, he pushed me back. "Now run, or this was all for naught."

"What will happen to you?"

"Foolish little Crow, you've unleashed the darkness onto these Golden Lands." His laughter shoved me from the hall. "They eat at my table, and tonight we will feast on the spoils of a Crow."

Nix pulled at my pant leg. "He is the only one here that doesn't need to run, Perdi. Let's go!"

"I'm sorry about the fire."

"What fire?" he asked, breathing in, smelling the air.

"I told you I'd burn this court to the ground," I answered and lit a match. Nix struck the next, my little creature soon followed. We lit bundles of wood and dry grass that was spelled to spread.

"I'll see you soon, my little Crow."

"I'm not *your* little Crow."

"Fear nothing," Solas whispered.

"Trust no one," I replied.

After one last glance to ensure we were all free, we left the darkness to swallow the cursed court, gold and souls and all. And for the first time since meeting Solas, I hoped he'd be spared the flames. Although I had known from day one that he was who Elphame feared most, I hadn't feared him a single day.

I ran along the trees, under cover of darkness, although I knew I could hide from no Fae, big or small. From the screams behind us, I knew I was the least of their troubles on this Crow-fated night. The earth shook below my feet as magick poured through the grounds. The battle for the Golden Court had just begun, and it would be a fight that all would remember for all times—the night a Crow brought the Golden Court to their despicable knees. I felt nothing for them. They'd gotten what they deserved…finally.

At the river bed, Elswyth stood, her eyes wild with fear. I knew she'd be foolish enough to wait for us, but I didn't stop running. I pushed Elswyth into the water, catching her off guard.

"You're free, Elswyth, at last," I called out to her and kept going along the banks.

I had already bargained, in secret, for her freedom. The same nymphs who had saved the others would get her to the Court of Less, to her well-deserved liberty. I hoped, if I saw her again, we would both be free of our prisons. And if I were captured, I prayed I never laid eyes on her again. I'd remember her as free, and that was enough.

I lifted the small, winged creature from my pocket and tucked him into a tree, out of sight. We didn't exchange words, just a simple nod. He scurried up the tree and out of sight. It was safer for him, me leaving him behind. To stay with me meant being hunted by all. I sent up a small prayer to the Gods for his survival. If nothing else, saving who I could would be enough if this were to be my end.

I looked back once to see Solas standing between me and the entire Golden Court. His voice rolled across my soul. "Run, little Crow."

Nix led the way through the woods, through the brush, and had to slow down for me many times. Although only a foot tall, he was faster than my eyes could track. It was how his people, the gnomes, are the oldest of Elphame, the oldest of Fae. They were creatures on quick feet. *"You can't kill what you can't catch,"* he'd once said. We both knew I wouldn't be able to keep up the speed for long and would need to rest long before Nix even broke a sweat. But we needed to get out of the Golden Court's territory before that could happen. I'd push myself to my limits. I'd crawl if I had to. One way or another, I would leave the Golden Court alive and of my own volition.

Once our plan had come together, I had found a map in the library. The king had boasted over his lands, and I'd swooned at his power. He took me on walks and showed me every square inch of his grounds. And when he questioned my desire to see more, I'd claim I didn't want to turn back yet, that I selfishly wanted to spend more time with him. When all else failed, I always reached for his ego and stroked it. He was an egomaniac, and the more I spoke of his wonderment, the more I saw. He was a foolish king, and I wasn't a stupid girl.

Locked in my room, away from prying eyes, we mapped most of Elphame. My creature crossed out areas on the map to stay clear of, and most of those places had welcoming names. She pointed at several locations on the map and dragged her fingers across her throat. We'd die if we went there. We plotted around the deadlier areas and would pray while we went through the others.

With Nix at the lead, my creature scanning for doom, I kept up. I would worry about one problem at a time. Right now, the focus was getting out of the Golden Court and steering clear of any Fae who would drag me back. The cramps in my legs and my side would need to wait until I had the luxury of time to complain. To the courtless lands we ran, because it was only there where I could finally taste freedom. I might be on the run for the rest of my life, in Elphame, but at least I'd be free for each day.

I'd killed one king for justice and uncaged the monsters for a chance in hell.

I'd do worse things to better for freedom.

I'd burn worlds before I spent another day as *their* Crow.

Want to see more from this author? Here's a taster for you to enjoy!

A Cursed Crow: The Court of Less

Lanne Garrett

Excerpt

"Foolish little Crow, you've unleashed the darkness onto these Golden Lands."

Solas' words echoed into the night and pushed me from the dead king and burning kingdom of those who had caged me. Behind us, the Golden Court trembled under the cruel touch of a long-caged hell released from its belly. They would be the last court to Take me—a promise I made to myself when I'd struck the match on my way out of the dungeons that had once held me. Setting it to burn had lit a fire within my soul.

A certainty fell over me as I ran. I wasn't afraid to die for freedom or what it would take to keep it. My fear rested in living, of being forced inside another prison and never tasting a choice that was my own. If Elphame had taught me anything, it was that nothing was free—not for Fae and not for a Crow on the run with a gnome and a fairy. And as we ran from Alfheim, I knew I'd pay for what I had done.

The Golden Forest plunged us into ominous darkness. The moon above and the carnage we left behind roused creatures, and the curious, rapacious beasts crawled out of their lairs, awoken by the smell of blood in the air, the promise of flesh and their duty to protect their cursed court. I muffled my screams, caught them in my throat and saved them for later, but I still jumped and twitched with each new squall and bloodcurdling cry that echoed through the forest and crawled up my spine. I watched as the trees came alive, transforming into a lethal playground. Whenever something bravely approached us, readying for a feast of traitors, they would be taken by something scarier, snatched off the ground and torn up through the treetops and into the sky above.

The lands around Alfheim, where no one freely ventured, were the deadliest. It was their first defense against invaders, and we willingly ran through them, through the monsters too fearsome and hideous to invite out of the shadows. I could feel them slowly pressing in around us, but I didn't stop running. I couldn't. The choices were to be eaten on the run or be caught and dragged back. I'd sooner become the next meal of a creature than ever step foot back into the Golden Manor. I could think of a dozen worse ways to die within the Golden Court, none of them as merciful as ending in the belly of a beast.

Tree branches grabbed at me, igniting my fear of being found. The limbs stretched out in front of me, blinding me to my way. The forest closed around us, forming a cavern of distorted arms and legs that reached for me as I passed. As I stumbled and staggered, tripped and skinned layers from my pants and soon, my bare knees, I didn't stop running. Running was the only power I had that was my own, the only thing that would grant me the remotest of chances. I turned the pain and fear and the months of becoming one of them—one of the hideous beasts of the courts—into fuel. I left that person behind—the monster—and ran from her as much as I ran from the court that helped create her.

Pain clamped my chest like a deadly vise, and my lungs begged me to slow. My legs felt like rubber after miles of jogging at a constant pace. I swallowed down selfish breaths of air, never getting enough. But not even my starving lungs caused me to stop. Each time I fell, Nix was there, pushing and pulling until I got back up. The fear on his face drove me to stand each time. My feet dragged noisily on the carpet of moss and leaves and kicked up an easily trackable route. I hadn't been worried about hiding my footprints, for it wasn't mere mortals who would be hunting us.

"Close, Perdi—almost at the border," Nix whispered from my side.

"Thank God," I groaned. Despite my weak state, I curled my mouth into a smile. We approached the border, and the realization that I had actually escaped the Golden Court finally struck me.

We were stopped twice before we were free of the Golden Court. Both times, those who had found us let us go, for no other reason than what we had done for two dozen prisoners. The creature I had freed from the muck had spread the word of what we had accomplished. We had risked our lives to save those who were weaker, and for that, they'd say they hadn't seen us. I took the freedom but left the gratitude behind. I didn't want to be a hero, but I didn't want to be a prisoner, either.

We climbed over a rock wall and landed on the other side—the Summer Court. The pace slowed, but the danger was not over and wouldn't be for several days. Yet, I still felt smug about my small win. I was free from the clutches of King Aelfdene and his court of subjects, those who were mirrors of their leader. Once we crossed out of Golden Territory, I breathed a little deeper. The stench of flowers was almost gone, along with the tightness in my chest. I hadn't realized how putrid the air had been until I took my first deep breath of something other than funerals.

The heat never changed as we crossed the border from the Golden Court—the capital of the Seelie Courts—into the Summer Court. The only difference was the cool breeze, and the stench of floral arrangements had almost disappeared. The grass was green but sunbaked in areas. The trees blossomed in brilliance but lacked the magick of the Golden Court. Where King Aelfdene forced perfection, the Summer Court allowed its natural flaws, and that's what made it beautiful. The broken flowers, too heavy to hold their heads high, its mud and rocks and ugly barked trees had made it feel more like home than the Golden Court ever could. The reality of my freedom sank in as I pressed my hands into the rough tree. I was free. Even if it didn't last, it was still worth it.

"We need shelter," I said through my gritted teeth. My legs began to shake and cramp. I was tired, scared, cold and hungry. "I'm not feeling too good here."

"We need to keep going. We can't stop, not yet," Nix called back. "We need to get away from the estate of the Summer King, Morrow. To save his court, he'll send us back."

I cursed under my breath. "I'm not Fae. I can't keep going." My body tingled. I had used up all my magick and energy to get as far as I had, and there was nothing left in me to give.

"Just a little farther… We can stay in one of the fox dens up ahead." He compromised once he saw me crawling through the dirt on my hands and knees.

I slinked on all fours, too tired to stand. I bargained with the gods and goddesses for just a bit more energy to make it to shelter. They hadn't ever heard my prayers before, but today they might just think it was funny enough to let me live. Nix walked at my side and griped that he wasn't big enough to carry me. He said he was strong enough, but my weight wouldn't be balanced, and I'd collapse around him, pinning him beneath me. The thought made me laugh.

"We're here," he announced and pointed to a dark hole in the ground at the base of a tree. "You rest, and I'll find food."

He didn't need to convince me to climb in. I maneuvered my body into the mouth of the den and scooted in feet first in case something was in there that needed a kick. Inside the dirt mound was a twenty-by-twenty room carved out of the earth by claws too big to think about. It was large enough for me to stand, jump up and not touch the ceiling.

"You probably don't want to see what an Elphame fox looks like," he said, to my surprise.

"What are the chances that it'll come home tonight?" I asked.

He shrugged. "I wish I could say zero, but the odds are extremely low. Mating season is here. They move up the mountain to find a mate. They'll remain there until they need to give birth. Then, they'll come home. We won't want to be anywhere near here when they're ready to birth."

"And what exactly do I do if it comes back and you're not here?"

He laughed. "It won't matter if I'm here or not. We'll all three be dead, one after the other."

"I don't know why I expected anything less than death," I replied.

Nix went to forage, and my creature hovered at the entrance, keeping guard. The shadows in the crevices eased my weary bones, and when they moved, I relaxed. I picked a spot on the straw in the corner and closed my eyes. The ground was cold, as was my body. I shivered until the familiar warmth of darkness settled over me, and for once since coming to Elphame, I thought I had a good chance of surviving. I wasn't scared. I was free. It didn't matter to me how long I remained free, as long as I died that way. With a sigh that vibrated against the dark, I slept deeply, sleeping to the hum of dozens of soft voices.

For three hours, not even the gods, who ignored me at a constant, could have woken me from my slumber. Not even Nix or my creature could get through the shadows to wake me. Each time they tried, they hit a solid mass of black. When I woke and crawled from inside my cocoon, the shadows were gone as quickly as they had come. Nix was pacing and had marched a dent into the earth in front of my makeshift bed.

"Do you know what that is?" Nix yelled at me. My creature sat on his shoulder, shrilling words I couldn't understand.

"The dark?" I asked.

"Yes, the dark. The mist. The bloody brick wall of shadows that I couldn't get through. Do you know what that is?" he asked again.

"No, not really," I answered. "They came to me when I first got to the Golden Court, then again when I was being lashed. They've been coming around since my first day. They helped me bring down the stone wall in the basement of the Golden Court."

"They are what our nightmares are about. We don't need any more nightmares, Perdi."

I knelt beside his mound of food and ate. I was starving. I stuffed my mouth full of berries and roots, leaves and fruits. Nix had refilled our canteens with fresh spring water, and it tasted like liquid gold. After filling my stomach, I leaned against the wall and smiled. I had eaten some of the best meals that all Elphame could provide, but this was the finest I had eaten in all my life.

"I couldn't get to you. Neither of us could. I couldn't smell you anymore. I couldn't feel you." He sat on my knee and hung his head. "It scared me. I didn't know what to do."

"I'm sorry. I didn't know. Solas was able to get to me before," I answered.

"Solas can reach into hell and pluck the wings off a demon," Nix replied. "You need to stop calling to them."

"I'm not calling them. They just come."

"You *are* calling them. You just don't realize it. The darkness has only answered to one, and you don't want him coming on the fires of hell next time. Perdi, he is feared by all, and we released him. He eats the souls of all. Do *not* call on his shadows, lest you wish him to follow them back to you."

"Who?" I asked. "Solas?"

Nix shook his head. His eyes darted from corner to corner. "No. Not even I will say his name in the dark. He is made of shadows and stolen souls, and you just busted him out of his prison. Just stop, okay?"

"What's the plan for today?" I asked, and he let me change the subject.

"Same as yesterday. More running, hiding, fear, the usual." Nix jumped off my knee and began to pack up our gear. "Perdi, we have to get to the Court of Less."

"I saw Solas in the hall before I killed the king. He told me to go to the Courtless Lands. That it was the only place where I won't be hunted."

"It's the only place the other kings will not venture and live," he replied.

"Besides Solas," I countered. "Something tells me he goes wherever the hell he wants."

"Well, there's that." Nix laughed.

"I freed his people, didn't I? Doesn't that buy us something? Won't they help me?" I asked.

He shook his head. "Don't count on it. And for the record, of those locked in the dungeon, not all of them belonged to Solas. What you freed—what terrifies us all—answers to no one, and you let it go without asking a favor in return, a payment for their freedom. He gave us a head start, as promised. Now he doesn't owe you anything."

"Great, let's add them to the list of people to run away from."

"Perdi, there is no list. We simply run from everyone, regardless of who they are. No lies or pretending, it doesn't matter who it is. We run from them until we get to the Court of Less."

"Remember all those survival classes they made us take growing up? Years of training on how to protect ourselves if ever we were Taken, and I can't wait to tell them it's a gigantic waste of time," I half joked. "Nothing I've learned has come in handy. Why would I build a fire and signal to all Elphame where I am?"

"It is to keep you warm so you don't freeze to death. The fire isn't what will show Fae where you are, Perdi. They can smell you long before they'd see the smoke."

"That's not very comforting," I muttered.

"It wasn't meant to be," he replied. "Least comforting of all is they will know where we're headed.

It's where everyone goes who is on the run. Courtless Lands are the only safe haven. Fire, no fire, smell or not, they'll know that is where we're going. If they were smart, they'd just wait for us at the border."

We finished our lunch, and my little creature lifted a small leaf of paste for the cuts on my hands. Once it touched my wounds, the burning stopped and brought a sigh of relief. She fluttered in and out of the den, bringing back plants and seeds, which I wrapped up and stuffed in my bag for her.

"I'm sorry, Nix," I whispered.

"It's okay. Just leave the dark alone," he answered.

"No, I mean, for everything. I'm sorry I brought you back here and for subjecting you to that awful place." My eyes watered and my nose tingled. My tears were close to falling. "I didn't think of how all this would affect you or hurt you. I'm so sorry you're in this mess. I'm sorry you had to watch all of that happen and be powerless to stop it."

He climbed onto my crossed legs. "You didn't drag me here. I choose to come. You didn't subject me to anything. *They* did. Do not take responsibility for them. Don't *ever* do that."

I nodded and wiped away the few tears that had escaped. "I know it may sound bad, but I'm thankful you're with me."

"Me, too. But the next time you plan to kill a king, let me know first. I'll be a little more prepared." He laughed. "I was in my sleeping gown, for God's sake. What possessed you to kill him, anyway? That was a pretty provocative move, even for you. We spent months building your lies, and in a hot minute, you made your final move."

"I bet no one saw that coming," I joked.

"Not even I did."

"Every single night, I could hear them scream. After the banquets, the parties, the dinners, Aelfdene would pick one woman, sometimes barely of age, and would force her into his bedchamber. He'd drag them down the halls by their hair. I'd hear them begging for help, followed by him laughing. They were just meat to him." I cringed at the memories of their cries, their pain and my own inaction. "I was always too scared to help. I was terrified he would pick me to replace them. I didn't want to take their place in his bed. I just wanted it to stop. I wanted *him* to stop. I needed to know he'd never do it again. The only way I could guarantee he'd stop was to kill him."

"Do you regret it?" he asked.

"No. Not even if I die because of it," I answered. "I'd do it again, only slower."

"He needed to die, Perdi." Nix patted my hand. My creature nodded.

"Yes, he did. Elphame is a better place without him."

"Let's hope the son who takes his throne doesn't revel in the same delights. I'd hate to have to return for you to kill him, too. It's a long journey back." He grinned. "It's time to go."

I pulled on my pack and started to climb from the den into the light. I much preferred the darkness, where I could hide. I followed him out of our false safety and back into the hunt for a Crow.

This time, we were walking and not running. I was thankful for the slower pace. My body needed the break. My wounds required time to scab. We stayed undercover and stopped when we heard the faintest of noises. Nix ran up ahead every so often and returned to tell us it was a bird or an animal or something to avoid. My creature zipped in and out of the trees, her wings as fast as a hummingbird's. At times, Nix would make us go back and find a different route, either because he had run across a farm with Fae in the field or because the animal was big enough to eat us. Other times, he would march us past a farm and farmers with bushels of food, a thank you for what we'd done. Nix had said the news had spread across all Elphame and likely into the mortal realm. A Crow had escaped with all the prisoners and killed a king who was feared by all on her way out.

"A Crow, a gnome, a creature and a slave escaped the Golden Court and freed everyone along the way." He was proud of himself. "I couldn't make this stuff up if I tried. If it weren't an immediate death sentence, I'd be shouting it from the rooftops."

"I certainly hope everyone is as happy about this as you are," I answered back and threw my apple core into the bushes. I stopped in my tracks. My apple hit something with a thud and a scurry. "Nix, we're being followed."

"Like I wouldn't notice? Nothing escapes the nose of a gnome. Give me some credit here. They're with her." He pointed his thumb to my creature. He jumped down from my shoulder and whistled. From every branch and fallen tree, small creatures came out from their hiding spots. "They travel in packs. They've never been too far away. But in the Golden Court, they'd have been killed, so they waited in the trees."

"They're so cute—terrifying, but cute." I laughed as I was swarmed. The joy I found in my laughter surprised me. It felt like a lifetime had passed since I laughed with the full force of my soul.

"You can't keep them, Perdi," he teased. "One is bad enough, and she's a pain."

For the next three hours of walking, the creatures didn't hide, but mine was the only one who rode on my shoulder. Her shrills, from her perch, sent the group up and down, left and right. She commanded them, tucked into my hair, warm from my body. When one strayed, she would grab them, scold them and come back to me. She was scary when she wanted to be, and not many of her people tested her patience. I likely wouldn't, either.

Nix told me stories of the Summer Court, ruled by King Morrow. He was as cruel as the next but wasn't feared for his dungeons or his taking of the unwilling. He was known for being vicious in war and protective of his people and family. The smallest slight was war, plain and simple. I could respect his ruthlessness. If he wasn't willing to do what it took to keep his people or family safe, no one else here would. His territory spread along the entire bottom of the Seelie Court, and there was no way around it. It edged the river that was used to bring me to the Golden Court on the barge of the dead. It was the river that separated the Seelie Court from the Unseelie, with the courtless lands spanning the top.

"How do we get over the water?" I asked. "I'm not getting in it. I know that much."

"I'm not getting in the water, either. What a waste of a trip this would be, only to be eaten," he answered. "That's not even our biggest problem. We have to get *to* the water first. The grounds won't be as deserted as they were on your arrival."

"Naturally," I grumbled under my breath.

"Perdi, we've come this far. We can do this. When we get to the water—and we will—there are a few bridges, and if the barge is there, I can bargain for transportation."

"I wish I had your confidence." I smiled weakly.

"If we were in the Court of Blood and Bones or the Court of Shadows, I would be more concerned about trying to sneak around. But once you've been to those two courts, this isn't nearly as scary. The first one, no one has ever made it back out of. The second, without an invite, is a quick death…no questions."

As the night sucked the sun from the sky, we took refuge in an old cabin no bigger than my old bedroom in Whitwick, that looked much like the abandoned cabins in the hills back home. I tried to ward the doors and windows, but each time I did, the creatures and Nix would be dragged outside by a wind of my making. There were too many cracks and crevices for my spell to work and not bounce wildly around, seeking something to grip. Nix tried to tell me to keep the wards and they'd sleep outside, but I couldn't risk them. If my friends died because of me—by weather, creature or Fae, when I could have given them a better chance at surviving—I'd hate myself. I wouldn't separate us. We were stronger together, no matter how big any of us were or weren't. In Elphame, size was not a deciding factor.

Together, we hunkered down in the farthest corner, under old and musty blankets that smelled of years of weather and animals. Together, I felt tougher, like we could take on whatever came through the door or walls. I tucked Nix and my creature into my jacket for warmth and willed my bones and muscles to relax. As hard as I tried, my muscles remained flexed, ready to bolt from danger.

"I feel strange here…like every nerve is alive." I twisted around. I felt antsy and restless.

"It's Elphame. You're feeling the constant thrum of energy and magick. The longer you're here, the more like here you'll become."

"I don't want to become Fae."

"Elphame doesn't really care much for what you want, Perdi. It's what happens to mortals of Fae blood who come here."

Another reason to hate the place was added to my list, which had grown into a book.

"Do you think we'll make it?" I asked, fearing the answer. "No lies."

"I hope so," he finally answered as if he'd weighed our options first. "If we don't, we died free, and there's no better death than a free one."

"Solas will find me. I can feel it. I can hear them, his people. I can hear the flap of their wings, their groans rolling across the clouds. They're not far from here." I said what we all knew and didn't want to acknowledge. "I can smell him on the wind from their wings."

"As do I. Together, they are the very darkness that haunts Elphame."

"How do I kill the darkness?" I whispered in fear that they'd hear me.

"You can't. You just hide."

"If Solas controls the Sluagh, why didn't I see any of them at court, protecting him?"

"They're always a few steps behind him and would have rained down like fire from the sun had Solas needed help. But he doesn't need help or protection. He's a force on his own."

I nodded. "If I'm caught, will they kill me for what I did to the king?"

He popped his head out of my sweater and hugged me as best he could. "Yes. No. I don't know. They'll either want your head or sentence you to prison. You killed their king, Perdi. How else should they respond? To do nothing would show weakness. As you've learned, weakness is not an affordable commodity in

Elphame. But honestly, no Crow has ever had the gumption to attack a Royal, let alone kill one. Though I'm sure they'll be adding that to the next negotiations."

"I'm not that brave. I was terrified to my core."

He kissed my nose. "Yes, you are. Bravery doesn't mean you're not scared. It means you still rise to the occasion. And as it turns out, sometimes that occasion is killing a king."

"You've read too many mortal books, Nix," I replied, my small laugh quieting into a yawn. "I killed someone. I've never killed someone with my bare hands."

"You should rest, Perdi. Don't think about things you can't change or things you don't want to change." He slunk back down into my sweater. "Tomorrow comes fast when you're exhausted."

I nodded but had one more question. "What about the oath? Will they kill me for leaving? Will the mortal world suffer for what I've done?"

"You didn't break any oaths since you're technically still in Elphame. The oath says you must remain here, as the Crow, for seven years, but it doesn't say where in Elphame you must remain. It's an agreement among the Fae where the Crow will live, not part of the oath with mortals. Teind, the tithe we pay to the Gods, is for a sacrifice to Elphame. You're still here, so I don't see how they could call you an oath breaker and ask for your life as payment. We're walking a fine line, but you haven't crossed it."

I had no more questions. He had no more answers.

I wondered if we'd make it through the night.

We scheduled turns to keep watch. We ate a snack, and I gave my creature a drop of my blood since she couldn't eat what we had. I offered her a leaf with several drops of my blood for her people as a thank you. She seemed surprised by the offer but eventually took it. The others, scattered around the room, each took a taste. With my blood on their lips, the creatures blanketed us while we slept. They kept watch in appreciation for my life essence.

I slept, finally, once my body realized it wouldn't be able to fight without rest. I dreamed of darkness, the cabin and its inability to protect us, with walls as broken as I. The howling from the forest had slinked into my dream and haunted me, followed me. Creatures I couldn't see nipped at my ankles. I dreamed of eating them, of letting my Malice out like twisted black roots and letting her feast on the souls of others. Rather than winding my Malice around their souls and forcing them to feel what I wanted them to feel, I pulled. I yanked with all my might and took away everything that kept their hearts beating—their very will to live—as I drank them down, refilling my cup of magick with their energy. The darkness from the dungeon watched from the shadows I had created with the souls I had taken.

"Why are you here?" I glanced to my right to see a man standing in swirling shadows.

"Because you are here. Save your energy. You cannot eat them all."

His mouth didn't move, but I heard every word as if he were whispering into my ear.

"I'm not here. I'm dreaming. I can feel it. I feel Nix curled into my neck as though he were here right now. I can hear my creature."

"Think, little Crow. Why do you hear your creature? What could make her shrill so loudly?"

I thought about it for a moment. *Trouble.* I only hear that noise when there is trouble.

"You need to wake up. The real games are about to begin."

"I don't want to play anymore."

"If you don't open your eyes now, when you do, you will play games you do not wish to play."

"Don't leave me."

About the Author

Lanne Garrett writes books. Considering where you're reading this, it makes perfect sense. She lives in Vancouver, here she spends her days getting lost in the beauty of reading and writing and can be found behind a mountain of books on any given Sunday.

Lanne loves to hear from readers. You can find her contact information, website details and author profile page at https://www.finch-books.com

FINCH
BOOKS

www.ingramcontent.com/pod-product-compliance
Lightning Source LLC
LaVergne TN
LVHW091039080826
845145LV00002B/560

* 9 7 8 1 8 0 2 5 0 5 3 3 7 *